THE BLACK MASK LIBRARY

THE EARLY YEARS (1920–26)

The Man in the Shadows: The Complete Black Mask
Cases of Terry Mack *by Carroll John Daly*

THE SHAW YEARS (1926–36)

Blood on the Curb *by Joseph T. Shaw*

Black Harvest: The Complete Black Mask
Cases of Jules Tremaine *by Norvell W. Page*

Boomerang Dice: The Complete Black Mask
Cases of Johnny Hi Gear *by Stewart Sterling*

Dead Evidence: The Complete Black Mask
Cases of Harrigan *by Ed Lybeck*

Laughing Death *by Raoul Whitfield*

Luck: The Complete Black Mask Cases of
Oscar Sail *by Lester Dent*

Murder Maze: The Complete Black Mask Cases of
Jerry Tracy, Volume 2 *by Theodore A. Tinsley*

The Price of a Dime: The Complete Black Mask
Cases of Ben Shaley *by Norbert Davis*

Somewhere in Mexico: The Complete Black Mask
Cases of Jerry Frost, Volume 1 *by Horace McCoy*

South Wind: The Complete Black Mask Cases of
Jerry Tracy, Volume 1 *by Theodore A. Tinsley*

THE LATER YEARS (1936–51)

Dead and Done For: The Complete Black Mask Cases
of Cellini Smith, Volume 1 *by Robert Reeves*

Dog Eat Dog: The Complete Black Mask Cases
of Cellini Smith, Volume 2 *by Robert Reeves*

It Happened at the Lake *by Joseph T. Shaw*

Let the Dead Alone: The Complete Black Mask Cases
of Luther McGavock, Volume 1 *by Merle Constiner*

Murder Costs Money: The Complete Black Mask
Cases of Rex Sackler, Volume 1 *by D.L. Champion*

Murder on the Midway: The Complete Black Mask Cases
of the Human Encyclopedia, Volume 1 *by Frank Gruber*

DOG EAT DOG

The Complete

Cases of Cellini Smith

1940

ROBERT REEVES

introduction by Kenneth S. White

illustrations by Peter Kuhlhoff

cover by Rafael de Soto

BLACK MASK
2022

Table of Contents

Introduction

IT'S BEEN A good many years since anything approximating the serial form has appeared in *Black Mask* and, frankly, we wonder if it's hitting the spot or not. We're familiar with a good many arguments—pro and con—regarding this business of continued stories and we'd like to conduct a sort of Gallup poll to learn whether the pros or cons have it in this particular instance. We'd like to be confirmed in our impression that readers brought up on *The Maltese Falcon, The Glass Key, Green Ice* and various other yarns that once ran serially in these pages and helped to make them memorable, will approve an occasional handpicked novel strung out over no more than three installments.

Now meet the author of the current Cellini Smith opus—Robert Reeves. Free, white and twenty-nine he is a transplanted New Yorker—like so many other Californians. Having acquired an A.B. at New York University, Washington Square Branch, where he majored in History, English and Anthropology. He promptly put his education to work as driver of an armored Post Office Department truck. Among the other activities that have engaged his attention from time to time are carpentry, cabinet-making, candy-making, reading for Fox Films and various and sundry Broadway play-brokers. He had several years experience in show-business as a casting director, play doctor, stage manager and assistant producer. Stage-managed for the Theater Guild at one time. Has forsaken his other interests now to concentrate on the problem of making Cellini Smith support him.

Dog Eat Dog

Pugs and wrestlers—gunsels and brain-guys—cops and private eyes—chiselers and chiseled—wenches and a lady—and Smith—Cellini Smith—who hated to be shoved around by any of them!

1

Hollywood Hangover

CELLINI SMITH INTRODUCED his lemon-haired companion. "This is Nina Saunders, Mr. Miles."

Morton Miles gestured toward the brassy music and the noisy diners and drinkers. He shifted slightly and cupped his hand to the good ear. The shapeless blob of pink meat representing the left ear of the one-time, light-heavyweight champion of the world was utterly useless. "Come again?"

Cellini Smith repeated the introduction into the right ear.

"Pleased to meetcha," muttered Morton Miles. His fleshy brows creased in the effort to add something gallant. "I'm always tickled to meet a good-lookin' dame."

Nina Saunders smiled conventionally, but the green in the eyes glittered with interest and the nostrils dilated faintly. There was something earthy, something elemental about prizefighters that was lacking in her Pasadena men—even the two-goal ones. Her voice, however, was almost indifferent. "I didn't imagine pugilists were such practiced fibbers, Mr. Miles."

Morton Miles shook his head so that the heavy, pendulous jowls shivered like Jello. Dating back to the bare-knuckle days when he had fought men like Fitzimmons and Philadelphia Jack O'Brien, Morton Miles was now sixty and stout. What had been muscle was now fat. "It's the truth, Miss Saunders," he said. "I throw it straight for everybody."

"For the Terrible Turk too?" asked Cellini Smith artlessly.

The Turk speared another oyster

There was just the barest tremor of suspicion in the tightening of the folds about Morton Miles' eyes. The former light-heavy said slowly: "Sure, the Turk too. We got enterprises together. We're pals."

"Sure you are," said Cellini unctuously.

Morton Miles eyed Cellini Smith speculatively, his good ear still cupped toward him. "How long you been in this town, Smith?"

"A couple of months."

"Well, take it easy."

Cellini Smith controlled himself with effort. He didn't like to be stepped on, but neither was it advisable to tell a man like Miles where to head in. He peeled the damp label off the beer bottle and made no reply.

Nina Saunders caught the tension between the two men and decided to ease things. "You have a nice place here, Mr. Miles."

MORTON MILES TOOK in his gaudy night club with an obvious, placid pride. The place was called the "Hangover" and here every up-and-coming and down-and-out, every would-be and has-been prizefighter came to buy and cadge drinks, to exchange news and hear gossip, to preen feathers and lick wounds, to wangle bookings and pick up mail, to borrow and—on rare occasions—repay money.

All thirty tables and wall booths squeezed into the tiny club were occupied at the moment. The bored musicians played on a platform that affected to be a boxing ring. It was roped off and canvas-padded save for a small hardwood area reserved for the specialty dance acts.

Around the bar congregated the broad-shouldered, long-armed men with cauliflower ears, mushroomed noses, and dragging, scraping feet—hallmark of the punch-drunk fighter. On the walls were typical, framed photographs of fighters from Gans and Ketchel to Louis, lithographs of fleshy chorines in various states of undress, and autographed gloves and ring-robes of the fistic great and near-great. The men's lavatory door said: *Heavyweights,* the women's: *Lightweights.*

The Hangover was redolent with the leather and smoke and sweat and stink of the ring. It was owned by one of the great old-time fighters. It was the Mecca of the boxing world. It was on the must list of every tourist to Hollywood.

Morton Miles told Nina Saunders that he thought it was a nice place, too, and that she must come more often.

She replied that she was a regular patron but that he'd never noticed her. Her tone implied that he was one of the few men guilty of such an omission.

Morton Miles barely heard out Nina Saunders. Abruptly he turned back to Cellini Smith. "Were you driving at some-thing, Smith?"

"Forget it. I was just trying to do you a favor and you jumped me."

Miles regarded him with expressionless face. Cellini Smith was about thirty. His mouth was too big, his face bones too prominent, and his black, abundant hair too much like the back of a protesting porcupine. He was not good-looking but the perennial, quizzical expression and the trick of flashing a quick, twisted, heart-warming smile helped a lot. He had never been a fighter, Miles noted—but he could have been.

Miles said placatingly: "You're all right, Smith. You were one of Moro's boys in New York and that's good enough for me. You're the only peeper I let in this place."

"I wasn't one of Moro's boys," said Cellini Smith.

"Sure you were. That's why I don't care if you're a dick now. I know your heart ain't in it. So open up."

"O.K.," said Cellini. "I hear lots of rumors in my business and I heard one about you the other day."

"What was it?"

"I heard that the Turk has hired a private operative to nose around and ask questions about you."

Morton Miles was silent. A sleek little bantam at the next table began to explain to an awed extra why a nose breather was much better than a mouth breather. Nina Saunders waved to one of her socialite friends slumming over a champagne cocktail at a ringside table. Finally Miles said: "So the Turk don't trust me. Who's the peeper he set on me?"

"The very best," replied Cellini. "None other than the great Ned Lyams." He gave a mirthless laugh as he remembered the time he had wasted attempting to cultivate Ned Lyams.

The Sioux City Slasher, formerly a borscht-circuit welter but now a good, rowdy master of ceremonies, silenced the band. "Folks, comes now jokes. Hump, tell that guy in the can to come out because the floor show's starting."

Hump was a small, hunchbacked waiter whom fighters once liked to have in their corner because they thought it lucky to rub his deformity before a fight. When four fighters in a row rubbed his hump and were knocked cold in the first round, he had to ask Morton Miles for a job. Nevertheless, he was a good second. Hump replied: "The guy in the can left because he couldn't stand the smell from the kitchen."

"Then we can start," continued the Slasher. "The first will be our own, buxom Kate Kelly singing, 'The First Time It's Love—The Next Time It's Two Bucks!' Sober her up boys, and bring her on."

THERE WAS A clatter of applause. Morton Miles' face settled into pleased creases and he turned attentively toward the ring. There was another burst of applause for the swirl of petticoat, lace, and bare thigh as Kate Kelly climbed through the ropes. She was in her late forties, jovial, and her figure was executed on a lavish scale. Her expressive black eyes sought out Morton Miles, she flashed him a loving smile and started on a series of ribald lyrics. As she sang, her body heaved to the rhythm of the music and the ungirdled fat under her dress quivered voluptuously. She completed her turn to an ovation, refused an encore, and headed for the bar.

Morton Miles ran fingers through his gray hair dyed black and sighed. What a woman!

The Sioux City Slasher leaped into the ring again. "And now, folks, the guy who pays my salary, the man who fought the best of them and after he fought them they were still the best—Morton Miles!"

Morton Miles got into the ring and started a routine of vaudeville jokes popular in the days of Corbett and Sullivan. Cellini Smith lost interest.

"Another drink?" he asked Nina Saunders.

She laughed aloud. Her yellow hair was in pleasant contrast

to ripe lips that hardly needed the lipstick that had been applied. Her body was pliant without being sinuous, her morality refreshingly simple: Do what you want but keep it out of the papers. Her family was filthy rich and she spent her time serving as

Cellini Smith

one of the managers of the Young Women's Aid Society—a charity organization engaged mainly in the furious distribution of Christmas baskets.

She said: "Thanks, no, Cellini. I don't like beer and you can't afford to get me drunk on scotch."

"That's right," he admitted ruefully.

"Cellini, who's the Turk?"

Cellini Smith pointed to a sign on the wall which read:

Who thinks THE terrible TURK STINKS?

Wall space under the sign was disfigured with myriad initials, signatures, and improvised drawings made with pen, pencil, chalk, and steak knives. It was the Hangover's guest book.

"Oh. That wrestler?" asked Nina Saunders.

"Right."

"They don't like wrestlers here, do they?"

"A fighter like a wrestler? Didn't you see Miles overheat when I mentioned the Turk? That's the eternal argument, Nina. Who can beat who—a fighter or a wrestler?"

MORTON MILES FOLDED his joke bag and crawled away to join Kate Kelly at the bar. A boy-and-girl tap-dancing routine replaced him in the ring. Someone at a nearby table grabbed a runt by the shirt front with one hand and began punching his nose with the other. The blood ran from the runt's nose as freely as from a spigot. A lithe, broad-shouldered fighter detached himself from the bar and hit the aggressor a heavy blow on the nape of his neck. The runt said that nobody could do that to a friend of his, swung at the fighter, and missed. The fighter clipped the runt over his ear, dropped him on top of his friend, and returned to the bar. The tourists gasped. A lady with a lorgnette applauded under the mistaken apprehension that it was part of the floor show.

Nina Saunders watched avidly. Her eyes shone.

"You liked that, didn't you?" said Cellini. "Life in the raw! The seamy side!"

"There's something about fighters—" She left the sentence dangling.

"I'm not a fighter. I'm just an operative looking for a client."

She leaned toward him and he caught the faint scent of an expensive perfume. "You're a happy compromise, Cellini. I like fighters but most of them are smelly and rude. You have the energizing vulgarity I admire in them and yet that minimum of civilization I demand in men."

"Don't let me fool you, Nina. Deep down I'm a gentleman."

Under the table she slipped her hand into his. He let it rest there without pressing or clasping it. She made a face and withdrew her hand. "The opposite," she said. "That's your technique, Cellini."

"Come again, Nina?"

"Forget it. Tell me something about fighters and the underworld and about the people in here. Make it gory, Cellini."

"Sure," he said obligingly. He pointed to a sad-visaged man at a rear table in earnest conversation with an exquisite brunette. "That's man's a thorn on my detective's mind. He sits at that same table every night, sometimes alone, usually with that gorgeous thing. His name is Earl Nikken."

"And the thorn?" asked Nina Saunders.

"Just that. Earl Nikken is here every night and he gets the same table every night. Why? Who is he?"

"Why not ask someone?" suggested Nina Saunders.

"No. I'd probably get a very simple answer and I'd be out another problem in detection. At the rate I'm going now I've got to hoard even the tiniest problems."

"What else?"

"Then you see that man at the bar with the steel brace holding his head in place? He was one of the best middles on the Pacific coast until he dropped on a spot where the canvas wasn't well padded and broke his—" Cellini stopped short as an overdressed man in his forties passed the table. "Hello, Joe."

"How's the Hawkshaw?" A Broadway byproduct of the days when Rothstein and Legs Diamond carved filets out of the Tenderloin, Joe Lucca had the sophistication and synthetic personality of that school.

Cellini said: "Miss Saunders here is interested in the underworld, Joe. Show her your profile."

Joe Lucca obliged. Nina Saunders voiced her disappointment in finding it a quite nice profile and the racketeer passed on to the bar. Kate Kelly entered the ring for another song. Nina Saunders watched Cellini listening to the raucous, whisky contralto. She said: "Take me for a drive."

Cellini stood up. He was five feet ten in height. His body was powerful and moved with a supple, feral confidence. Cellini Smith didn't believe that the pen was mightier than the sword. He didn't believe that anything was mightier than the sword. He led the way out of the smoke-filled club.

THEY CROSSED THE street to a Plymouth roadster parked in front of the Professional Building. Cellini started the bronchitic motor and they headed for the hills. When he reached Sunset he turned right into Laurel Canyon and then left into Lookout Mountain Road and they started climbing. Nina Saunders lit two Parliaments and placed one between Cellini's lips. As the car banked around S curves she took advantage of them to lean heavily against him. He could gather the perfume more distinctly now. It reminded him of columbine. When the car leveled out she continued to lean against him.

As they gained the crest of the hill and cut into a clearing they suddenly confronted a panorama of pyrotechnic splendor. As the eye grew accustomed to the prodigal millions of lights, details of anatomy became discernible—broad boulevards ablaze with street lamps and shop windows, byways crawling with automobile headlamps like moving columns on a gigantic ant heap, downtown office buildings looming black and menacing in the overhanging haze and, from oceanward, a hungry fog that crept inland, swallowing the hills and oil fields in its path. There it sprawled at their feet— what cynics called "Seven villages in search of a city"— Los Angeles.

Duck-Eye Ryan

Nina Saunders tamped out her cigarette without removing her head from Cellini's shoulder, but when he remained wooden and unresponsive she abruptly sat up. Cellini drummed with his fingers on the steering wheel and thought of all the murders, shadow jobs, crimes, and investigations in that city below them—and none of it, he reflected bitterly, came his way. Not even by chance.

He grew aware of light, feminine fingers brushing against his side and then he felt some clinking metal object drop into the right-hand pocket of his jacket. He gave no indication that he had noticed anything.

They sat in silence for a quarter-hour when he finally stirred and said: "Let's get back."

She suddenly voiced her pent-up annoyance. "You're a past-master at this sort of thing, aren't you?"

She felt the shrug, but could not see the amused smile in the dark. "How's that?" he asked.

"You're a past-master," Nina Saunders repeated. "You know what I'm talking about. I'm talking of the art of seduction—as practiced by Cellini Smith."

"I don't understand," he said. "Is this some patter you've picked up in the Beverly-Wilshire lobby?"

"It must be after ten now, Cellini. We've been together over three hours now. In all this time you haven't missed one opportunity to size up every pretty girl that passed. You made a point of it!"

"Well, this is where you find them," he said apologetically.

"We nursed beers for an hour," she continued without heeding him, "and you were very polite, very gentlemanly—and oh so bored. You kept looking past my shoulder with a vague, detached air and never once did you size me up! Why do you take me out? Why? What do you call it, Cellini? The resistance-breaking technique? Why you've never even tried to get me drunk."

He remembered he hadn't been to his office that day. And Duck-Eye Ryan hadn't been able to watch the phone either because he had a match tonight. But nothing lost. Probably a few more collection hounds.

Her voice rose slightly. "Don't think I'm piqued. Just tell me, Cellini, do you think the system is working?"

He switched on the ignition and pressed the starter. He slipped into gear, backed the car around, and they headed down the tortuous road from Lookout Mountain.

After a while Cellini said: "You're a bit on the neurotic side, aren't you, Nina?"

"No, I'm not," she replied slowly. "I'm just very curious about how the male ego functions."

Cellini gave no reply and they were silent until presently he turned into a quiet street lined with palm trees of alternating height and stopped at one of Hollywood's less famous but more distinguished apartment hotels. A beautifully trimmed pomegranate hedge across the front lawn spelled out the name: *Sheraton Manor.*

They stepped out of the car and Nina Saunders extended a gloved hand. A nearby street lamp highlighted her youthful, lovely face. He took her hand, pressed it casually, and said: "Good-night."

With ill-concealed exasperation in her voice, she said: "This is a case in point. I'm not being suggestive, Cellini, but, as an example, you've never once tried to kiss me good-night."

Cellini patted her backside briefly. "Run along and be a good girl."

Nina Saunders gave a chagrined laugh, said, "That's what I get for going out with a crude detective," turned, and went up the broad steps of the Sheraton Manor.

CELLINI GOT INTO his car, drove south till he reached the Professional Building again, and parked. It was two-story, pseudo-Spanish, and situated directly across the street from Morton Miles' Hangover. Cellini Smith's office, the West Coast branch of the Sampsel Agency, was on the second floor over the immense Japanese fruit market.

He paused, undecided whether to go up to his office or to

return to the Hangover. He looked at the dark windows of the office and a scowl settled over his face.

Not one single job, not even a divorce case, since he'd taken over the place. Only ten weeks ago he was a free man in New York. He had money in his pockets, friends to talk to and fight with, and—why not?—even the chance to grab the pin-marble racket on the lower East Side. Though he was never one of Tony Moro's henchmen, yet by some paradox he was regarded as Tony's crown prince and he knew that that empire of graft, shakedowns, and sluggings could have been his for the taking.

But Tony was dead and somehow he had allowed Old Man Sampsel to talk him into the West Coast branch of his detective agency. There it was, behind the two dark windows, with its wire tray full of unpaid bills. He shrugged and crossed the street.

Cellini said, "Hello, Jo-Jo," to a newsboy in front of the Hangover.

The "boy" was thirty-eight, a former Golden Glover out of New York. He looked tough and he was tough. Because of his background he was the only newsboy allowed at that stand by Morton Miles.

Cellini asked: "How's business tonight, Jo-Jo?"

Jo-Jo spat into the gutter. "Sour as hell. They think they need a prescription to buy a paper."

Cellini entered the club, looked around, spied a table that had just been vacated, and made for it. It was between floor shows and the customers were drinking and talking, paying scant attention to the band. Hump came with a damp cloth and one beer.

"Has Duck-Eye been in?" Cellini asked.

The hunchbacked waiter shook his head. "Nope. Where'd he fight tonight?"

"At an Elk's smoker near Pomona."

"Taking a dive?"

"No," said Cellini. "He's winning. I'm building Duck-Eye up till I can get Miles to put him on a decent card. Then I'll bet my roll against him."

"Tell me when and I'll get on the gravy train."

The promise was made and the waiter left. Finally Cellini Smith reached into the right-hand pocket of his jacket. He pulled out a key and metal tag. His eyes exulted under narrowed slits as he read the stamping on the metal: *Sheraton Manor— 3-B.* He rolled it in his fingers slowly, stoking his imagination. The beer went flat. After a while he returned it to his pocket.

CELLINI SAT AT the table, watching the activity for a half-hour. Alky-drunk and punch-drunk fighters came over and put their strangulating arms around him and said he was all right because he had been one of Tony Moro's boys. Cellini irritably told them he had never been and they left when he wouldn't buy drinks.

At last Duck-Eye Ryan arrived. He was an enormous man of phenomenal strength. Tabbed by the fighting fraternity as a "has-been," the term was strictly a method of classification as he had had neither the brains nor agility to achieve any sort of reputation during his prizefighting prime. He was a dullard, though a kindly one. His large, round, battle-scarred face was usually innocent of expression and his protruding unblinking eyes rarely betrayed any glimmer of thought. At the moment, one of them was blown up, the lower lip split, and the nose red from bleeding. The customers paid little heed to Duck-Eye. A bruised fighter was a common sight in the Hangover.

Duck-Eye Ryan sat down and pushed two tens and a five across to Cellini. He said: "That's our split. I give half to Peanuts for the Brodey."

Cellini had pangs of conscience as he saw the bruises. "How's it you got hurt?" he demanded angrily.

In his halting, monosyllabic way, Duck-Eye Ryan explained that Peanuts had taken the dive in the third round, as prearranged, but that later in the dressing-room he had claimed that Duck-Eye had hurt him in the process. Then and there Peanuts beat him up.

Cellini scowled. It galled him to be kept in food and drink by the few dollars Duck-Eye earned at county fairs or rural smokers. After Tony Moro's liquidation in the East, Duck-Eye, who was Tony's most devoted strong-arm, had followed Cellini to California with the unreasoning tenacity of a stray dog. Cellini was sentimental about him. He shoved the money back.

Duck-Eye returned the bills to his pocket without comment. It never occurred to him to question Cellini. "Did you ask Mr. Miles when I fight next?"

"No. You're not fighting any more."

"I ain't fighting?" His split lips parted in surprise.

"That's what I said. I'm through with your chicken feed. I don't want it. You're too dumb to get away without a beating if the match is on the level."

Duck-Eye Ryan said that he was only thirty-one. He said if Cellini didn't want the cabbage he could use it. Then he evidently left a few connecting thoughts unvoiced for he next announced that he liked Hollywood women. Finally, he begged Cellini to get Mr. Miles to book him a couple of good fights—maybe hundred-dollar ones.

"All right, shut up," Cellini barked in a heavy, grating voice. "I'll get you your fights but you get it through your thick head I take no part of the kitty. I'll get you fights but if you come back marked up again I'll beat you senseless myself."

Duck-Eye Ryan gave a pointless grin. In his vague way he sensed that Cellini was fond of him. "Cellini, a U.C. frat is puttin' on a few fights tomorrow night. Maybe if it ain't all booked Mr. Miles will give me one of 'em."

"O.K., I'll ask." Cellini flagged Hump. "Is it too late to stick Duck-Eye on tomorrow night's card at the frat shindig?"

"Maybe there's still a chance. Why don't you go speak to Morton Miles?"

"Where is he?"

"He's home," replied the waiter. "Everybody always wants him when he ain't here."

"Where does he live?"

The hunchback supplied the address, observed Duck-Eye, and said with a good deal of heat: "When the hell will you learn to roll with a punch? You want to remember you're so big and so damn slow you can't help getting hit so your only chance is to learn to go away when you're belted by—"

The catechism continued as Cellini threaded his way outside to the Plymouth roadster.

2

X-Champ

CELLINI SMITH CRAWLED down Maple Grove Lane until he approached number 2385, waited for a dark red De Soto to pull away from in front, then parked in the same spot.

Morton Miles lived on the east side of the modish duplex. From the open windows of the other half came the blare of a radio, the clinking of glasses and ice, and drunken laughter.

The door to Morton Miles' apartment was ajar. Cellini pressed the buzzer. He waited and pressed it again. From somewhere back in the service pantry he heard the mechanism respond. But nothing else stirred. Only then did it strike him as odd that the apartment was completely lighted. Without waiting further, he padded into the low-ceilinged living-room. The room, a bachelor's idea of solid comfort, was indeed lighted by every floor and wall lamp. Cellini whistled but there was still no reply. He crossed to the heavy portieres over an arched opening beyond the fireplace, parted them, and looked into the den.

For a while he stared at what he saw near the far wall, then he returned to the apartment door, and shut it. He made a quick tour of bedroom, kitchen, dining-room, butler's pantry, and bath. He looked into closets, behind furniture, under beds. He could find nobody.

He returned to the den and kneeled over the fleshy body of the elderly, ring-scarred Morton Miles. The ex-light-heavyweight champion of the world was dead.

Morton Miles lay on his back and the bloodstained shirt, tie, and jacket attested to at least one bullet buried somewhere in his chest. The bullet or bullets had probably told swiftly as the fat, wrinkled face was not constricted with pain. Still clutched in the right hand was a small, .25-bore automatic. To the right of the body, and at a wide angle, a bullet had plowed through the dove-colored rug and lodged in the flooring.

Near the head lay a packet of twenty-dollar bills. Cellini dropped a handkerchief over the packet and, through the linen, counted twenty-five bills—five hundred dollars.

He was puzzled. He stood up and took note of the open wall safe above the body. Inside were more packets—probably several thousand dollars—and neat, apparently undisturbed bundles of papers. A gumwood secretary stood in one corner. Cellini tried the drawers. All were locked securely and no attempt had been made to force them. The murderer, it seemed at first glance, had been interested in nothing but murder.

Cellini curbed his first inclination to phone the police. He needed time to make sure of his alibi. His background and recent arrival in the city made his position sufficiently precarious. Why draw police suspicion to himself? Besides—though he did not admit it was the most important reason—there might be some gravy in this for him if he had a little time to find out a couple of things first. He left the apartment, crossed the vestibule to the other duplex. By now the party hit crescendo and Cellini had to lean on the buzzer.

Finally a small man, fierce with drink and wearing thick bifocals, opened the door. He said: "Friend, nobody's crashing this party. Already there's five men to two dames."

"Not interested," replied Cellini placatingly. "I'm studying to be a sky-pilot and forgot to reverse my collar today. I'm just looking for an airdale."

"Oh." The inebriate became less belligerent. "We got a couple of other kind of dogs here, Reverend, but not that kind."

"You sure? How long has this shindig been going on?"

"We come in a half-hour ago from a show. You're O.K., Rev. Want a drink?"

"Certainly not," said Cellini, offended. "Maybe someone who was here earlier saw my airdale. Someone with a De Soto coupé," he added illogically.

The little man said nobody with a De Soto had seen no airdale. Cellini thanked him, went out to his car, and drove off.

TEN MINUTES LATER Cellini Smith parked at the Hangover. The air inside was thicker now, the people drunker. He waited till Hump had a free moment, called him to one side, and asked without preface: "What did you mean before when you said that everybody always wanted Morton Miles when he wasn't here?"

"Nothin'. Miles just had a call a couple of minutes before you come in asking where he was."

"Who called him?" asked Cellini.

The hunchback squinted suspiciously. "Why you wanna know?"

"This may mean a lot to me," evaded Cellini.

"That ain't no answer."

"Hell," said Cellini impatiently. "You ought to know me well enough by now. I'm just trying to figure something. It has absolutely nothing to do with you."

"O.K. Jesse Lee Ward phoned, asking for Miles."

"Thanks, Hump. And one more question. How long after Miss Saunders and I left here did Morton Miles leave?"

The waiter rubbed his stubbled chin as he thought. "Well, about five minutes after you went he made a phone call. Ten minutes later he went home."

"Thanks, Hump. Forget we discussed this."

Nina Saunders

The waiter moved off. Cellini beckoned to Duck-Eye Ryan who was straddling a stool at the bar and the two went outside where Jo-Jo still hustled his papers.

"Who's Jesse Lee Ward?" Cellini asked the newsboy.

"Jesse Ward does all the figgerin' for Morton Miles. He runs all the books for the Hangover, figgers out where to promote fights and all that stuff. He's up in Palm Springs now."

Cellini nodded thanks and crossed the street to the Professional Building with Duck-Eye. They walked up the flight of stairs. Cellini unlocked the door to his office and snapped on the ceiling lights as they entered.

The office was a single, medium-sized room furnished with a small, Carolina pine desk, a few chairs, and two tremendous and empty filing-cabinets intended to impress clients. On the desk were the customary stationery items, with the addition of a beautiful example of a perforated stone hammer of the Neolithic age. Duck-Eye Ryan threw himself on a worn settee in one corner.

Cellini sat behind the desk, fished for a cigarette, and turned to the day's mail. It consisted of two dunning notes and a special six month subscription offer from *Motherhood Stories*.

He dropped the letters into the wire tray on his desk and then looked at his calendar pad. It was virgin of appointments and the memoranda consisted of the one word "Gymnasium." He crossed this out and wrote it in for the following day. It was a daily ritual. He had yet to visit any gymnasium.

All in all he had wasted about ten minutes before he reached for the directory and searched for the number of police head-quarters.

From the settee, Duck-Eye apologetically intruded: "Did you get me a job? Did you get Mr. Miles to book me?"

"Mr. Miles," said Cellini, "has been booked himself—by Gabriel."

"You mean he was killed dead?"

"That's right, Duck-Eye. He was killed dead."

"Jeez! That's tough. It means no job."

"No job for you but if we work this right and stick around maybe I'll get a job." He dialed and waited for his connection. "Hello, this is Cellini Smith of the Sampsel outfit.... I said Cellini Smith!... No," he said wearily, "It's 'C' like in Cellini and 'S' like in Smith.... No, I'm not a wise guy...." Fists clenched. He said: "I'm not kidding anybody and that's my name and I don't like any insinuations about it." He smashed down the receiver.

Within a few foments the phone rang. It was the police department again. A voice asked: "Did you call us before?"

"Yes. I was waiting for you to call back."

"Did you say you were from the Sampsel Detective Agency?"

"Yes."

"All right. You didn't have to get so excited. It's not good policy to try it with us. What did you want?"

Cellini said: "I wanted to report a murder at 2385 Maple Grove Lane."

There was a faint pause before Cellini heard the voice again. "Listen, you

Haenigson

Cellini Smith, I don't know who you are but I think you're very smart. I don't like you one bit. Who was murdered?"

Cellini said: "That's all right. I like you enough for both of us. Morton Miles was murdered. It's his house."

"The fighter?"

"Yes."

There was another pause. Then, "Where are you?"

"At my office opposite the Hangover in the Professional Building."

"Well, thank you for the information, Smith. It was kind of you to ring us. Suppose you stick around a while. We might want to see you."

Cellini said: "You know damn well you want to see me." He cradled the receiver and leaned back in the chair, lost in thought.

SEVERAL TIMES DUCK-EYE Ryan attempted a conversation but lapsed into discouraged silence when there was no response. Cellini Smith smoked and stared at nothing. He checked his watch and thought over the evening's events. It was now twelve fifteen. When he and Nina Saunders left the Hangover it could not have been more than ten—possibly a few minutes earlier. Immediately after, according to Hump, Morton Miles made a phone call and fifteen minutes later went home. About ten fifteen. Then somebody named Jesse Lee Ward phoned for Miles at the Hangover at perhaps ten thirty. A half-hour later he had found the ex-fighter dead. At the time, the party in the duplex adjoining Morton Miles' was in swing a half-hour already and had there been any shooting during that time it would certainly have been heard.

Therefore, Cellini calculated, the murder had occurred sometime between ten thirty and eleven.

He wrinkled his nose as if smelling something unsavory, reached for the phone, and dialed the Sheraton Manor.

"Hello, Nina?"

There was a note of asperity in Nina Saunders' voice as she asked: "What is it, Cellini? More of your technique?"

Cellini laughed. "That's what I like about you, Nina. Your subtlety."

She said in a steely voice: "Well I can't say I like your lack of it. I didn't expect this phone call and I don't want to be bothered again."

"Listen before you talk, you psychopath. If you're trying to tell me to forget about that key then it's O.K. with me. I simply wanted to say that I ran into a dead body after I dropped you at the Sheraton. The cops will be wanting to know what

I did this evening so you can expect a visit from them to check if I was really with you tonight."

"I don't understand, Cellini. Who will be here?"

"The cops."

"Do you mean I'll get mixed up in a murder?" Her voice sounded small and frightened.

Earl Nikken

"I mean they'll just check with you to see that my story's straight," he said patiently.

"Cellini"—her voice was strange and unnaturally high—"are you mixed—I mean did you really kill somebody?"

He said: "Sure I did. I put my trusty bolo across my victim's neck but it was so thickly encrusted with dirt that I couldn't cut deep enough. So I—"

"I'm sorry, Cellini. It was a foolish question. I was just worried for you."

"That's nice, Nina. I knew that deep down your motives were beyond human reproach."

"That's not the point, Cellini."

"Whatever the point, just don't let your memory slip. We were together from six thirty to a quarter after eleven or so, and between ten thirty and eleven we were star-gazing on top of Lookout Mountain. Ten thirty to eleven. Remember it."

"But that's just it, Cellini. Don't you understand?"

"Sure. I understand that you wouldn't like it known you went out with an ordinary detective who's not in the social register. But that can't be helped now."

"Cellini, listen to me. I can't get mixed up with the police on anything like this."

Coldly, he asked: "Why?"

"My family. *I* wouldn't mind, Cellini, but they're terrible snobs. You know how old families are. A scandal that touches one touches all. They never pay attention to me till they read my name in the papers. I hate it myself, Cellini, but I don't want to hurt them. They feel I have a family dignity to maintain and even the remotest mention of my name in connection with a murder would be a terrible blow to all of—"

He said brutally: "Let's get this straight. You're willing to sleep with me but you're not willing to alibi me. Is that the way it goes?"

"Chel-*ee*ni! Please don't talk like that. All I want is to stay out of any mess that—"

He had heard enough. He dropped the receiver back into place. But for a twisted smile, his face was expressionless as he searched for a small memorandum book in his pockets. He found it, flipped the pages till he had the number he wanted, and dialed.

"Hello, is Joe Lucca there?"

"Who wants to know?"

"Cellini Smith wants to know."

"Oh, hello, Cellini," said Joe Lucca. "I was just being careful. With elections coming on you never know when to expect the shams to get civic-minded. Say, that was a tasty tidbit at your table tonight."

Cellini said: "Never mind the tongue-twisters, Joe. I've got to be someplace between ten and eleven tonight."

"Uh-huh. How tight a spot are you in?"

"Don't you want to do it?" asked Cellini sharply.

"You know it's nothing like that," hastened Lucca. "I just want to know how good an alibi I should make it."

"Make it good."

"Weren't you at the Hangover?"

"Not during that time. Too many people saw me go out."

"Well, what if I talk to Nate?"

"Who's that?" asked Cellini.

"He runs a steer joint called the Blue Chip on La Brea— roulette and stuff. He's got about two dozen croupiers and hangers-on there who'll do anything he wants. If necessary they'll swear you came riding up to the door on a penguin's back."

"That'll be all right, Joe. Better make it that I was there from ten fifteen on so's I'd have the time to get there. I'll stay here in my office waiting for the O.K."

Lucca said: "Check."

CELLINI WALKED OVER to the window and stood there looking down on the street. Kate Kelly's voice was thick and sensuous in the night air. From the settee came Duck-Eye Ryan's snores in counterpoint. Jo-Jo hawked his news to passing motorists. Each time anything resembling a prowl car cruised by, Cellini's eyes narrowed. Twenty minutes later the phone rang. He crossed and answered it.

"Hello."

"Cellini," said Joe Lucca rapidly, "I phoned the Blue Chip

but Nate wasn't there yet. He's expected and they'll ring me as soon as he's in and tell me if the proposition's O.K."

"I haven't got much time."

"Then you'll have to cover," replied Lucca. "Use the spare only if I don't call you back in time."

"I'll do it that way, Joe. Try me at my apartment if you can't get me here."

Cellini hung up and paged through the telephone directory till he found the number of the Translux Newsreel theater. He flipped the dial.

A highly nasalized, feminine voice said, "Translux, just a moment please," and before Cellini could speak she put her holding key down.

He waited some time before he heard the voice of the box-office girl again. He said: "What's the idea of giving me that 'just a moment' business and then keeping me waiting for a half-hour?"

"I'm very sorry, sir, some people were waiting to pass through the turnstile."

"You must have a fine manager there, lady. I had trouble tonight when I caught your ten o'clock show and you short-changed me."

The cashier said: "I'm very sorry, sir, but some people were waiting to pass through the—"

Cellini raised his voice. "I heard that once, you broken record. I want help, not criticism."

Cellini heard a "God give us strength" sigh and then the voice said: "I'm so sorry about all the trouble, sir. What is it you want, sir?"

He said: "My name is Cellini Smith. I caught your ten o'clock show tonight and sat about fifteenth row center. I stayed for the whole newsreel—that's about an hour, isn't it?—and now I find a small roll of one dollar bills missing from my pocket. It must have dropped when I took my handkerchief out. I want it back."

"We'll do our best to find it, sir. What is your address, please?"

Cellini gave her his home address and replaced the receiver. He roused Duck-Eye and told him to get out of the office and to stay away from the apartment for a few hours. He snapped the lights off, locked the door, and they left. Downstairs, Cellini paused a moment to say to Jo-Jo: "You didn't see me come in, go out, or anything. You're just a poor, near-sighted newsboy supporting an old Ziegfeld girl."

Duck-Eye ambled back to the Hangover and Cellini got into his car and drove off.

3

Alibi Trouble

CELLINI'S APARTMENT WAS off Melrose near La Cieniga and a two-mile drive from his office. It was on the ground-floor rear and consisted of a large living-room with wall bed, kitchenette, and bath. The building had fourteen such units and the rental on each was forty-two fifty a month including mythical maid service.

It was nearly one when he let himself into the apartment. A Capehart, the only item of furniture that was his, occupied the position of honor in front of a prop fireplace. The albums of records were stacked on the floor nearby. A large army cot—though hardly big enough for Duck-Eye Ryan—stood in one corner, but more often than not Duck-Eye slept elsewhere. It was his habit to remove his shoes and sleep where the night found him. In another corner was a rickety end-table which Cellini euphemistically called his bar. The bottles on it were mostly empty, though there was a quantity of rye and a little scotch left. A steel-spring wall-exerciser was fastened against the closet door and many books were piled haphazardly about the room.

Cellini dropped the wall bed, undressed, and donned pajamas. He went into the bathroom, returned a few minutes later, and chose a book at random. It was *Up From The Apes* by Hooten. Cellini fancied himself an amateur anthropologist.

With a wry smile he crossed to the apartment door and took

it off latch so that it would open from the hall. Then he got into bed and began thumbing the volume.

THE ANTICIPATED KNOCK came a half-hour later. Cellini called: "It's open," and the visitor entered and said: "I'm Ira Haenigson—Detective-sergeant of Homicide." He was six feet two inches in height and nearer fifty than forty. His movements were slow and decisive and his build was comfortable but by no means soft. The only soft things about Ira Haenigson were his voice and manner—both misleading.

Cellini made to rise but Haenigson waved him back, drew up a chair, and sat down next to the bed.

Apropos of nothing, Haenigson said: "He's mad at you."

"Who?"

"Our desk man. He says you got tough over the phone. You shouldn't have done that, Mr. Smith. After all, he's a policeman. The law is to be respected," Haenigson added sententiously.

"He started getting tough first and just because he's a cop I don't have to take it."

"Now, now, Mr. Smith," the detective-sergeant said mildly, "you mustn't take the Bill of Rights too seriously in this town. It will get you into trouble. Another thing you shouldn't have done was to leave your office when you were told to stay there and wait."

"How about a drink?" asked Cellini.

"When I'm on duty I mix it with a lot of seltzer."

"Do your own mixing. The stuff's on the end-table there."

Haenigson did his own mixing and returned to the bed with a glass of rye and vichy. He said: "If we're going to be friends in this town don't do too much of that sort of thing."

Cellini said: "I waited in my office a half-hour and then I got sleepy. I figured it was all right to blow because you boys would be spending all night looking over Miles' house."

Ira Haenigson suppressed an unbelieving smile. "I just made sure that Morton Miles was stiff and left. Frankly, I don't believe in getting down on all fours and looking for cigarette ashes and hair strands. I just get in the way of my men. Besides, it's easier to read reports than help make them."

"I'm lazy too," replied Cellini. "I'm also sleepy. Suppose you start asking."

Haenigson thoughtfully tapped the glass against the edge of his teeth, then asked: "What were you doing at Miles' house?"

"Well, I handle a fighter called Duck-Eye Ryan."

"Sure."

"Don't you believe me?" asked Cellini.

"Of course. It's natural for a private op to handle a prize-fighter. I once trained fleas. Go on."

"Well, that's the way it is. Morton Miles ran the boxing game out here so I went around to his house to see if he'd book my boy on a card tomorrow night. When I got to his house the door was ajar so I went in and found the body. Then I went back to my office and phoned you people."

Haenigson beamed brightly. "That sounds like a nice, straightforward account. I don't think there'll be much trouble with it. Do you know who killed Morton Miles?"

"No."

"We'll put it this way. Do you suspect who killed Miles?"

"No."

"Sure," said Ira Haenigson. "The doc made a rough, offhand guess and said that Morton Miles was fogged about ten fifteen to eleven. Now just to get the records in order, where were you at that time, Mr. Smith?"

"I took in the ten-to-eleven show at the Translux. The cashier will remember my name because I lost a few dollars while I was inside. When it was over, I went to the Hangover, met Duck-Eye Ryan, and then went out to Morton Miles' house."

IRA HAENIGSON PULLED at the lobe of one ear and looked at Cellini Smith dubiously. Very seriously, he said: "That sort of alibi is a good idea. They give no ticket stubs there and so many people pass through the turnstile you could show the cashier anybody and she'd say he was a patron."

"That's right."

"That's almost as good as the January second alibis. You probably know that every mug we pick up the day after New Year's claims he was out watching the Pasadena Rose Parade. And it can't be checked. Many thousands go."

"I'm glad you like it."

"Of course," continued the Homicide man with professional detachment, "the flaw in your Translux alibi lies in its very self. By the same token you can't prove that you *were* there even if we can't prove that you weren't."

The telephone rang. Haenigson was closer to it. He raised a polite hand, blandly said, "I'll take it," and picked up the receiver. He listened for a few moments and hung up. "That was Mr. Lucca," he informed Cellini confidentially. "Joe Lucca says that the Blue Chip alibi is O.K. He finally got in touch with Nate."

Cellini said nothing but eyed Haenigson with frank dislike. He threw back the bed covers, went over to the end-table, poured himself four fingers of scotch, and, glass in hand, returned to the bed.

"Now you have no worries at all," Haenigson said, "because this alibi will stand up much better than the Translux."

Cellini drank the liquor and kept his silence.

Suddenly Haenigson laughed. "Forgive me if I call you a sap, Mr. Smith, but *I* wouldn't play patsy for any twist. I wouldn't care *who* she was."

Cellini spoke carefully. "What are you talking about?"

"About Miss Nina Saunders of course. Granted she's a beautiful woman and you like her but still you should have told us you were out with her since—"

"So that's how it is," interrupted Cellini. "You tap the wires in this town."

Ira Haenigson nodded. "After a phone call about a murder such as you gave us? Of course we keep tabs on that wire. It's an automatic rule."

"I'll remember that one."

"I like you," Haenigson said unexpectedly. "Are you sure you don't want to tell me anything else about Morton Miles?"

"Uh-huh. I'm sure."

"How is it you know a gangster like Lucca well enough for him to take care of you, Mr. Smith?"

Cellini said: "I used to work for Tony Moro back in New York."

"Slot machines?"

"That's the one. He was chopped down by the cops one day so I tied up with the Sampsel outfit and they sent me out here. A couple of my friends gave me letters to some of the boys. One of the letters was to Joe."

Haenigson shook his head disapprovingly. "A letter of recommendation from one gangster to another. A fine thing. Well, I imagine it's a help though."

"Far from it," snapped Cellini with a sudden bitterness. "The peepers like Ned Lyams—and all the other operatives in this town—won't have anything to do with me. The boys down on Spring Street all know I was tied up with Tony Moro and because of that they think I can get them off whenever they plug somebody. For the same reason I never get a break from you people. The shams that know me think I've got the yellow pazooza. It's getting hard to pay the bills."

"Well, I'm sure you'll get along out here, Mr. Smith, though you have a lot of things to learn. Yes sir, I like you."

Cellini said: "You've got a nice line."

"What do you mean?"

"Being so damned sympathetic about my troubles."

Haenigson beamed delightedly. "You have caught on! Well, I find it usually works." He pointed to the wall-exerciser. "That thing any good?"

"I don't know. I've never tried it," said Cellini truthfully.

The Homicide man patted his midriff. "I guess I could use one. Bella—my wife—says I'm obese."

Cellini asked impatiently: "How do you size it up?"

HAENIGSON THOUGHTFULLY WORKED his chin with his fingers. "It's hard to say just yet till I get complete reports. It doesn't look like robbery though. The papers'll probably call it a revenge slaying. Morton Miles had a gun at his side with one shell missing. He must have shot it out with the murderer."

"Will you want to see me at Miles' house in the morning?"

"Oh, I wouldn't mind," said Ira Haenigson, "but I don't think you'll have the time to get there."

"Why?" asked Cellini.

"Because you'll be explaining things in the D.A.'s office," confided the Homicide man. "You'll be saying why your operative's license shouldn't be revoked. You might even be in jail."

"You don't say."

"Now it's nothing to get excited about, Mr. Smith. As I told you, I like you. I suppose you'll be able to explain things easy enough and keep your license. Just keep cool. That's all I ask."

Cellini said: "I'm keeping cool. Why will I have to explain things?"

"Because you acted very suspiciously."

"Come again?"

"Now I wouldn't pay much attention to it normally," soothed Ira Haenigson, "but this is a murder case. Look at it this way. You find someone murdered and instead of calling the police immediately you don't do so till you're in your office at least a half-hour later. That adds up to only one thing for me. You were fooling around to see what you could get out of it. You were first trying to see if you could promote any business for yourself and that should be sufficient cause to get your license revoked."

Cellini said: "I didn't."

Haenigson rose, went to the improvised bar, replenished his glass, and returned to his chair. He said: "You certainly did. You had enough time to go next door and start asking questions but not to call us. You wasted so much time that it might make the difference between us getting the murderer or not."

An unfriendly smile played over Cellini's face. He said:

"Suppose I'd thought I could catch the murderer. Would that have given me sufficient cause not to waste time phoning the police?"

"Maybe," said the Homicide man warily.

"Well, that's what happened. As soon as I saw the body I remembered that I had seen a maroon De Soto coupé pull away from in front of Miles' house just as I arrived. So I ran next door and asked if the car had been visiting there. They said no and I went cruising down the boulevard looking for the De Soto but I couldn't see it. By that time I was near my office so I went up there and phoned you."

Haenigson bent over, grabbed Cellini's hand, and pumped it. "By God, sir, I said you'd get along in this town. You certainly make sure of yourself before you step out of line! You and I both know you were trying to cook up a client but you've also got explanations ready."

Cellini Smith grinned. "I'll bet you say that to all the detectives."

"Of course," continued Haenigson, "you had time to drop over to the Hangover to find out who had phoned Miles. Do you think Jesse Lee Ward owns that DeSoto?"

"You get around quick," said Cellini with honest admiration. "But I don't know about Ward. Did Miles have any servants?"

"Give us a break, Mr. Smith. You must be one of these dynamic operatives. We found the body only a couple of hours ago."

Cellini yawned noisily.

"O.K. O.K.," said Ira Haenigson. "You don't have to do that. I'm going." He gave one of his beaming smiles. "I look forward to seeing you again. I wouldn't miss cultivating our acquaintance for any money."

"Thanks."

Haenigson set his glass on the floor and moved for the door. "Incidentally, I also have a Launcelot complex. I'll leave your Miss Nina Saunders alone—for the present." He opened the door. "Well I'm certainly glad we won't have to revoke your license. I hope you're not mixed up in the killing."

Cellini said: "You're a liar."

The Homicide man shook his head sadly and left.

CELLINI SMITH LAY in bed for a long time, smoking and blowing rings at the ceiling. Then, suddenly, he threw the bed covers back. He dressed hastily, slipping trousers over pajamas. He went outside, started the car, and drove to the nearest all-night drug store. He searched in a telephone directory, found his number, and dialed. After a few rings he heard a response.

"Mr. Ward?" asked Cellini.

"Yes," said Jesse Lee Ward.

Cellini said: "I'll make it short and sweet. My name is Cellini Smith. I'm a private operative. I went to Morton Miles' house this evening and—"

"Where are you calling from?" interrupted Jesse Ward.

"Oh," said Cellini, "you know that habit, too? Well don't worry. This is an outside phone."

"Go on."

"I found Morton Miles dead." Cellini waited for a reaction from Ward. There was none forthcoming. "Then I found out that you were looking for Miles this evening. The shams know it too."

"What do you want from me?" Ward's voice was cold.

Cellini said: "I suspect you're in the soup, Mr. Ward, and that you'll need an operative. Since I happened to get in on this at the beginning, why don't you hire me to protect your interests?"

Jesse Lee Ward carefully said, "If you start fooling around with me, Smith, you'll be the sorriest man that ever lived," and quietly rang off.

4

The Terrible Turk

CELLINI SMITH AROSE at eight, showered, and donned a sedate, double-breasted Oxford gray which represented fifty percent of his wardrobe. Duck-Eye Ryan, who overflowed the army cot, heard his movements and with a sudden burst of energy changed over to the bed. There was a grunt of contentment followed shortly by explosive spasms of snoring.

Cellini went out to his roadster, parked overnight on the street, and drove to a nearby drug store. Over orange juice and coffee he read a newspaper.

Morton Miles had made page one. Sandwiched between another bombing of Paris and the record handle at Santa Anita was the news that Morton Miles, prominent fight booker, night-club owner, and one-time world's boxing champion, had been murdered during the night. He was, the paper said, probably killed by some marauder and the police predicted an early arrest. There followed a mass of misinformation concerning the murder and Cellini noted with satisfaction that his discovery of the body had not been revealed to the press. He paid his check, went out to the car, and headed for the Professional Building.

As Cellini parked his car he paused to observe the commotion in front of the Hangover. A half-dozen reporters huddled together in conference on the sidewalk. A score of morons, attracted by the news of Miles' death, awaited developments. A press photographer took shots of the club's exterior. The reporters were apparently considering methods to get by the two pugs stationed at the door to keep them out. Cellini crossed the street, nodded to the guards, and entered the Hangover.

By now the news of Miles' death had reached his family of fighters to the last man and they gathered from all quarters of the city to mourn. Rarely abroad till late afternoon, now in the early morning they glumly crowded the bar in the chilly, unlit interior.

Cellini found an empty stool at one end of the bar and sat down. Silently, automatically, the red-eyed bartender set a pony of whiskey in front of him.

An old-time boxer called Denver Ed raised his glass and said: "To Morton Miles. He ain't comin' up for the next round."

Cellini glanced at the clock over the bar, shuddered, but politely sipped his drink.

"Yeah," muttered another. "The Great Timekeeper give him the bell."

"He turn in the towel," Amened the Sioux City Slasher.

Kate Kelly's chins dropped over the bar and heavy sobs shook her body. Strands of her hair swam in the alcohol drippings and the inspiring bosom chugged like an outboard motor. "He was a man," she moaned. "My man. There ain't none like him made anymore."

"Easy does it, Kate," said one of them.

She sobbed. "I'm gonna keep his memory green so long as I live. And all on accounta that Turk. That stinkin' Turk! He killed him! I know he killed him! Oh that stinkin' Turk!" she bleated.

They felt that embarrassment before unrestrained grief characteristic of men who use their fists more readily than their brains. The bartender refilled the glasses.

A promising welter called Tim Moore suddenly leaped to his feet and gave voice to their brooding thought. "Well what are we waitin' for? Christmas? If the Turk did it, we know how to take care of him."

There was an ominous murmur of assent.

Sharply but kindly, the Sioux City Slasher said: "Hold it! Let's be sure about the Turk before we get hyped up. We got to take it easy and figure."

The murmur subsided. They drank and figured. One of the fighters said that Morton Miles was watching them from heaven and demanding revenge. They all drank again and the bartender refilled the row of empty glasses.

Hump was next to speak. "The Slasher's right. Let's go easy or we'll get winded. I think the Turk did it, too, but I want to be sure." The little hunchback paused impressively, then suddenly stabbed a finger at Cellini Smith. "First, let's ask *him* a couple things. Like what he did after I gave him Miles' address last night and why he come back and asked me who phoned Miles."

Glinting, merciless eyes bored into Cellini. He said smoothly: "That's just what I came here to explain, boys. I knew you'd want to know exactly what happened." He then proceeded to detail his discovery of the body as he had related it to Detective-sergeant Ira Haenigson.

HE SPOKE SYMPATHETICALLY and persuasively and slowly the suspicion faded. They returned to their drinks and their already apocryphal memories of Morton Miles' great fistic prowess and kind heart. Jo-Jo, with a batch of newspapers under his arm, had come in while Cellini still spoke. He now said: "Smith's O.K., guys. He was one of Tony Moro's boys."

The others, somewhat maudlin from drink, agreed with Jo-Jo and added that it was too bad that a nice guy like Smith was a dick. A new flood of torrential weeping engulfed Kate Kelly and she staunched it with bourbon. Hump turned to Cellini again. "Why were you so interested to ask me who called Miles last night?"

Cellini replied: "After I found Miles dead I naturally wondered who had been so interested in seeing him. So at least we know Jesse Lee Ward wanted to see him and—" At mention of Jesse Ward's name, the faces froze on him. Ward, Cellini perceived, was one of them and he instantly tacked. "—and that might be a break because he may be able to help us."

"Of course he'd help us," a pug said.

Kate Kelly wailed: "Oh that stinkin' Turk!"

Tim Moore brought his fist down on the bar and upset several glasses. "Well, let's get the lead out of our pants. If it's the Turk why don't we do something?"

"That stinkin' Turk! He hated my man's guts."

Again they toasted Morton Miles and then looked to the Slasher as their natural leader. The master of ceremonies pondered and said: "I figure it this way. Instead of sittin' around and shootin' the bull why don't we first see the Turk and put it to him straight—"

It was action he proposed. They chorused approval.

"—and ask him a couple of questions. Then we'll see. So supposing me and Denver go, and we'll take Mike because he's got the gift of gab."

A derelict of a man, who had the shot, sandpaper voice of the discarded fight announcer, reluctantly pulled the whiskey glass away from his mouth and said: "Gladly, gentlemen, but what you require is not an aptitude for grammar but the logic of fists."

"Sure, sure," said the Slasher vaguely, "you're right, Then maybe we ought to take Smith because he knows about this kind of thing."

Cellini felt tremendous relief as he saw the possibility of a client, but he said casually: "Sure. I'd like to help you boys. I guess I can take off a couple of hours."

Denver Ed said mockingly: "Don't try to kid us, Smith. You ain't got any business. You could take off a couple a years and not miss it."

Cellini didn't trust himself to reply. Without further talk, the Slasher, Denver Ed, and he, rose and walked out on the gratuitous admonitions regarding the Turk's treacherous nature.

Outside, the riled reporters nailed them. The Slasher started conciliating. A fighter, he remembered, was as good as his Press. He apologized for barring them, their grief was sacred-like, he couldn't give them a handout because he knew nothing himself, but he was sure that the death of Morton Miles was a disaster to the community. That they could quote.

They piled into a large touring sedan standing in the no-parking zone, Cellini and the Slasher in front, Denver Ed in back, and moved off.

THEY REMAINED SILENT as the Sioux City Slasher took Sunset at sixty. Cellini glanced at the steering post where, as required by the law, the owner's registration card was fastened. He could read the name—*Earl Nikken*. He gave a start as he remembered the sad-faced man who sat nightly with that stunning brunette at the same table in the Hangover. He asked: "How come this bus is owned by Earl Nikken? I didn't know he was tied up with you boys."

"Smith, there's a helluva lot you don't know," was Denver Ed's measured reply from the back.

Cellini shrugged, lit a cigarette, and settled back into the mohair until presently they sighted the distended building that housed the Turk's bowling alleys. The Slasher pulled into the curb. A huge, three-faced sign that could be seen for blocks, announced simply—*The Terrible Turk*. Under it was the information that there were twenty-eight bowling alleys, forty billiard tables, and unlimited cocktails at the bar.

The three men left the sedan and entered. Barely eleven in the morning, the alleys and tables in the rear were unoccupied. To their right was the cashier's desk, to their left a lunch counter that joined with the ornate bar. A Filipino was mopping the tile floor.

Led by the Slasher, they rounded the end of the bar and, without knocking, pushed through a small door.

They found themselves in the Turk's combination office and living quarters. In place of chairs the floor was littered with damask-sheathed pillows of offensively matched colors. The Grand Rapids ottoman was narrow and uncomfortable and the goatskin draped over the floor safe was not, as the Turk imagined, from the hills of Anatolia. Stars, crescents, and scimitars scintillated on the walls to hurt the eyes. To assault the nose, the Turk kept a shelf full of madder, mother-of-pearl, valonia, coffee, and sponges sick with mildew. It was a burlesque producer's conception of a Turkish harem and handed Cellini his first real laugh in weeks. It was a pity he couldn't accept it.

There were three men in the room, of whom the Turk was easily the most arresting. He was seated cross-legged on a mammoth sofa pillow and sucked on a Turkish water pipe. When standing he achieved nearly eight inches over six feet—but he usually squatted on his pillows. A masterly politician, the overlords of wrestling had allowed him to keep the heavyweight title into his late forties. But he was still stringy and powerful. His mouse-gray hair was sparse and his face a testing ground for ambitious sportswriters who used it to try new adjectives. At various times in his career they had called him Spawn of Frankenstein, the Gruesome Monk, and Nature's Mistake but, best of all, he liked the Terrible Turk. He liked it so well he threw himself into it—water pipes and all. For a while, he even tried a harem but discovered that he wasn't quite terrible enough to manage four women at the same time. But taking it burlesque and all, one thing was certain—the Turk was nobody's fool.

The Terrible Turk said: "I'm glad you come. Sit down." He didn't bother to introduce his two companions. They were Ned Lyams, the affluent detective, who was sprawled over some pillows and a wrestler called the Siberian Adonis who did his bag of tricks in the hundred-seventy-five-pound class.

Cellini hastily made for the ottoman and Denver Ed and the Slasher were stuck with the ubiquitous pillows.

"I heard the news," continued the Turk, "that Morton took his last fall. It's tough. He was a swell guy."

Cellini repressed a smile with difficulty. He remembered the many stories, some true, some false, of the lifelong enmity between them in Cleveland, New York, Philadelphia, and latterly Los Angeles—of those reconciliations which were terminated with a doublecross by one or the other—of the struggles of each to dominate the professional sporting world—of the contempt in which all fighters and wrestlers hold each other.

Denver Ed may have been thinking something of the same, for he said: "We'll bury our own dead, Turk. We're here to find out who killed him. Maybe you know."

The Siberian Adonis gave a grunt and moved in closer. The Slasher waved him back with a contemptuous gesture. "Now don't start thinking you're good. Any time a wrestler thinks he can beat a fighter, I'll be there to show he stinks."

"This ain't no time for fighting," said the Turk sharply.

"Then tell that toe-holder not to get tough," snapped the Slasher.

The Turk raised a restraining hand. "Hold it! I want just as much as you to find out who fogged Morton Miles."

Denver Ed spat out a four-letter word.

THE TURK'S COLORLESS eyes narrowed and he drew on the tubing. The water in the bowl gurgled. "Sure I want to find out," he said deliberately, "because I know that if I don't your outfit'll think I did it and it'll be curtains for me."

"You called it," the Slasher observed blandly.

"I also know you got a lot of argument on your side. You remember that for fifteen years me and Morton put the double-O on each other, you remember the time he shoved a ringer on me in a tank town, and you remember the time he kidnaped a boxing commissioner because I got the guy to ban his fight. You remember a lot of things like that but we always made up and we were really friends. I'd say it in front of him if God let him out long enough."

Denver Ed gave a short, barking laugh.

"So what?" asked the Slasher.

"This much," said the Turk. "In all the rookings me and Morton did we never killed each other so why should we start now? Now, when we both were making out O.K.? If I never killed him before, why should I kill him now? Tell me."

Denver Ed and the Slasher shrugged a grudging acknowledgement of the argument. As Cellini lolled on the ottoman he seemed bored but he was listening intently. And wondering why they had come in a sedan owned by Earl Nikken.

The Terrible Turk drove home the clincher. "On top of that, me and Morton buried the hatchet a few weeks ago. Look!" He displayed the pair of golden gloves dangling from his lapel. "Maybe you don't know, but he gave me that when we made up and I give him a small scimitar made out of Damascus steel. Kill him? I'm doin' all I can right now to find out who did."

"Maybe," remarked the Sioux City Slasher less belligerently.

"Look," said the Turk with vast patience, "you could take my word for it I was right here all the time the papers say Morton was plugged. Hell, we been gettin' together in business lately. Poor Morton. He thought we'd make a lot of dough shipping scrap iron. But he don't need dough any more. You know as good as I do we had this business deal."

Denver Ed nodded and the Slasher said: "Yeah, I know."

The Turk made a final gurgle in the bowl and put it aside. "Then why don't we get together and find out who did it instead of fighting each other?" He extended a hand.

The Slasher hesitated perceptibly, then shook hands with the Turk. "O.K. I think you're dealing it from the top—for a change."

"Fine," said the ex-wrestler. "Now, before we go on, how about some fine coffee? I get it sent to me direct from Ankara. That's in Turkey."

They didn't want coffee direct from Ankara.

Cellini stirred and caught the Slasher's eye. The Slasher nodded permission and Cellini said to the Turk: "Maybe Ned Lyams there will think I'm letting out a trade secret but I happen to know that he's been doing a lot of gumshoe work on Morton Miles for you the last couple of weeks. How come you were checking on Miles if you two were supposed to be such great friends?"

"Who's he?" asked the Turk harshly.

Ned Lyams spoke. Still in his early thirties, he was head of the most important detective agency in Los Angeles. His was the carefree, grand manner of the successful. He liked money, women who liked money, and liquor. He said contemptuously: "That's a two-bit operative, Turk. His name's Cellini Smith. He blew into town a few weeks ago and he's been trying to chisel coffee and doughnuts ever since."

Cellini's face clouded and his lips twisted into a joyless smile. He flexed his fingers tentatively and stood up.

Irritably, the Turk said: "Oh for Chrissakes, don't let's start it again. If you two want to beat up do it some place outside. We're trying to get together here. We got work to do."

The Slasher nodded agreement. "Yeah. Morton Miles is still dead." He waved Cellini back. "You, Smith, sit down and you, Turk, answer the question. Smith said you been, putting a peeper on Morton Miles. How come if you were such great friends?"

The Terrible Turk stalled a moment before replying. "Slasher, me and Morton Miles knew each other a long way back—at a time when you didn't know what gin or women smelled like. And all the years we'd fight and then make up. Sometimes he'd come to me with a gilt-edge proposition and sometimes I'd go to him with one. If we watched careful we both made cabbage out of the deal but usually we'd try and rook each other. So a few months ago I buried the hatchet with Morton. Then a little later he comes to me with a proposition. He tells me he ain't got the sugar to swing it and I should put it up."

"We know all that," said Denver Ed impatiently.

"The Slasher asked. I'm answerin'."

"Go ahead," said the Slasher.

"The proposition," continued the Turk, "was to buy up a lot of scrap iron and ship it to Japan. With the war it's twice as valuable like before. So Morton shows me a lot of figures that this Jesse Lee Ward, this friend of his drew up and a contract with a Jap outfit. It looked solid like Man Mountain Dean and I agreed to back the proposition after my men checked with this Ward. Then, like you know, a bunch of lousy Chinamen and unions stopped the ship from sailing and I lost all the dough. It wasn't penny ante stuff so I got Ned Lyams here to check if Morton was dealing from a cold deck. Do you blame me for checking?"

"And what did Lyams find out?"

"Nothin'. Strictly nothin'. It ain't important now, anyways. When I found poor Morton got his I called in Lyams again and I was just telling him to get me the man who did it. He's the best peeper in the city and if anyone can do it he will."

The Slasher stood up. "O.K."

"Don't you want to talk it over with Lyams?" asked the Turk.

"We don't need you, Turk. Something stinks. We'll get our own peeper to find out what it is."

"Sure, sure," said the Turk placatingly. "And when you pick one I'll send Ned Lyams over to cooperate the fullest."

The Slasher walked out. Denver Ed and Cellini followed. They went out to the sedan with Earl Nikken's registration card and rode to the Hangover in a silence that would have been complete without Denver Ed's repetition of his favorite four-letter word.

5

Cellini Gets a Client

THE REPORTERS WERE gone and traffic on the sidewalk in front of the Hangover was normal. Inside, the bruisers still cluttered the bar mournfully and discussed the tragedy in subdued tones. The buxom Kate Kelly slumped over a table in an alcho-nostalgic stupor.

The Sioux City Slasher said, "You wait here," to Cellini and he and Denver Ed went back to the bar to face the fusillade of questions.

Cellini docilely sat down at one of the tables and thought of what the Turk had told them. In all fairness, he decided, there was a reasonable possibility that the wrestler spoke the truth. After a while, Mike wandered over. The washed-up announcer pointed a tobacco-stained finger toward the bar and in his shadow-voice said: "They're discussing you, Cellini. They're debating whether or not they ought to hire your detecting services."

"I know."

"I told them I thought you had the minimum of brains required to ferret out the murderer."

"Thanks. Mike, the Turk said that Morton Miles didn't have any money when he got bumped."

"That's quite correct. Pugilists shouldn't try to outguess the stock market."

"How's that possible?" insisted Cellini.

"Well, he did have some," admitted Mike. "As this is between us, a man who engaged in as many shady rackets as Miles had to have *some* money. That is, it was money in my sense of the word—a few thousand dollars perhaps—but according to his definition he was stone broke."

"But he owned this night club, Mike. It's a gold mine."

"He never owned the Hangover, Cellini. He didn't have the money to open it. He just came in for a share of the profits for being the nominal owner and glad-hand artist for the tourists."

"That's a new one. Then who does own it?"

"Earl Nikken. He owns the Hangover."

"Ah." Cellini said, "Ah," again and stared contentedly at the ceiling. Small wonder that Earl Nikken owned that sedan and little mystery in his nightly presence at the same table. If Nikken knew Morton Miles well enough to back his business ventures he might also know some interesting things about him. Now, dreamed Cellini, if he could only manage to get the damned job of finding who had consigned Morton Miles to the worms.

"You seem surprised," remarked the announcer.

"Just astonished. Where did Earl Nikken get his dough?"

Mike hesitated. "I'd rather not say. You know how it is. These bruisers regard it as a secret and I'd never be able to cadge another drink if they thought I—"

"Forget it. Could you tell me what this scrap-iron business between Miles and the Turk was about?"

"That I could. As you may know, the Japanese are engaged in saving the Chinese from the horrors of self-government. In that process they require a good deal of scrap iron and Morton Miles with Jesse Lee Ward managed to snag an order from a Japanese firm for a large amount of this iron. To finance the purchase and the delivery of the scrap a great deal of money was needed and the Turk agreed to put it up. Which is about all, excepting that I might add that the patient died. The scrap never left San Pedro harbor and the Turk lost a lot of money."

"I gathered that," said Cellini, "but if Earl Nikken financed Miles' opening of the Hangover why didn't he also back his excursion into scrap iron?"

"I wouldn't know about that," said Mike noncommittally. "Here comes your news."

THE SLASHER, WITH several pugs in his wake, approached the table. "We decided," he said. "We decided to make you our peeper on this thing. Some of the boys think you want to know a little too much but you were with Tony Moro so we know you're O.K., Smith."

Cellini stood up. "Fine. What are your instructions?"

"No instructions."

Jo-Jo entered and cast about the club, then called to Cellini: "There's a sham outside, Smith. He says for me to tell you he wants to see you."

"Thanks," said Cellini. "I'll be right out." He turned back to the Slasher. "That's another angle. What about the cops?"

The Slasher picked a hundred-dollar bill from his wallet and handed it to Cellini. "There's nine more of those coming to you if you turn the trick. And what do you want to know about the cops?"

"They may have their own ideas about the murderer," said Cellini.

"The cops ain't done nothing yet," replied the Slasher, "and we don't want them to. They work hard," he said with heavy sarcasm, "and they got long hours so we don't want to bother them. We'll take good care of Morton Miles' killer ourselves—you just find him."

THE POLICEMAN CELLINI Smith found waiting outside the Professional Building was a porcine rookie named Boggs. He described himself as Ira Haenigson's assistant, ushered Cellini into a waiting prowl car, and they drove off.

Fifteen minutes later they stopped at the late Morton Miles' duplex. Two department cars were parked in front and a patrolman was stationed at the door. They passed into the living-room and Detective-sergeant Ira Haenigson came over, took Cellini by the arm, and politely introduced him to the other two men in the room.

The medium-sized man was Max Cushman, one of the better-publicized lawyers in the city. He was near fifty and a nervous breakdown. His speech was rapid and offensively barbed. He had a reputation for carping honesty. He represented Jesse Lee Ward, the other man in the room. Ward was fortyish, well-fed, beautifully dressed, and consciously handsome with a thin, blond mustache. He sat in an overstuffed and looked mighty worried.

When the grunted introductions were over, Haenigson said: "I'm glad to see you, Smith. How are you?"

Cellini told him that he was just fine.

Haenigson was pleased. He explained that he was seeing people here because they were still going over the house for prints and what-all.

Max Cushman interrupted irritably: "All right. Now that Mr. Balzac Jones understands, let's get on."

"It's Cellini Smith," said Cellini Smith through thinned lips.

Haenigson patted Cellini's shoulders. "No matter. Suppose you give Boggs a whirl. He's learning the art of dactylography. We're trying to identify the prints we picked up here."

Cellini followed the rookie to a desk where the inked pad and paper waited. He pressed his fingers on the pad and planted a set of prints on the sheet. He wiped his hands on a tea towel and sank into a leather club chair.

"As I see it," said Max Cushman to Haenigson, "you want to find out where Jesse Ward was yesterday evening. Right? We've been here for a half-hour and you still haven't asked him so let's cut out the red tape and start from there."

Ward smiled wanly. "Better let the inspector handle it his own way, Max."

Haenigson said: "Now, now, Mr. Ward, your attorney knows your rights."

"I haven't any time to waste," snapped the lawyer. "If you don't need me here, say so. If you do, let's get ahead."

Ward sighed. "Sometimes I wonder if Max is in my corner or the opposite. As for my story, it's simple and straight. Morton Miles and I were very good friends. Everyone knows that."

"Know him long?" asked Haenigson.

"Many years. Believe me when I say that we were the strongest of friends." His voice broke and he made a pretext of clearing his throat before continuing. "Morton came out here from the East and I followed him a couple of years later. The market had taken him for a ride so we hunted up a backer and I opened the Hang-over. Things were going well and about a month ago I took a vacation in Palm Springs. Yesterday afternoon Morton phoned me there and told me to come right back because a business problem had come up. I arrived in town around ten and drove to my apartment. I phoned the Hangover—about ten fifteen, I suppose—but Morton had gone for the night so I went to bed without leaving the apartment." He smiled bleakly. "That's my alibi."

"Well," said Max Cushman, "that's settled. I can get back to my office now and you, Jesse, you don't seem very anxious to get out of here. I thought you were going to get married this afternoon."

THE HOMICIDE MAN took time off to deliver congratulations and several bromides on the theme of wedded bliss. Ward thanked him and disclosed that the girl's name was Olive Fain, that she was beautiful, and that he'd known her a long time. Cellini stopped admiring Ward's robin-egg-blue tie and thought of an embarrassing question to ask him at the opportune moment.

"Well," the lawyer finally asked, "will that be all, Inspector?"

"I like being called 'Inspector'," the Detective-sergeant said. "It makes me feel like Scotland Yard. We'll be through in a minute. Mr. Ward, you mentioned a business problem that had come up. What was it?"

Jesse Lee Ward seemed to welcome the question. "Well, we were having some dealings with that wrestler who owns the bowling center—the Terrible Turk." His voice hardened with the evident hatred he felt for the wrestler. "There's the man you should be questioning at this moment."

"I will," said Ira Haenigson mildly. "Thanks for the tip. And the business?"

"The three of us got together—"

"Us who?" put in Haenigson.

"Morton Miles, the Turk, and myself," replied Jesse Ward. "The idea was to buy scrap iron cheaply here, ship it to Japan, and sell it at a big profit. Morton and I had the contacts and the Turk put up the money. It was a legitimate proposition."

"Except that it didn't work, I bet," murmured Haenigson.

"No it didn't," allowed Ward. "The contract with the Seiicha Sawamura Export Company called for delivery by a certain date. And we couldn't deliver. We were stuck with a lot of scrap iron on hand and our dough was gone."

"Why?" It came from Cellini Smith.

The lawyer gazed in Cellini's general direction. "May I ask what authority Mr. Smith has to question my client? He represents nobody and I see no reason why Mr. Ward should be subjected to a quizzing by him."

"I guess that's so," conceded Ira Haenigson.

Cellini kept silent and thought of a second embarrassing question to ask Jesse Lee Ward. He wondered if the bruisers at the Hangover would believe him if he concluded that their good friend Jesse Ward was the murderer.

"And while we're on the subject," continued the attorney, "Mr. Smith phoned my client last night and offered his unsolicited services. I resent those ambulance-chasing methods and I resent the implication that my client needs a private detective."

"None of that is my business," said the Homicide man wearily, "but I think you're right in what you say. If you want Smith to leave—"

"A correction," interrupted Cellini. "Mr. Cushman was wrong when he said I represented nobody."

"No!" said Haenigson with admiration. "So you managed to chisel your way in. You're a good man, Smith. Who's your principal?"

"I'm responsible to the Sioux City Slasher, though I guess I'm working for all the pugs at the Hangover who were friends of Miles."

An involuntary sigh of relief escaped Jesse Ward. He gazed at Cellini piercingly and his handsome face gave a friendly smile. "Well, I guess that puts us on the same side of the fence, Smith."

"I guess so," said Cellini without too much conviction.

"I'm glad the boys hired you even if I wasn't consulted. That's the thing I want most right now—to find out who killed Morton Miles."

"Then you shouldn't mind answering a couple of questions."

Ward was instantly alert again. "There's nothing I know that could conceivably help you. You ought to be talking to the Turk. That's the only help I can give you. Besides, we don't want to take up the inspector's time here."

"I don't mind," said Haenigson graciously.

"Then we'll talk here," said Cellini. "I just want to clarify the situation. How do you expect me to work for you if I don't understand what it's all about?"

Jesse Ward capitulated. "Sure. Let's work together. What do you want to know?"

"What's the ship's name that was supposed to carry the scrap to Japan?"

"The *City of Kobe.*"

"Why didn't it sail?"

"Because the day she was supposed to leave, every Chink's

mother's son in the world went down to San Pedro to picket. It looked like Chinese dragon day. On top of that, the long-shoremen wouldn't load on final supplies and half the crew walked off. They kept that up for a few days and by that time it was too late for the ship to arrive in Japan in time to meet the contract date with the Sawamura outfit."

"Wasn't it insured?"

"We submitted it to Lloyd's but the rates were prohibitive."

Cellini nodded. "As I see it, you and Miles got the contract and figured things out and Miles approached the Turk on the proposition. Miles told him you two had an order from—what was that name?"

"Seiicha Sawamura Export Company."

"That's the one. Where are they?"

"Their United States branch is on South Hope Street."

"Then," said Cellini, "Miles told the Turk that this Jap concern had placed an order with him for scrap iron to be turned into bullets to civilize the Chinese. But since the Turk's not a complete idiot, Mr. Ward, he asked for proof of those statements before he financed the deal. What was that proof?"

Ward said: "The Turk was careful. He sent his accountant and attorney over to see me. It was all on the level. The Sawamura Corporation gave me and Morton a contract to deliver scrap to Japan by a certain date. But before we went ahead we saw to it that they put the money in escrow in the Seamen's National pending delivery of the consignment. It was to the tune of a hundred eighty thousand dollars and the Turk made sure it was there before he agreed to finance the purchase of scrap from the jobbers."

"I like this," grunted Ira Haenigson. "It saves me a lot of spade work."

"And how much money did the Turk put out to purchase the scrap iron?" asked Cellini.

"Seventy-eight thousand."

"Well over a hundred percent profit. Right?"

"Yes."

THERE WAS AN impressive silence that was broken by Max Cushman as he turned to the Homicide man. "I'm sure this can all be aired some other time, Inspector, so let's drop it. All you want to know is whether my client killed Miles."

"O.K., then. *Did* your client kill Morton Miles?"

"I don't know. Ask him." Ira Haenigson did.

Jesse Lee Ward said: "No." He lit a cigarette with steady hand and said, "No," again.

Cellini thought the time was ripe. "Just two more questions, Mr. Ward, and I'll sign off. Now, you said you cut your vacation short in Palm Springs because you got a phone call from Morton Miles who told you to return to Los Angeles. If that's so, why—"

"Hell," interrupted Haenigson in an aggrieved tone. "I caught that one too, Smith, so I deserve to ask it. The point is this, Mr. Ward. If your return to Los Angeles was accidental, as you seem to claim, how is it you're getting married this afternoon? Is this marriage of yours so unimportant that it depended on your haphazard return to town or did you know all along that you would return last night?"

Max Cushman suddenly stood up and looked at his watch. "Well, here's where we came in. Jesse, you've given your alibi so let's leave. For the present you're not answering questions."

"Sure, leave," urged Ira Haenigson blandly. "I can't force you to answer my questions. Go ahead—if you want to give the impression that you have something to hide. It'll look mighty bad when some ambitious deputy D.A. goes to work on you."

Jesse Ward hesitated. His blond, pencil mustache trembled. "It's nothing like that. I've nothing to hide. What do you want to know?"

Through clamped teeth the lawyer mumbled something that sounded like "You dumb oaf" and sat down again.

The Homicide man rephrased the question. "How is it you're being married this afternoon if you hadn't planned on being in town in the first place?"

"Well, Miss Fain and I had planned to marry as soon as I returned from Palm Springs. We'd been thinking of it for a long time. So when I knew I was coming back I phoned her and we decided to get married this afternoon."

"There," said Haenigson sympathetically. "I knew you had some such logical explanation."

Max Cushman grunted suspiciously but kept his angry silence.

Cellini said: "There's still my second question. If Mr. Cushman hadn't mentioned my phone call of last night I wouldn't have brought it up. Mr. Ward, when I phoned you last night why were you concerned where I was calling from—before I told you Miles was dead?"

There was a sharp reflex but Jesse Lee Ward was mute.

"I'll tell you why," continued Cellini. "Because you already knew Miles was dead and you were afraid I'd mix you up in it if my phone were tapped."

Ira Haenigson drawled: "Maybe I'll break this case sooner than I thought."

Jesse Ward whirled on Max Cushman. "You're a hell of a lawyer!" he shouted.

"That's what I am," flared Cushman. "I'm not a magician. You'd need another Houdini to make your alibi stand up. I told you to get out of here while the getting was good."

Ward muttered something low and vicious. Perspiration mixed with the barber's talcum on his forehead.

Haenigson took the lead again. "Smith saw a dark-red De Soto coupé leave here shortly after the murder. What kind of car do you own, Mr. Ward?"

Jesse Ward lit another cigarette. This time his fingers weren't steady.

"Come on. Tell me. I can check easy enough. You've probably got it outside right now."

"A maroon De Soto auxiliary coupé," said Ward heavily.

Max Cushman's voice sounded tired. "God, how dumb you are, Jesse. You should have been a congressman. Now that you've done enough damage I suppose you're ready to leave. Come on."

The affability in Haenigson vanished. His voice beat a merciless ratatat. "Ward, you were in Miles' house about the time of the murder. You knew he was dead. You probably returned from Palm Springs to kill him. Your return wasn't accidental because you knew all along you'd get married today. You knew Miles was dead when Smith called you last night, and he saw your car leave this house. You were not—" He stopped short. Jesse Lee Ward and his attorney were already out of the room.

The Homicide man smirked and turned to Cellini. "Well, Smith, do you think we can make a murder charge stick against him?"

"Of course we can make it stick," said Cellini. "But that won't necessarily mean that he did it."

"Let's not quibble, Smith. Let's not quibble."

6

Fujiyama Run-Around

CELLINI STOPPED AT Mario's on La Cienega for lunch. When he finally reached his office it was two in the afternoon. Duck-Eye Ryan sat on a chair rubbing the eye that was still blown up and gazing vacantly ahead of him with the other. "Nothing doing," he said in response to Cellini's query.

"No calls?"

"No. Oh, sure. Joe Lucca called. He called twice." The mound of swollen flesh was raw from rubbing.

"As a secretary your beauty is exceeded only by your efficiency," remarked Cellini. He dialed. "Hello. You've been calling me. What is it, Joe?"

At the other end, Joe Lucca said: "I don't think you should have asked me to do it without me knowing what it was for."

"What was for what?" parried Cellini.

"The Blue Chip alibi. I wouldn't have set it for you if I'd known it was for the Morton Miles killing."

"As it turned out I didn't need it, but it never entered my mind you'd be scared of the Hangover outfit."

"I'm not scared of anybody. I just like to keep my nose clean. That's how I get along in this town."

"Joe, do you know who killed Morton Miles?"

Joe Lucca laughed. Cellini asked the funniest things!

"There must be someone important mixed up in it for you to

steer clear of this mess, Joe. Is it the Turk? Is it Earl Nikken—the guy behind the Hangover? Who is Earl Nikken?"

The laughter continued.

Cellini said, "Take it easy," and dropped the receiver.

There was no mail, and he carried over on his pad the gymnasium reminder for the following day. Now that there was money coming in, he reflected a bit glumly, he really had to go to a gymnasium. Exercise was healthy.

"I talked to the boys," Duck-Eye Ryan said.

"Yes?" prompted Cellini.

"They told me the Turk fogged Mr. Miles."

"Maybe, Duck-Eye, but I saw the Turk this morning and I'm not so sure."

"You know the Turk?"

"Yes."

"That's swell."

"What's swell about it?"

"Well," said Duck-Eye Ryan hesitantly, "I been thinking maybe I should become a wrestler. You know how it is. When you begin to get on in years those twenty minute rests on your back begin to look good to a man."

"Forget all that penny-ante stuff, Duck-Eye. We're out of that class now." He took the hundred-dollar bill out of his pocket and flashed it for the benefit of his large companion. "See this C-note? It's a retainer to find out who put the slap on Miles. You'd need a half-dozen fights to clear this much."

"Jeez!"

Cellini carefully replaced the money, then handed Duck-Eye a ten-dollar bill. "Here. I want you to stock my apartment with this. Make it two scotch, some rye, and a bourbon if you have enough left. And if there's still something left, buy yourself some Sterno. But first go down to the Hangover and get Denver Ed to razor that eye. He knows how to do it. Then buy the shellac and come back here and watch the office."

DUCK-EYE STUMBLED OUT as the phone jingled. The caller was the pedigreed Nina Saunders. Cellini grimaced into the phone but said: "How's the Queen of Sheraton Manor?"

"What have you been doing, Cellini? I've been waiting to hear from you."

"What's the matter?" he asked. "Want your key back?"

"Cellini, let's not have another argument. I want to say how gallant it was of you."

"What was?"

"That you didn't embarrass me by mixing me up in that murder case."

"Oh," he said. "It was a cop with a Launcelot complex. Thank him."

"No, I know it was you, Cellini. You're just being sweet about it. It would have been horrible if my family had seen my name in the papers coupled with—"

"Me?"

Unexpectedly, Nina Saunders laughed. "I guess you're right. You're just a tramp, Cellini, but I like you. You're a type."

"Patronize me," he said dryly.

"Cellini, was it Morton Miles—the man you introduced to me? That old fighter?"

He could detect the subdued excitement in her voice. He

said, "You've talked enough to the lower classes for one call," and replaced the receiver.

He lit a cigarette and began to trace figures on the thin film of dust that covered his desk. He had nearly completed his bacterial conception of a scrap-iron ballet when Ned Lyams strode in.

The successful operative coolly examined the office. A faint, contemptuous smile appeared on his lips. "Not as pretty as yours, is it?" asked Cellini.

"It'll do for a start," was the reply. "Only a plump blond secretary missing. Nothing like a plump blond secretary to take your mind off women."

"How many have you got in your office?"

"Two. And a brunette to do the work." He sat in a chair facing Cellini and produced two fat Havanas. Cellini accepted one of them. "Too bad about the floor though," continued Ned Lyams. "It'll be hard to rip up."

"Yes," said Cellini.

"For God's sake ask me why."

"All right. Why?"

"Well, I want to bury the hatchet under it."

"I guessed all that when you came in so can the boyish charm."

"Good. Don't chew the end of that cigar off. It ruins it. Use this knife. I heard Miles' friends hired you so, like the Turk said, I'm here to cooperate." He waited to see if Cellini would speak, but had to continue. "I know what you're thinking of. You're thinking of a couple of months back when you opened this office and called on me and I'd have nothing to do with you, of the time I tried to get your license revoked because I said you were a New York torpedo—and a couple of other things." He paused to clip his cigar tip. He then inserted it carefully into a meerschaum holder and lit it. "But you can't blame me. There are too many dicks in this town already and when a nobody like you horns in with Duck-Eye Ryan—a hood from way back—what can you expect? The freeze, of course. But now it's different. You're in and I've got enough drag to see that all the other peepers work with you. So let's get together. The Turk told me to see you and that we must get Morton Miles' killer because he's scared the pugs'll gang up on him if we don't."

"That's not what I was thinking of," said Cellini.

"What then?"

"I was wondering how willing you'd be to cooperate with me if we found that the Turk killed Miles."

Ned Lyams's voice was suddenly hard and cold. "If I found that the Turk did it I'd sell him down the river so quick he'd catch pneumonia from the breeze."

Cellini pursed his lips and essayed a smoke ring. "O.K.," he finally said, "but remember this. I intend to make some sugar on this deal so don't try to put the double-O on me. Double-cross anybody you want—and I guess you're good at it—but not me. Lyams, remember that."

THEY SHOOK HANDS. "You won't be sorry," Lyams said. "I can do a lot for a new fellow trying to get along in this town. I got a job just this morning that I can turn over to you. A Mr. Weatherly wants to find out how his private phone numbers get on the sucker lists—"

"Forget it," said Cellini. "Who do you think did it?"

"I don't know."

"How about your client—the Terrible Turk?"

"Why should he?" asked Ned Lyams. "You've got to have motive for murder."

"He found out that the scrap-iron deal with Miles and Ward wasn't on the level and that peeved him because he dropped a big wad."

"But that's just what he didn't find out," said Ned Lyams. "The Turk hired me to work on that angle for two weeks before the murder and it all looked above-board."

"How do you know?"

"Well, I found out that the Seiicha Sawamura outfit really put the sugar in escrow with Seaman's National pending delivery of the scrap by a certain date. Then, while I didn't actually see the scrap, I know Morton Miles bought it with the money the Turk gave him because I saw the *City of Kobe* loaded down to the Plimsoll mark with cargo."

"Why didn't you see it?"

"The skipper wouldn't let me aboard."

"Maybe it was on the level," said Cellini slowly, "but if it wasn't, then the Turk had a swell motive for murder."

"It's possible," commented Ned Lyams. "Anyone else you can think of?"

"There's Jesse Lee Ward," said Cellini. "If he didn't kill Miles he was there shortly after the murder."

"That's something to follow up."

"The shams are whittling away on him but what you can do is send one of your men up to Palm Springs. Tell him to find out if Jesse Lee Ward had a phone call from Morton Miles before he left and also whether he made a long distance call to L.A. to somebody called Olive Fain."

"Check. I'll have the report by to-night. Who's Olive Fain?"

"Some twist that Ward is marrying this afternoon."

"Ward's a good bet. I'll check with the cops to see how they get along with him."

"Fine," said Cellini. "Do you know who owns the Hangover?"

"Earl Nikken, of course."

"Where'd he get the dough to back Morton Miles?"

"You don't know?" marveled Ned Lyams. "You, one of Tony Moro's boys?"

"I don't know."

"Do you remember the poultry racket in Chi during the twenties? Do you remember the guy who ran it? Do you remember Chicago Earl?"

Cellini blinked and gave a long, low whistle. He thought of that sad-faced, elderly man sitting at the table with that stunning brunette and whistled again. Chicago Earl had been the Capone of the poultry business.

"That's right," said Ned Lyams. "Chicago Earl is Earl Nikken. He's in real quiet retirement out here. In the first place he doesn't want to remind the government to start looking up his income-tax returns and, secondly, there're still a couple of old Chicago pals who'd like to find him—pals who were left holding the sack when he blew. If I were you I'd forget about him. He and Miles were old friends so you can chalk him off your suspect list."

"If they were such old friends," said Cellini, "why didn't Nikken put up the dough for the scrap iron? He must have loads of dough."

"Because—" began Ned Lyams.

Cellini finished it. "Because the deal wasn't on the level."

Lyams shrugged. "I'm young and healthy and I'm not going to start investigating Earl Nikken. I've got too many women dependent on me."

"All right. Let's break it up. I've got things to do."

"Where're you going?" asked Ned Lyams.

Cellini shook his head. "I don't expect much help or information from you, so don't expect too much from me."

Lyams shrugged, waved a good-bye, and left, closing the door behind him. Cellini pulled the phone over and dialed Joe Lucca's number. "Joe," he said, "I've got to bother you again. It's something I know but I've got to double-check. I have to be sure. Is Earl Nikken, Chicago Earl?"

Joe Lucca said: "Uh-huh."

Cellini cradled the receiver and called out: "That's all for the present, Lyams. You can go home now."

Only the faintest rustle beyond the door told Cellini that he had guessed right.

CELLINI CUT INTO the curb on South Hope Street in front of a squalid building and stopped the motor. He took the dirty, ill-lit flight of creaking steps, holding his breath. The dust he kicked up was choking. By the skylight above the second-floor landing he read the letters, *S. Sawamura Exp. Co., Inc.*, on the corrugated glass door. He rattled the knob. The door was locked and nothing stirred within. He scowled at the Yale night latch which disallowed keyhole peering. He left the building, picked up his roadster and headed north.

Ten minutes later he parked as near as he could to 1151 South Broadway, entered the building, and went up to the Japanese consulate.

A young, male secretary, who introduced himself as Masato Kazuichi, thrust a handsome travel brochure into Cellini's hand and flashed him the standardized toothy grin. "Concerning what may I help you, please?"

"I should like to have some information on scrap-iron exports to Japan."

The grin diminished perceptibly. Mr. Kazuichi said: "And the information, please?"

"To begin with," said Cellini, "I'd like to know exactly how much scrap iron the Seiicha Sawamura Export people manage to send to Japan over the period of a year."

The grin was now nowhere in evidence. "The Sawamura Export—they are a very fine people."

Cellini said: "Yes. What of it?"

Mr. Kazuichi said: "This is not my department. I am just a secretary. Could you wait a moment, please?"

Cellini sat down on a bench and studied the dozen different views of Fujiyama in the brochure. He discovered that there were over four hundred and fifty varieties of the cherry blossom. Fifteen minutes later another Japanese appeared from an inner office. He too had a travel folder in his hand and he introduced himself as Mr. Masunaga. He was not of the grinning variety.

Cellini showed his brochure. He said: "I've got one already. It's nice."

"Your name, address, occupation, please?" asked Mr. Masunaga.

Cellini supplied the information and added: "A man who was interested in scrap-iron exports was murdered and I'm investigating the case. That's all."

"Yes? Our purpose is to be of assistance."

"About this Sawamura Export Company. Who is this Mr. Sawamura to begin with?"

"A fine man," said Mr. Masunaga.

"Do you know him?"

"I can not say I do."

Cellini said: "That's reasonable. Do you know where this Mr. Sawamura lives? Can you give me his address?"

Mr. Masunaga said that he would look in the files and excused himself. He was away a half-hour. When he finally returned he said: "The best I could find out was that Mr. Sawamura went back to Japan some time ago. Anything else, please?"

"Plenty," replied Cellini. "For example, how much scrap iron is there exported to Japan each year?"

Mr. Masunaga's reply was considered. "I would not like to hazard a guess, sir. Those kind of statistics are handled at the Consul General's office."

"And where's the Consul General's office?" asked Cellini.

"In San Francisco."

Cellini took a deep breath and began again. "Is this Mr. Sawamura a Japanese or an American citizen?"

"I am not sure."

"I should think you could check easily enough."

"Well," said Mr. Masunaga hesitantly, "I think he is a Japanese citizen."

"Good. Did a man called Morton Miles ever have any business here?"

"I do not recollect the name. Please remember this is not a business concern. These are government offices."

"I know that. Who's in back of the Sawamura Company?

Who financed them? How long have they been in business? Exactly what is their business? Who do they buy scrap for or does the Japanese government just buy anything they can deliver there?"

Mr. Masunaga shrugged. "I am just one of the many government clerks here. I do not have the facts in hand. Perhaps one of our vice-consuls could help you—if you care to wait."

Cellini said: "I care to wait."

ANOTHER HALF-HOUR PASSED before Cellini was ushered into a delicately furnished office and introduced to a Mr. Hazama, one of the vice-consuls.

"Concerning what, please?" asked Mr. Hazama.

Cellini said: "Scrap iron. And I've got the description of Fujiyama already."

"Well," began the vice-consul, "the Consul General in San Fran—"

"I know," interrupted Cellini. "He's in San Francisco and I'm here. Can you tell me what the set-up of the Sawamura Export Company is?"

"Set-up, please?"

"What sort of organization?"

Mr. Hazama said: "Oh. I don't know much of them but I have heard they are a fine, solvent company."

"What else?"

"Have we your address?" asked the vice-consul. "Could we mail you the information?"

With surprising patience, Cellini said: "Yes, you have my address. Suppose I had an idea to export something like scrap iron to Japan. How would I go about doing it?"

The vice-consul suddenly threw his hands up with a show of annoyance. "But that was nothing to do with *me*. That stupid clerk! He should not have sent you to me. I am so sorry. All that is handled by our under-secretaries in the statistical department. I am so sorry."

Cellini said, "Not at all," and was shown out. An under-secretary approached him. It was Mr. Masato Kazuichi again. "Scrap iron," said Cellini through his teeth.

"But didn't we discuss that an hour ago?" asked Mr. Masato Kazuichi.

Cellini thrust the travel folder into his hand and said: "All right. Take back Fujiyama. I get it. It's the brush-off. Sorry I didn't recognize it before,"

He strode out as Mr. Kazuichi said: "Please be sure to drop in if we can ever be of assistance again."

Cellini wasn't angry as he drove for his office. He had hardly expected to get much information at the consulate. There were other sources, such as checking on the *City of Kobe* down at San Pedro harbor. Nor was he surprised that scrap iron was a delicate subject for investigation. Too many elements were interested in either shipping or sabotaging the shipments and now that a European war was in full swing it would be even more difficult to trace what was and what was not true. Yet, trace it he must if the Terrible Turk was to have a motive for murder. And the Turk had to be considered. Identification of Morton Miles' murderer from the facts at hand, he thought, would not be too difficult. It was pretty apparent and the problem now was to eliminate those other suspects and to check on a couple of the more interesting angles. One of these interesting angles was Earl Nikken—that gangster of another decade. Where did Chicago Earl stand and why had he not backed Morton Miles' venture into scrap? Also on the interesting side of the ledger was the question why Joe Lucca, after first setting an alibi, had shied away from the entire affair when he discovered it concerned Morton Miles. Had it been on Chicago Earl's account? Lucca and his followers were not the kind to shy away from anything. Only on the rarest of occasions did Joe Lucca consider discretion preferable to valor.

7

Chicago Earl

AS CELLINI SMITH reached his destination and put the car into the parking lot next to the Professional Building, he was accosted by a thin, worried little man with pallid skin stretched tight over the cheek bones.

Cellini regarded him fondly and said: "Hello, Gopher."

The Gopher flipped his hat with the jerky, scared movements typical of him and leaned against a lamp post for support. He had jake-leg from the denatured alcohol of prohibition days and he derived his name from the circumstance that he was a stir bug. "I heard you was out here," the Gopher croaked. "How you doing?"

"Lousy. And how are you getting along?" Cellini asked politely. "They picking you up much lately?"

The Gopher's face twisted with hatred. "I ain't important enough," he said. "And just because I ain't important enough the bulls pick me up when they catch me and beat me up on general principles."

"*Tch, tch,*" clucked Cellini sympathetically. "Just out of stir?"

The Gopher nodded. "Meat-ball rap. Eight months."

"You know your way around these parts," said Cellini, "so tell me if you've ever heard of Jesse Lee Ward."

The Gopher shook his head.

"How about Earl Nikken?"

"Jeez!" exclaimed the Gopher in his peculiar grating voice.

He pointed thumbs down. "Lay off. Don'tcha know who he used to be?"

"Sure. Chicago Earl. Now how about a woman named Olive Fain who's getting married this afternoon?"

The Gopher said slowly: "That frill ain't marrying nobody. Keep your mitts off her—she's dangerous."

"You're better than Winchell," commended Cellini. "Why do you think she won't get married?"

But the Gopher didn't hear the question. He was looking past Cellini's shoulders. "I'm dusting," he suddenly announced.

Cellini grabbed his arm. "What's the hurry?"

"I don't like the smell of peepers. You're the only one I talk to. I'm dusting."

"You'll dust in a minute. Why won't she marry?"

He squirmed in Cellini's grip. "I knew when to stop singing. I'm getting out of here now. Lemme go!"

Cellini released him and he hobbled off rapidly. Cellini turned to seek the cause of the Gopher's sudden fright. Twenty yards away a man idled conspicuously in a delicatessen doorway. He watched Cellini steadily, with no attempt at concealment.

Cellini walked toward him and the man backed off, keeping his distance. Cellini began running but the man sprinted ahead. Cellini stopped and the man likewise stopped—still twenty yards away. There was little likelihood of overhauling him. Cellini wondered how long he had been tailed. He regarded his shadow speculatively. The shadow childishly put thumb to nose and spread four fingers fanwise in Cellini's direction. Cellini's face became grim. He turned his back completely on his shadow and, with leisurely steps, strolled back toward the Hangover.

Jo-Jo was hawking his wares at his stand in front of the night club. Cellini took a paper, casually glanced at the headlines, and said: "I want you to do something."

"Yeah?" asked Jo-Jo.

"I've got a shadow. Five-six and your age. Sports a light gray kelly with brim down. Credit clothing with wasp waist."

Jo-Jo began waving his newspapers and bellowing, "Oh, get your paper here! Hitler threatens world! Read all abaht it," as he made a complete turn-about. Facing Cellini again, he asked: "Cigar?"

"That's the stoop."

"O.K. I got him tabbed."

"He interests me, Jo-Jo."

"Glad to do it."

CELLINI STARTED OFF. He went the exact twenty yards before he heard the shout that whirled him around. As he raced to close the distance, the shadow tried desperately to squirm out of Jo-Jo's scientific head-lock. To the pass-er-by it looked as if Cellini were joining in innocent horse-play. To the shadow it felt as if his arm were being wrenched from its socket as Cellini expertly pulled it back and up with paralyzing effect. The struggle ceased. The youthful face was vicious and unkempt. Ugly hairs curled from the flaring nostrils.

"Hold it, crumb," soothed Cellini. To Jo-Jo he said: "Do the same for you some time."

"No trouble at all." The newsboy waved airily.

With his free hand, the shadow jammed his cigar butt against Cellini's trouser. Cellini shot the arm up. There was a yelp of pain and the cigar dropped. Cellini brushed at the charred cloth till it stopped smoking.

"You shouldn't ought to let him do those things," reproved Jo-Jo.

Holding the arm taut, Cellini steered the shadow into the Hangover, walked him quickly to the rear, wedged him into a vacant booth, and sat opposite.

Hump came over and watched interestedly.

Cellini said: "I'll have scotch and soda with a twist of lemon peel. What do you want, crumb?"

The shadow plumbed his stock of latrine English and told Cellini at great and obscene length exactly what he wanted.

"Well, well," said Hump, "your little boy wears long pants now, Smith. Why don't he take that Fuller brush out of his nose?"

Cellini said: "Don't mind him. This is the guy that writes the limericks on toilet walls."

The shadow began again. Cellini's left hand reached across the table and grabbed him by the lapels. With his right he slapped the shadow's face back and forth like a metronome till he shut up.

"So he's the guy who writes 'em," mused Hump.

Cellini said: "Give him a drink. Best in the house. Make it a Hangover Express."

"Check." Hump left.

Cellini seized the lapels again and slipped a wallet out of the shadow's breast pocket and released him again. He spread the contents on the table. It contained the usual debris of crumpled pieces of paper, the cards of a bail bondsman and mouthpiece, an old pari-mutuel ticket, a French postcard, a few shady

addresses, a rusty nail file, and an embossed card that read—
Ned Lyams Detective Agency.

The money consisted of five greasy singles. Cellini palmed them and said: "I'll keep this as payment on account for ruining my pants. I know where to collect the rest."

The shadow stared stonily at the bronze plaque of a bruiser over the bar. His face was livid from the slapping. Hump returned with the drinks. The shadow sank his in one quick swallow. Cellini shoved the wallet and its contents at him. He stuffed them into his pockets, slid off the bench and hurried out.

Hump stared after him and sucked on an imaginary lemon. "Smith, when you back-slap keep your thumb down or you'll fracture it. I know that guy. He's a peeper. What'd he want from you?"

"He was tailing me. What do I owe you for the drinks?"

"Two bits for your scotch. Nothing for the mickey finn."

Cellini paid. "Fair enough."

"What you doing about Morton Miles' killer, Smith?"

"Give me time, Hump. I accepted the case only this morning."

THE HUNCHBACKED WAITER left and Cellini scanned the club as he sipped his drink. Barely five in the afternoon—an hour when the Hangover was normally empty—there were only a few unoccupied tables.

Talk was subdued, appetites were whetted by the murder of the night club's nominal owner. Earl Nikken sat alone and, at a ringside table, sat Nina Saunders with something elegant in males. Cellini could not place Nina's escort but the supple carriage and set of the shoulders betokened the fighter. The bar still supported its complement of sorrowing, semi-drunk bruisers.

Cellini dallied over his drink and thought of the shadow. No matter—it was part of the game. He would take it up later with Ned. What did annoy him was that he hadn't expected it. But he should have. In the future he'd be more careful.

The Sioux City Slasher parted the ropes and entered the ring. "Folks," he announced somberly, "as a rule there ain't so many suckers around at this time of day. But this afternoon it's somethin' special. You're here because a great guy took the count last night. He was my friend and your friend and the greatest fighter that ever lived. Guys like him made fighting a great game. If heaven is like the sky pilots say, he's booking fights up there right now. Death don't stop guys like Morton Miles. Folks, the reporters asked if we would close down. No! He would want us to go on like nothin' happened. Though we ain't prepared we'll put on a floor show right now. And drinks on the house—with the compliments of Morton Miles!"

There was a cheer and the Slasher launched into his routine and drinks were set up. The jokes rang unfunny and the applause hollow.

Nina Saunders caught sight of Cellini and gave an audible squeal of delight. She hurried over to his booth. "You termite! How long have you been here?"

"Not long."

"I've had a wonderful time, Cellini. Everybody is so jittery on account of that murder. Cellini, what's a round-heel?"

"Pushover. Why?"

"The way he hit him was a work of art. Cellini, I don't understand. What do you mean?"

"A roundheel," explained Cellini patiently, "is a frill with heels so round the slightest push sends her over. Now what are you talking about and who hit who—or is it whom in your circle?"

She pointed to Earl Nikken. "Well, he started it. Two men were discussing a marriage that took place this afternoon between Ward or something and somebody else."

Cellini became alert. "Between Jesse Lee Ward and Olive Fain?"

"That's it. At any rate, one of the men said he wouldn't marry a girl like Olive Fain because she was a round-heel. Mr. Nikken overheard him but before he could do anything Mr. Slasher grabbed hold of the man and hit him. Mr. Slasher just held him by his shirt and kept hitting him. When he became tired another one of those fighters took over. He had a ring on his left hand and he hit downward and ripped the man's face open. They took him away. It was wonderful."

"And what did Earl Nikken do?"

"Nothing. He just stood there, and then he told them it was enough and they called an ambulance. A woman fainted. I didn't," she added proudly.

"And who was the guy dumb enough to shoot his mouth off?"

"I don't know but the man at my table says it was an eastern fighter who got into town yesterday and didn't know what was what."

"Ah," said Cellini. "The man at your table knew the guy they beat up on?"

"Yes."

"He saw it take place?"

"Of course. He was with me."

"And who is the man at your table?"

"Cellini! You're jealous."

"That's right. Love is gnawing at my heart like a hungry rat. What's his name?"

"It sounds like a cigar. He's called Juan de Rico. He once killed a snake with his bare hands on the Pampas."

"Call him over. I want to talk to him."

SHE WAVED TO de Rico and the dark Latin made his way over. Introductions were performed and drinks ordered. "He's rather dumb, but pretty," said Nina Saunders. "I thought it was worth buying him a drink just to look at him while I waited for you, Cellini."

Juan de Rico took it as a compliment.

"Too bad he's a fighter," she sighed. "He'll get all messed up. He's fighting tonight."

"No I won't," declared the boxer. "Me, I'm smart. I don't take 'em if they're on the level."

"Diving in the tank tonight?" asked Cellini politely.

"No," replied Juan de Rico. "I'm fighting to a fast draw."

"Look," said Cellini. "That guy who was pushed around before. Was he a friend of yours?"

De Rico seemed reluctant to speak but with Nina's urging he said: "Sure. I blew in from the East with him a coupla days ago."

"Why'd he make that crack about Olive Fain?"

"I guess he don't know any better. Me, when I crash a new town I make no cracks until I know the lay of things. I'm smart."

"How'd it happen?" asked Cellini.

"Well, my friend was pretty liquor-stunk and a couple of guys at the next table was talking about the marriage and they toasted this Fain dame and he butted in and got his lumps." He decided to sidetrack the conversation. "You know that reminds me one time down on the Pampas—"

"Drop it," said Cellini wearily. "I'm an old billiard drinker. The only Pampas you know is the Brooklyn veldt."

Juan de Rico grinned. Nothing ventured, nothing gained, the grin said.

"Cellini," pouted Nina Saunders. "I'm the only one who can be rude to him. I've got a drink invested."

"Did you invest a key, too?"

"Oh!"

"You," said a voice. They looked up to see Denver Ed poking a stubby forefinger at Juan de Rico. "You were drinking with that dung who steamed outa turn before."

Juan de Rico's lips moved but no sound issued.

"We don't like him and no friends of his. Get!"

Juan de Rico slid from behind the table and half walked, half ran till he was out the door. Denver Ed sat down and finished de Rico's drink.

The Sioux City Slasher cued in Kate Kelly. She stumbled into the ring, large, red-eyed, and slatternly.

"What'd you want with that guy?" asked Denver Ed abruptly.

Cellini shrugged. "I heard there was a fight. I wondered what it was about."

"You got your job, Smith. Work it."

"O.K., Denver, but take it easy. I'm not a Pampas pimp."

Denver Ed stayed his reply as Kate Kelly made an announcement. Her bosom heaved under turbulent emotions. "Fellow mourners, I ain't gonna say much. I just want to tell you I'm gonna sing *My Man* now and I'm dedicatin' it to Morton Miles. I'm dedicatin' it to Morton Miles because I want to keep his memory green. I'm gonna keep it green so long as I live." She choked a sob and *My Man* seemed in imminent jeopardy. To stall for time, she spun the piano stool to various levels and fussed with sheet music she didn't need.

"Somebody wants to see you," Denver Ed said to Cellini.

"Who?"

"You'll find out."

"Listen, Denver, I know damned well who wants to see me and I want to see him. I just don't like being shoved around. Why don't you guys get it into your heads I'm working for and not against you?"

Denver Ed wagged a menacing forefinger at Cellini. "Chips on shoulders," he said. "They're my specialty—"

Cellini captured the finger and stilled the wagging.

"—I take them off," completed Denver Ed.

They stared at each other for a long moment. The fighter suddenly relaxed and Cellini released the finger. It was a draw. Nina Saunders gave a happy *"Aaah."* These men were so vital!

"And who did you think wants to see you?" asked Denver Ed.

"Earl Nikken, so let's go."

THEY MADE THEIR way to Nikken's table as Kate Kelly finally began. Her voice was whiskied and grating, but possessed of a certain poignancy that managed to arrest attention.

Oh my Miles I loved him so

He'll never know....

"Please sit down," invited Earl Nikken in a velvet voice. The ex-racketeer and semi-legendary figure did not show his fifty-five years. He was over six feet, impressive, perfect type-casting for a retired bank president. The haunting sadness in his face lingered even as he smiled and offered Cellini a cigarette. Denver Ed returned to the bar. Chicago Earl's privacy was invaded only by invitation.

Cellini took the cigarette and they waited for Kate Kelly to reprise the song to vociferous applause.

Earl Nikken said: "Is it true you were connected with Tony Moro in the East?"

"Yes."

"Moro was O.K. in his way," he mused, "but his kind had to go. Their ingenuity was limited to putting people into bathtubs filled with cement and dropping them in rivers. It's no longer necessary to build up a gang with armored automobiles and Thompson subs when you can make much more money legitimately or semi-legitimately. The modern racket is run like any other business."

"Such as scrap iron?" asked Cellini bluntly.

Earl Nikken gazed at Cellini with friendly curiosity. "What do you know about me?"

Cellini said: "I know who you were and where you came from. I know you don't like publicity about it and I know why. I also know that you opened this place for Morton Miles and that you own it. I can also guess that the century retainer the Slasher doled me came from you, as would the remaining nine hundred if I cracked the case. Shall I go on?"

"By all means."

"Well, the rest I can't understand. A while back I met a grifter on the street who told me that Olive Fain would never marry anybody—this despite the fact that she married Jesse Lee Ward this afternoon. Then I come in here and find out that you had some poor poop dusted off for making some out-of-line remark about her. Mind you, all this about the wife of one of my chief suspects. All this about a marriage between Ward and Fain which I swear the groom never knew about as late as yesterday morning."

"Most of which is correct. I like frank people, Smith—but I like them only if they toe the line."

"Our interests are the same," said Cellini. "To get Miles' murderer."

"I'll grant that. I also want you to realize that I'm not quite as one-tracked as the boys around here. Much as I'd like to see the Turk fry for the murder, I also realize it's wish-thinking and that you must of necessity investigate every conceivable angle."

"I'm doing that and if I don't the cops will."

"The cops have," corrected Earl Nikken. "I had a long talk with someone called Haenigson. It's only natural that the first place they should turn to is Morton Miles' place of business."

"That's just what I'm getting at, Mr. Nikken. You've got to explain everything to the cops so why hold out on me—the person who's working for you?"

"The police were very satisfied when they left here," said Nikken quietly. "I know how to deal with them."

"And how to deal with me, too?" prompted Cellini.

"Exactly," said Earl Nikken. "Jesse Lee Ward was a friend of Morton Miles and the way you put him on the spot this morning in front of the police was inexcusable. I—"His voice trailed off as he noticed Hump circulating among the fighters at the bar with a hat in his hand. Nikken wagged a finger and the hunchbacked waiter hurried over. "What's that for?"

Hump lowered the hat and they could see that it was full of bills and change. His reply was embarrassed. "Well, the boys kind, of thought it would be nice to give Morton Miles a real send-off."

"How?"

"Well," said Hump, "we were thinking of one of those bronze-plate caskets if we could get enough cabbage together. You know the kind—with platinum handles. We want the best."

"How much have you collected?"

"Over two hundred and eighty-six bucks already."

"Well buy five dozen orchids with it and another five for me and send it over to the Englebrecht Mortuary. You can have them made up in six foot horseshoes. And forget about the bronze casket."

Hump was more puzzled than surprised. "Forget about it?"

"Yes, you damn fool. Bronze-casket-full-dress funerals were repealed with prohibition. They're not," he added with a wry smile, "supposed to be in taste any more. Now beat it and do as I say."

HUMP LEFT AND Earl Nikken picked up the thread of his conversation with Cellini. "As I said, there was no excuse for the way you directed suspicion to Jesse Ward this morning. He also is a friend of mine and I want you to leave him alone." His voice became milder but somehow more menacing. "I want you to leave him alone—both him and his wife, Olive Fain."

"I just want to do my job."

"Good. Do it."

"Do you mind if I ask a couple of questions now?"

"Not at all. I want to help as much as I can."

"Well, if I'm to get after the Turk I must know whether the scrap-iron dealings he had with Ward and Miles were on the level."

"They were."

"Were you in on it?"

"No."

"And it was on the level?"

"Yes."

"I see where I'll have to work hard for that thousand bucks," said Cellini.

"I guess that's enough for now," said Earl Nikken in dismissal. "I don't expect miracles from you, Smith, but I do expect fealty since I'm paying for it. I'm sorry for you if I don't get it."

Cellini Smith left the Hangover and stopped at the large Japanese fruit store which comprised most of the Professional Building's street floor. A pretty, little Japanese girl pertly asked him what he wanted.

"Did you ever hear of a Japanese called Seiicha Sawamura?" he asked.

Her tilted nose bobbed up and down. "Certainly!"

"Who is he?"

"Mister," she countered, "have you ever heard of John Dillinger?"

Cellini said: "Yes."

"Well, please, what was he?"

"I guess you could call him a typical American gangster," he told her.

"Then," she said triumphantly, "Seiicha Sawamura is a typical Japanese gangster."

8

The Bride Who Didn't Blush

THE TERRIBLE TURK'S bowling center was operating at near capacity when Cellini Smith walked in at seven. The disciple of exercise for other people paused to take in the clamorous spectacle—rubber-shod, sport-sweatered bowlers annihilating the pins with 16 lb. balls, ping-pong players counterfeiting masculinity with 4 oz. paddles, and finally, the hollow-chested, consciously sinister pool players, sinking pool balls with enormous science.

Tight-bodied waitresses in peasant dress displayed alluring clefts as they leaned over to decant beer for the players, thus stimulating orders for more beer. Cellini laughed. The Turk got them coming and going.

Next to the cashier's booth a big-boned, middle-aged man with close-cropped hair stood doing nothing. He was a typical, small-time hood. Cellini began to walk up the length of the bar toward the small door that led to the Turk's quarters. The hood left the cashier's booth and intercepted Cellini.

"I want to see the Turk."

"He's feedin'."

"That's O.K. My name's Cellini Smith. I just want to see him for a few minutes."

"He don't see nobody when he eats."

"I heard you the first time. Go in and tell him I want to see him. Jump."

The man with the close-cropped hair grunted: "Go smear yourself with vanishing cream, sister."

Cellini said: "I see your shoulder holster bulge and it doesn't impress me, I've taken too much back-talk today to let a hood with bad teeth worry me. Now just go and do what I say."

The bouncer squinted at Cellini a few seconds longer, then suddenly marched off. In a short while he reappeared at the opening of the small door and Cellini followed him inside. The hood shut the door and leaned against it.

Like a Nero of old, the Terrible Turk reclined on a mound of cushions and stabbed at the remains of a shrimp salad on a tea-wagon. He wore a brilliant, vermillion fez. Sprawled next to him was a girl in a dotted print dress and little else. She was very young and very drunk. Her one hand clutched a tall drink and the other kept replacing a loose shoulder-strap that slipped down twice a minute.

"What do you want here?" asked the Turk. "Didn't Lyams see you?"

The girl giggled and said: "He's cute. Maybe he wants me."

"Shut up," said the Turk with more sincerity than anger, "before I slap you stupid." He turned to Cellini again. "You got your job, Smith. What's the matter? Ain't Lyams cooperating?"

"Sure he is. We're getting along fine. I just want to talk to you for a few minutes."

The Turk speared his last shrimp and, with an elegant flourish, brushed the plate off the wagon on to the rug. With perfect timing, the waiter marched in with a dozen oysters imbedded in cracked ice. They were large and meaty, probably flown in from the East. The Terrible Turk spiced one and, with the slurping sound of a whirlpool, absorbed it. To Cellini, it looked like osmosis.

"What do you think, chief?" asked the bouncer. "Want to throw him out?"

Cellini cut in: "And get that pest away from here. He couldn't scare a gazelle."

The Turk waved an oyster shell and the bouncer left. "Maybe I should get out, too," remarked the girl.

"You stay," said the ex-wrestler. He leaned over the plate. "O.K., Smith."

"When," asked Cellini, "did you hire Ned Lyams to check on your scrap-iron deal with Ward?"

"A couple weeks ago."

"Did he find anything wrong?"

"No." The Turk fumbled under some cushions and came up with several sheets of paper which he pitched to Cellini. They proved to be daily, confidential reports by the Ned Lyams agency. Cellini glanced through them. They showed only that the investigation of Morton Miles had revealed nothing dishonest or suspect in the abortive deal.

"Swell," said Cellini. "Were the cops around to see you today, Turk?"

The Terrible Turk nodded to the girl. "Now you can scram, sugar." He waited for the door to close behind her. "So it was you steered the shams on me."

"No. I just happened to be there when Jesse Ward blew off about you."

THE TURK ANNULLED three more oysters before he said: "I don't think it was Ward. You sent the cops here and I don't like it."

"All right," said Cellini, "have it your way. I steered the bulls on you. What happened when they got here?"

"Smith, don't get the idea that you or the shuffle-feet down at the Hangover have me scared. I know this town and I pay off. If they start anything my toe-holders will break them in two."

"You weren't talking like that this morning," Cellini reminded him.

"Only because I want to know who fogged Morton Miles. I want to know that more than anything else."

"Why?"

"Because I'm being framed for the job. When I find who's doin' it I'll—"

"You'll do what?" prompted Cellini. "Kill him?"

The Turk found a tainted oyster. He swore, hawked, and spat it on the rug. He speared another and examined it critically. He asked: "Where were we?"

"On your eleventh oyster," said Cellini. "Stop horsing me, Turk."

The waiter brought in a dish of ravioli and meat sauce.

"Three seconds too soon," Cellini reproved the waiter. "Turk, what alibi did you give the cops for last night?"

"Why don't you talk to Ned Lyams like you're supposed to? He'll tell you."

"Lyams is working for you," said Cellini. "I'm not. I'd like to know what your alibi is for the Miles murder."

"It would be funny," mused the Terrible Turk, "if an ambitious snoop like you tried to pin it on me."

Cellini said: "I'd split a gut laughing. Scoop some of that ravioli out of your mouth, Turk, and tell me if you were visiting Miles last night after ten."

"Yes, I was," replied the Turk.

"Did you see Miles?"

"Yes," said the Turk.

"Did you have a fight with him?"

"Yes."

"Did you pack a gun?"

"Yes."

"All right, Turk, I'll ask it. Did you kill Miles?"

The ex-wrestler said: "Yes."

Cellini shrugged. "I'm getting tired of this. You're as funny as a baby's open grave."

Again, the Turk grunted, "Yes," through the ravioli.

Cellini said: "Close your mouth when you masticate. It looks like a cement mixer in there. What's the story you told the cops?"

"Yes."

Cellini turned to go. When he was at the door, the Turk said: "Stick around, Smith. I like to be entertained when I masticate."

"I'll do my entertaining to the shams," replied Cellini hotly. "And if they won't do anything about it, I'll come back here in a couple of days and you'll tell me plenty!"

The Terrible Turk smacked a cushion with the palm of his hand.

"Don't try to kid *me*, Smith," he shouted in sudden anger. "You're just an ambitious snoop. I could pick you up right now and throw you through that door. But you might figure that meant I knew something so I won't do it."

"Anytime you want to square off, say the word," interposed Cellini brashly.

"Smith, I'll just say I don't like you. I could hire your services to get you on my side but you ain't worth it. You ain't dangerous enough and when you are I got plenty ways to take care of you. You couldn't prove anything about me, Smith. You couldn't prove I was alive.

"Name any spot in the city and I'll get you fifty citizens to swear I was there all the time. I'm one guy you'll stop thinking about, Smith, because it don't do you any good and because I'll make a daisy pusher out of you if you don't watch out. This is my town, Smith. Don't forget that!"

Cellini went out, paged through a directory, found Jesse Lee Ward's number on Carew Drive, sat down to the counter, and ordered a sandwich which the menu proudly called *The Turk's Turkey Special*.

Wedding night or no wedding night, Jesse Lee Ward was the only logical person to see next, thought Cellini. The handsome Ward, friend and associate of Morton Miles, had an unsatisfactory alibi for the murder time.

Cellini noticed the waiter carrying a planked T-bone and fried onions to the Turk's seraglio. The girl of the slipping shoulder strap trailed behind. Cellini flagged her and asked her to tell the Turk that Earl Nikken and Chicago Earl were one and the same. Just that. No harm in fishing in the dark, he thought, especially if he could worry the Turk. He finished the sandwich and glanced at his watch. It was almost eight. He went out to the Plymouth roadster and pointed it for Carew Drive.

CELLINI PARKED THE car in front of the Spanish bungalow and walked up the few porch steps as the front door opened and a man and a woman appeared. The woman was dressed for departure. The man said, "Good-bye," but the woman paused as she saw Cellini.

Jesse Lee Ward muttered something to the woman and curtly greeted Cellini who walked past them into the living-room. They exchanged glances, followed Cellini inside, and closed the door. Ward virilely handsome in dinner jacket, scowled. "Have you spoken to Earl Nikken, Smith?"

Cellini nodded and said nothing as he studied the woman standing in the center of the room. She was dressed in an informal cardigan jacket with beige skirt. The form-fitting woolens enhanced the contours of a figure that was pliant yet full. Her face was framed squarely by the long black hair draped over her neck with "pageboy" effect. She carried herself regally, conscious of the desire of men and the envy of women.

Ward repeated the question.

"Yes, sure I saw Earl Nikken," said Cellini, "and he told me that you were a friend of his and that I shouldn't try to pin the murder on you. He was pretty serious about it, too. But I still think there are things you can tell me and here I am."

"Well, it's a very inopportune time. I was married this afternoon and while I realize that clearing this case up would be to my advantage as well as yours, please don't bother me now. I'll gladly make an appointment with you."

"I'm here now," said Cellini. "Besides, your bride was just leaving."

A dull red appeared on Jesse Lee Ward's sun-bronzed face. However, when he spoke, his voice was mild. "We were going to take a walk."

"You're Olive Fain," Cellini said to the woman. "That is, you were before your marriage today."

She said: "Yes."

"Why should you be dangerous?" he asked.

She smiled. "Dangerous, Mr. Smith? May I ask you a question? Don't you think it's in questionable taste to flirt with another man's wife on her wedding day?"

"I wasn't," said Cellini. "I don't like flirting. It's a pastime that always lags behind my imagination."

"Then what did you mean?"

"Somebody told me you were dangerous. And that you wouldn't marry anybody. Why?"

"Was anything else said?"

"No. But I wonder about this sudden marriage which your husband didn't seem to know anything about when he was vacationing in Palm Springs two days ago. Then I wonder about the extremes that Earl Nikken went to, when someone called you a roundheel. The man was carted off in an ambulance."

Jesse Lee Ward gave a sickly laugh. "Swell guy, Earl. He'd do a lot for Olive and me."

Cellini examined him with unconcealed distaste. "Mr. Ward," he said, "you're either as yellow as the Terrible Turk's teeth or scared as hell of me."

"I don't get you."

"The hell you don't," replied Cellini. "You don't have to take any of this from me and you don't even have to talk to me. I know that one word from you to Earl Nikken or the pugs at the Hangover would be enough to put me out of commission. But you're still scared of me. Why? The only answer I can see is that you're mixed up in the murder so damned deep you're afraid of your skin—afraid I'll stumble on something."

Jesse Lee Ward shook his head and a lock of brilliantined

hair fell picturesquely over his brow. "You have me wrong, Smith. All I know is that you're trying to find Morton's killer and I want to help. What's the use of blowing up?"

Olive Fain said: "I think we ought to let Mr. Smith ask his questions, Jesse, so he can leave."

"I get it," said Cellini. "I'm interrupting cupid. Yet you were going away when I came in. But no matter." He turned to Jesse Lee Ward. "You still claim you weren't in Morton Miles' house last night?"

"That's what I said."

"How do you make a living?"

"I'm a business man."

"I imagine that's a euphemism," observed Cellini. "You still claim your scrap-iron deal was on the level?"

"Of course."

"My hunch is you're a liar but it's only a hunch yet and we'll go into that some other time. Mrs. Ward's a stunning woman. I'll leave soon. I don't know, but wasn't seventy-eight G's a lot of cabbage for the Turk to invest for a mess of scrap?"

"That included the ship."

Cellini said: "That's fine. Now we've got a ship. If somebody would trouble to sit down for a minute and tell me the whole story it'd save me a lot of asking."

"It's the *City of Kobe*—the ship I mentioned this morning. We bought it intending to sail it to Japan and then sell it as scrap along with its cargo."

"American registry?"

"Yes."

"Will this go on for long?" asked Olive Fain with exaggerated sweetness.

Cellini shook his head. "No. I've got my car outside. I'll leave shortly."

Uneasily, Jesse Lee Ward said: "We'll be finished in a moment, dear."

"Now for the very last time I'll ask this question," said Cellini. "Why didn't the *City of Kobe* sail with its load of scrap?"

"I told you this morning. Those Chinese picketers. They cost us the deal. That kind shouldn't be allowed in this country."

"Sure," agreed Cellini. "That kind should be sent back to China so's the Japanese would need more scrap iron from you to kill them off. But you and I know there isn't an ounce of scrap iron on the *City of Kobe*. My compliments on your platonic marriage and good-night."

HE SAT WAITING in his car no more than fifteen minutes before Olive Fain came down the short flight of steps and picked out the roadster parked three houses down the road. She walked over, opened the door, and sat in next to him.

"I gathered your meaning," she said, "when you said your car was outside."

He started the motor.

She said, "My hotel is the Langley," and asked for a cigarette.

Cellini supplied it and set the car in motion. "I wonder why you're not with your husband tonight," he mused.

"Mr. Smith, I'm in this car to say only one thing to you."

"And that is?"

"To warn you not to bother or browbeat my husband. As you surmised, he's spineless and gutless and that may give you the idea you can do anything you want with him. Don't try it."

"I don't like warnings," said Cellini, "even from lovely women."

"We're not discussing your likes or dislikes, Mr. Smith. When you said I was dangerous, did you know why?"

"Yes, Mrs. Ward. Earl Nikken makes you dangerous. You're the gorgeous brunette who sits with him almost every night in the Hangover."

"Exactly, Mr. Smith. Don't worry about my marriage to Jesse Lee Ward. Tread lightly or I'll see that Earl takes care of you."

"We'll see." He took a deep breath. "You're the first lovely woman I've met who doesn't stink from some high-class perfume and doesn't paint her fingernails."

"Mr. Smith, I don't give a damn whether you like something about me or no. I'm only trying to do you a favor."

Cellini said: "Flattery isn't my line. I was just remarking on some feminine phenomena."

She gave a small laugh. "You're right. Flattery demands some degree of subtlety. I wish I had the sense to leave you to your blundering fate."

"This isn't the time for fencing," said Cellini abruptly. "Your point is that if I don't leave your pretty husband and you and Earl Nikken and everybody else alone I'll be picked up in a ditch."

"Exactly," she said.

"Why do you bother warning me?"

Olive Fain said: "Because, before you were found in that ditch, you might succeed in making things uncomfortable for myself and my friends."

"Fine," said Cellini. "My answer is that I'm understudying to be a hero—a latter day Frank Merriwell—and that no combination of sinister mugs and beautiful women could make me run. Do you mind telling me how long you've known Earl Nikken?"

"Quite long."

"And why did you marry Ward?"

"Shall I be facetious?"

"No. I'd rather you didn't reply. This wedding night you two spend together two miles apart worries me. Where did you meet your husband?"

"Out here."

"Do you think there's a possibility he murdered Morton Miles?"

She said: "I imagine the possibility exists though I doubt if you'd be able to prove it."

Cellini sighed: "Mrs. Olive Fain Jesse Lee Ward Earl Nikken, you set me on fire."

"Mr. Smith, let's understand each other. On account of what some moron said you may have the wrong impression of me. Mr. Smith, I'm not a roundheel. Whatever I may be I'm selective."

"You mean," asked Cellini, "that you'll keep the field limited to Earl Nikken and Jesse Ward?"

She gave her small, tinkling laugh again. "In a way—a very remote way—I admire you, Mr. Smith. This is the place. Thank you for the ride and goodbye now."

Cellini cut into the curb at the Hotel Langley. He said: "You've been able to twist every man you've ever met around your fingers, haven't you?"

"Yes," she admitted. "Every single one. Unwind yourself, Mr. Smith."

9

When Op Meets Op—

CELLINI LAY ON his bed listening to recordings of string quartets. He had sent Duck-Eye Ryan on a busman's holiday to see the fights at the Olympic and the last requisite for good, clear thinking was filled and even justified by the scotch highball in his hand. For now he thought he had the solution to Morton Miles' murder.

Yet, as he examined this solution in the light of the facts that inescapably drove him toward it, his better judgement declined to accept it. Again he told himself that it was impossible. He remembered the gun still clutched in the fight promoter's stiffening hand, the open wall safe with the undisturbed monies in it—yet his deduction remained the same. The murderer didn't budge.

He cauterized his thoughts with more liquor and was ready to try another tack when the buzzer sounded and he went to the door to admit Ned Lyams.

Lyams threw his topcoat over the bedstead, snapped on the ceiling lights, and reached for the bottle.

"Sure," said Cellini after his visitor had half-filled a glass, "why don't you have a drink? I insist." He lay down on his bed again.

Ned Lyams sat on a chair and examined Cellini's face keenly through half-lowered lids. He thought he detected a flush on his host's face. With a few more drinks, he decided, the man would be talking freely. He sipped on his glass and said: "It's bad when a man drinks alone. I've got to catch up with you now."

"You're right," said Cellini absently. He did not miss Lyam's comprehensive glance nor did he fail to note that his guest sipped the liquor slowly. So Lyams had the bright idea of getting him drunk. "You're not drinking much, Ned," he added.

"I've got a half-dozen under my belt from dinner," lied Lyams. He simulated a drunken whoop of good cheer, undid his tie, and removed his jacket.

Cellini decided to play it straight. "State the purpose of your visit," he said blurring the sibilants. "Speak your piece and leave me alone so's I can think of what an unlucky man Ward is tonight."

Lyams said: "I came to tell you I'm sorry I put Fred on your tail."

"Fred?" queried Cellini. "Ah, yes. My shadow." He buried his nose in the glass but neglected to drink. "You ought to tell Fred to clip his nose hairs. Or is it hair noses? No, that doesn't sound right, either."

Ned Lyams said that it was probably nose hairses.

"Anyway," continued Cellini, "forget about Fred. It was no trouble at all."

"It's nice of you to take it like that," said Ned Lyams. "Not that I don't trust you but—The Turk's a good client and with a little luck I can get a lot of cabbage out of him for this job. I didn't want you beating me to the tape."

"Forget it," repeated Cellini.

Lyams said: "I'm glad it happened, though, because you showed Fred how wrong he was. He had a very interesting theory that it was much easier to tail someone if that person knew he was being followed. He said ninety percent of the shadows lose their man because they're too careful. So he said the only way to stay out of trouble was not to be careful and to let the guy know he was being shadowed. Then all you have to do is keep up with him."

"Interesting," commented Cellini.

"I'm glad you disproved his theory. That was the only thing that made Fred a bad man."

"No trouble at all, Ned."

"I like both of you," said Ned Lyams heartily. "You and your liquor."

"While we're on the subject, Ned, and before you get too pickled—can you see this cigar burn in my pants?"

"I can honestly say I do, Cellini."

"Well, I want to see twenty-five bucks. The suit's ruined. It cost thirty. I collected five from Fred so I've got another twenty-five dollars coming from you. Fred's interesting theory did that."

Ned Lyams sadly downed one very thin finger. "It's an outrage," he said.

"No it isn't. I just want the twenty-five bucks."

"Twenty-five bucks! That's an old suit."

"Sure, Ned. That's what makes it valuable. I've got all kinds of expensive gravies and sauces on it."

Ned Lyams said: "I checked like you told me and I found out that Jesse Lee Ward never received a long-distance call in Palm Springs from Morton Miles. What's more, Ward never put a call through to Olive Fain from his hotel as he claimed. The chippie at the hotel switchboard says that Ward got just one call—a call from Earl Nikken and then he returned to town."

"You're sure?"

"Dead sure. We double-checked."

"What about the twenty-five bucks?"

NED LYAMS DIDN'T reply. He allowed another thin trickle of liquor down his throat and Cellini met it with a like amount. "You're a hell of a peeper," Lyams finally said. "Haven't you ever heard of the fraternity among private detectives?"

"No."

"Neither have I," said Ned Lyams, "but you'll hear now. You're trying to cheat a fellow professional man. You know as well as I do that you can buy pants to match for five bucks."

Cellini said: "It wouldn't be an exact match. Not sartorially perfect."

"Sartorially perfect my patella," scoffed Ned Lyams. Suppose you tell me why Jesse Lee Ward is an unlucky guy according to you."

"Because his wedding night is not according to the traditional pattern of connubial bliss."

"Hell," said Lyams. "You give out information with an eye-dropper."

They drank cautiously. Each felt the other was not drinking half enough.

Cellini said: "The shams must have checked on Ward's story at Palm Springs by now and found that it stank. Do you think they've pulled him in?"

"I don't know. I don't think so."

"He was a free man when I saw him this afternoon but he seemed pretty nervous. That reminds me. I have a job for Fred.

Get him to find out if Ward was ever part of Nikken's outfit in the Chicago days."

"I don't think he was. I've asked some questions about Nikken and there was never any mention of Ward."

"Good. Then send a man up to Palm Springs again and find out who visited Ward there and why."

"Right," said Ned Lyams and asked what had been happening. Cellini told him all he deemed advisable, then said: "I want that twenty-five bucks."

"You asked for it before," Ned Lyams reminded him.

"That's right. So I did. I remember it as if it was yesterday. You were sitting right there and I was lying here and I asked you for the twenty-five smackeroos."

"How time flies," sighed Ned Lyams. "Those were the days. Then when you asked me for the money what did I say?"

"That you wouldn't give it to me."

"Also right." Cellini put his glass down. The lines on his face hardened as if set in concrete. "O.K., Ned. Fork over or I'll beat the hell out of you."

"You can't," said Lyams equably. "I'm a guest."

"And I'm a creditor. You've done me a lot of harm in this town, Ned, and if you think I'd let you get away with ruining one of my two suits you're crazy." He began to rise.

Lyams waved him back. "All right. Relax. This'll come out of Fred's salary. God, what a temper!"

HE TOOK OUT his wallet and counted tens and a five into Cellini's hand. They picked up their glasses again and Lyams solicitously filled Cellini's. "Now we can talk shop," said Cellini. "How do you size it up?"

"Ward," said Lyams, "explains phoning Miles that night by saying that Morton Miles had ordered him in from Palm Springs. It was all very urgent but when he got back to town he says he didn't go over to Miles' house. On top of that we find that Miles didn't even phone him at Palm Springs but that Earl Nikken did. And there's that De Soto in the woodpile. Now what do you think of it all, Mr. Hawkshaw?"

"It looks like a case of blackmail."

Lyams chuckled. "That's good. The blackmailer killed Miles for his money, then wouldn't take it when it was right in front of him in the safe."

"I still think it was blackmail. The murderer went to Miles' house not to kill but to blackmail. Money was his only motive. So when he killed Miles he left the money there because that way no one could prove he had a motive.

"I know what you're thinking, but outside of Earl Nikken no one involved in this case is so wealthy that he can afford to ignore a windfall of a few thousand bucks. Why shouldn't he commit robbery when he was already guilty of murder? The reason why he didn't was because the money was his only possible motive—the only thing could hang him."

"Look," said Ned Lyams. "I like to see a young fellow come along in this business. I had to start like you once so I know. But just take it easy and don't rush to conclusions."

"O.K. I won't."

"Why is Ward unlucky?"

"Ah," said Cellini. "Olive Fain. I like that type. She's got that sloe-gin look. Calm outwardly but the kind of calm to let you know that tempestuous passions are seething underneath. Why should two people take the trouble to get married, then separate immediately?"

Ned Lyams rubbed the palms of his hands together. "You've come to the right man, Cellini—the proper authority. I'm probably the only man who can give you all the answers to that one. In the first place—"

"And what has Chicago Earl to do with them and they with him, you windbag?" continued Cellini.

They lapsed into a somber silence for some minutes until Cellini suddenly leaned over and lifted the telephone onto the bed. He jiggled the switch-hook and dialed Ira Haenigson's home number.

The Homicide man said: "It's in the bag, my friend."

"Sure," replied Cellini, "the laundry bag. I suppose you'll tell me that Jesse Ward's confessed."

"Not yet," was Haenigson's satisfied reply, "but he'll crack by tomorrow. Ward's story rings up phony. I checked his alibi in Palm Springs. I just have to find out a couple of more things before I pull him in."

"Good for you," said Cellini and replaced the receiver. "Hurry up with your drink," he told Lyams, "because we're beating Haenigson to the punch. He knows that Ward's yarn is phony so we've got to go down and see Ward now to get his revised alibi."

"Now?" exclaimed Lyams. "It's after eleven and you've got a lot of scotch left."

"Come on. Don't be afraid of a little work. Besides, at the rate we're going it would take us a week to drink a fifth of scotch."

Ned Lyams reached into his memory and said: "Work is the curse of the drinking classes. Let's go then."

"No use at all," agreed Cellini.

10

Fire Without Smoke

THE NIGHT WAS cool, the fog overhanging Ned Lyams' LaSalle. Lyams trained his eyes to the foglight as they sped for Jesse Lee Ward's home in beam and kept a truculent silence to remind Cellini that it was way past his normal working hours. Presently, they sighted Ward's home on Carew Drive.

"He's still up," said Cellini. "There's a light in his living-room."

Ned Lyams pulled to the curb opposite the house. As he cut the motor and set the emergency, the lights in the living-room went out. That was no coincidence, thought Cellini. Someone had heard the car motor. Almost immediately, from between the divided slats of the venetian blinds, dancing tongues of flame began spreading, lighting up the interior of the living-room.

Cellini said: "What the hell!"

Now they could make out a figure crawling past the low French windows on hands and knees. The weird play of lights and shadows in the growing fire gave it a werewolf quality. Crawling nimbly like a ferrety animal, it finally vanished into the interior of the room.

"Maybe we'd better go in," suggested Cellini.

THEY RACED ACROSS the street, up the gravel path and porch steps to find the front door unlocked but set on the night chain. They put their shoulders to it and on the third heave ripped the chain from the door trim and burst into the room.

The fire was localized in a coat closet, first consuming several cedarized garment bags, then spreading to the woolens, emitting billows of thick, black smoke. Cellini Smith and Ned Lyams wrenched the burning garments off the hanger pole, kicked them into one pile, smothered them with more coats, then quickly threshed over the smoldering heap with their feet, their eyes and throats smarting from the acrid smoke.

They stood there in the dark, silent and motionless and straining their ears. Over the blaring radio in some house up the Drive they could hear no sound.

Cellini said, "What the hell," again, went over to the door, and snapped on the ceiling lights.

Then they saw the body lying just a few feet from the coat closet where the heap of clothing still smoldered.

Mechanically, Cellini said: "The back way, you damned fool."

Ned Lyams ran for the pantry door. Cellini's stare stayed on the body but he made no move toward it. There was a neat bullet hole in the center of the forehead that precluded even the remotest possibility that Jesse Lee Ward was still alive.

Cellini shook his head sideways and muttered: "Impossible."

Ned Lyams returned. "Whoever it was, he got away. He must have run for it because he had no car."

"Impossible," said Cellini again.

A half-smile twisted Ned Lyams's lips. "Why?"

Cellini walked over to the body. There was remarkably little blood—only a slight trickle of crimson across the bridge of the nose to film Jesse Lee Ward's eyes. That too-handsome face

was unmarred. He no longer wore dinner clothes. His open jacket revealed a spotless white shirt underneath and Cellini automatically registered approval of the expensive pair of nile-green suspenders. The hands were clenched as if Ward had anticipated the bullet.

Cellini quit the body and walked to the coat closet. With the toe of his shoe he kicked apart the pile of clothing on the floor till he saw the charred garment underneath that had started the fire. It was a man's buff-colored lounging-robe.

"That's why we didn't hear the shot when we drove up," said Cellini.

"What?" said Lyams stupidly.

"The murderer took that robe from the closet and wrapped

*"Well?" asked Joe Lucca almost politely. "I've got four
rods to your four, Gimp. Do you feel tough?"*

it around his gun hand and shot Ward through it to muffle the
sound. That's how it caught fire."

Lyams nodded. "That sounds reasonable. I guess I ought to
call the cops."

Cellini said: "That guy who was crawling on the floor—the
murderer—I wonder if he found what he was looking for."

Wordlessly and methodically, with careful attention to the
distribution of their fingerprints, they searched the room. They
could find nothing that might possibly have been the object of
the murderer's search.

Cellini paused at the sofa where the pillows had evidently
been pulled off and hastily replaced wrong end out. He said:
"The guy probably found what he was looking for. He even
had the time to look under the sofa pillows."

Ned Lyams was poking through the drawers of a mahogany writing desk. He held aloft a tiny jeweled scimitar. "I see he got one of these from my client."

"That's what I heard," said Cellini as he looked into the cold fireplace. "One of those things from the Turk is equivalent to burying the hatchet."

They searched for several more minutes without discovering anything of value.

"So the murderer did it again," said Ned Lyams reflectively. "Before we mess things up we'll call the department and let Ira Haenigson worry about it."

For a third time, Cellini said: "Impossible."

"Maybe Jesse Lee Ward only thinks he's dead," said Ned Lyams with top-heavy sarcasm. "After all those things are only in the brain—like the bullet in Ward's."

Cellini made no reply. He ran his fingers under the edge of the rug. If only he could find what the killer had searched for!

FOR A MOMENT Ned Lyams stared at Cellini perplexedly, then he shrugged and dialed Ira Haenigson's home number. When, at last, several minutes of ringing managed to rout the Homicide man out of bed, he had only to make a few words of explanation before he cradled the receiver. Cellini finished his circuit of the rug and straightened up. He decided that if the killer hadn't found what he wanted, then either the thing was too well hidden or he hadn't recognized it.

"Did you call Haenigson?" asked Cellini.

"Yes."

"When will he get here?"

"A few minutes, I guess."

"Well, that's mighty comforting."

"What are you driving at?" asked Ned Lyams suspiciously.

"Nothing. I was just wondering what you were in such a hurry about."

"Why?"

"Nothing you don't know, Ned. I had one idea that you'd think this murder of Ward was a special gift from God to you. I had the idea you'd first try to get the guy who did this and have him fry for Morton Miles' murder as well."

There was a long pause before Ned Lyams replied. When he did, his voice was quiet and emotionless. He said: "How long have you known that I killed Morton Miles?"

Cellini shrugged. He strolled over to the window, adjusted the blind, and looked out. It was a starless night but in the distance he could see the lights of the houses in the Hollywood hills. He wondered what Nina Saunders would say if she saw him sport a pair of nile-green suspenders. Plenty, he supposed. In a car parked across the street a couple of college kids giggled nervously as the preliminary to some heavy necking. He turned to Lyams again and said: "I wonder what the connection is between Miles' murder and Ward's."

"How long have you known?" pursued Lyams harshly.

"Pretty much from the start."

"Why didn't you let on?"

"There were a lot of other things worrying me." Cellini nodded toward the body on the floor. "There still are. Now I've got Ward's murder on my hands—a job I know you couldn't have done."

"How'd you find out?"

"Why do you want to know, Ned? No one will suspect you.

You own the most prosperous detective agency in town. Don't you remember?"

"I'm serious, Cellini. It means everything to me. A —————— —— ————— like you would turn me in for the Miles killing," he said bitterly, "especially if you found a way to make a sawbuck out of it—so I want to know. How'd you find out?"

"To begin with, no one else had a motive. The Turk would have had a motive if he'd known that Miles had rooked him on the scrap-iron deal. But he wasn't sure. I saw those daily, confidential reports you handed the Turk. Up to two days ago you reported nothing out of line. And the same lack of motive applied to Jesse Lee Ward. Ward was a friend of Morton Miles and his leaky alibi proved only that he had visited Miles and found him dead—not that he murdered him. Jesse Ward didn't have an appointment to meet Miles at his home because Ward first had to find out where Miles was by calling the Hangover. In other words, Ward had expected to find Miles at the Hangover.

"But the point is that Morton Miles left the Hangover unexpectedly, that night, after making a phone call to someone and arranging to meet that person at his home. Earl Nikken stayed at the club. That left Earl, and others like him out of the picture. Besides, Chicago Earl was like Ward. He had no motive. The thing is, Ned, that Miles' phone call was to you."

"All right," said Ned Lyams heavily. "I don't know how you found out he called me but that gave you plenty to go on."

"It did. And starting with that I was able to figure how it happened."

"Then you know I did it in self-defense?"

Cellini nodded. "What of it?"

"Nothing. Go on."

"I was in the Hangover that night," said Cellini, "and I told Morton Miles you were checking on him for the Turk. That was the first he knew about it, and he must have been afraid you'd discover something—I don't know what—about his dealings with the

Ned Lyams

Turk. He had no dough. He couldn't afford to pay the Turk back. So he called you and asked to meet you right away."

"I'm not a killer, Cellini. It was justifiable homicide."

"You're not above blackmail though," Cellini remarked.

"Blackmail doesn't rate the gas chamber."

"Miles," continued Cellini, "had a visitor and he went to the wall safe to get money to give that visitor. Money was the only important thing he had in it. But Miles had no intention of paying off. He had a gun in the safe and as he took out a packet of dough with one hand—remember the money was found on the floor by his body—his other hand came out with the rod."

NED LYAMS NODDED, with eyes closed, as if he were conjuring up the scene and reliving it in his mind.

"But you weren't born yesterday. Ned," said Cellini. "Before he could bring his gun into line you had a bead on him and plugged him in the chest. Miles' finger pulled the trigger as he fell. That's how the slug from his gun went into the rug.

Blackmail was the only possible thing and you were the only one who could have anything on Miles because you were hired for that purpose by the Turk. Of course you beat it without touching the money on the floor or in the safe because money was your only motive for the murder and if you left it there you were automatically freed from suspicion."

"Well?"

Cellini stared at the corpse. "What about him?"

"You know damned well I don't know anything about it. I was with you all night."

"I know that, but somebody killed him. Why? It wasn't a coincidence. It had to have something to do with Miles' murder."

"I don't know," said Lyams. "I wish I did. Are you going to try to turn me in to Haenigson?"

Cellini's head snapped up.

"Try?"

"All right, then. *Will* you?"

"The Miles murder was an isolated case. I wonder why Jesse Ward was killed."

Ned Lyams began to plead casually, almost disinterestedly, as though urging Cellini to change his brand of cigarette. He said: "You would have done the same as me. I just saw a chance to make some easy money. I never had any intention to—"

"I know," interrupted Cellini. "You're so good Jesus wants you for a sunbeam."

"—kill anybody. Miles called me up and said he'd found out I'd been checking him for the Turk. He asked me if I'd uncovered anything and I said yes."

"Had you?"

"No," replied Lyams. "I just took a shot in the dark and it worked. Miles told me I'd better not report it to the Turk. I told Miles I protected my clients and that the only way he could expect me to listen to him was to hire my agency and that it would cost him five G's. Miles agreed to it and went to his safe and tried to plug me. I guess he figured on claiming that he had caught me prowling through his house and shot me. But I got him first. I'm not a killer, Cellini. I had to plug him. It was me or him. If I've got to, I'll take a blackmail rap. And it wasn't even that because I was just trying to sell my services to the highest bidder—but don't turn me in for murder."

"I don't know yet," said Cellini.

"I'll pay you off if that's what you want."

"I know you would."

"All right, Cellini. I'll never mention it again. Do what you want but I'd like to help you find Ward's killer. Maybe we can stick him for both jobs."

"Maybe we'll do it that way," said Cellini. "I don't know yet. I'm not promising anything."

THERE WAS A squeal of brakes as a car turned into the driveway and a moment later Ira Haenigson erupted into the room. The detective-sergeant stared at the two men, walked over to the body, and then made for the phone. The bogus air of geniality was missing. He barked orders, replaced the receiver, and then whirled on Cellini. "Now, by God," he yelled, "this is too much, Smith. I was willing to call it an accident when you walked in and found Miles' body but two in a row is too much!"

"Take it easy, Ira," cautioned Ned Lyams.

"Take it easy hell! This guy's in it up to his neck. I've been suspicious of him and his stories from the first. He's got a shady record with gangsters in New York. He comes out here and gets a dick's license by the skin of his teeth. And then, he tries to kid me around and pull the wool over my eyes."

"Cool down, Ira," said Lyams. "I don't think he's mixed up in this. He's got a good alibi."

"Alibi!" snorted the Homicide man. "I didn't think anyone as smart as you, could be taken in by any alibi of his."

"I mean it. Don't be down on Cellini just because he's a newcomer. Cool down and think it over. Sometimes he's too smart for his own good and he's got a lot to learn but that's no reason to accuse him of murdering Miles and Ward. You see, Ira, Cellini's got phoney ideas about this business and the way we do things out here but basically he's O.K."

"You're very kind, Ned," Cellini murmured. "Thank you."

Haenigson said: "You're too good-hearted. Ned. You've always been a sucker for bums. I still want to know where he was tonight."

For the succeeding fifteen minutes, the detective-sergeant plied Ned Lyams and Cellini Smith with questions. He asked the identical questions a dozen different ways and went over the evening's chronology, step by step, a dozen different times. Cellini and Lyams answered him truthfully though they both neglected to mention that they had poked about the house for some time before calling him.

Photographer, doctor, fingerprint man, and others from headquarters arrived and swarmed over the place. Finally, Ira Haenigson threw up his hands. He was disgusted. He said: "I've got only this to tell you, Smith. You're the luckiest man in the world that you've got Ned to alibi you for tonight. Now beat it, both of you."

The two operatives left.

"I'll drive you home," said Ned Lyams.

Cellini shook his head. "No. But let's sit in your car, Ned. I've got something to say to you."

THEY CROSSED THE street and got into the La Salle. The college kids were gone. They sat in the car for a few moments, smoking cigarettes, before Cellini suddenly grabbed Lyams by the arm. "So I'm too smart for my own good and I've got lots to learn, have I?"

"You didn't take me seriously, Cellini? I had to—"

"So I've got phoney ideas but basically I'm O.K., am I? *You* have to alibi *me!* What a laugh! All I had to do was sing about Miles' murder and you'd be on your way downtown in bracelets. Still you shot your mouth off about me."

Lyams sounded beaten. "I know you've got me hooked. I talked that way so that Haenigson wouldn't get suspicious. It was the only way to cool him down."

"O.K.," said Cellini. "Forget it. Have you got one of those confidential memo blanks that you give clients?"

"Sure." Lyams reached into the glove compartment and pulled out a sheet. "What do you want it for?"

"I want you to fill it out on the Miles case, sign it, and give it to me."

Ned Lyams gave a gasp of amazement. He leaned forward in the darkness to make out Cellini's face. "You're crazy!"

"Won't you do it?" asked Cellini.

"Of course not. I'd be signing my own death warrant. I'd have to get my head examined."

"O.K. I just wanted it for my own protection." Cellini opened the car door. "Since you're not signing, I'm going across to Haenigson to spill the story."

Lyams pulled Cellini back and shut the car door. "What are you trying to do?" he asked urgently. "I told you it was self-defense and I thought we agreed to try and pin it on Ward's killer. I'm not a killer, Cellini, and you don't need anything like that for your protection."

"I said *maybe* we'd pin it on Ward's killer," corrected Cellini, "and we didn't agree to anything. I want that report to make you stay a good boy and I don't want to ask you again. Decide right now because I'm going in to see Haenigson."

Lyams surrendered. He had no alternative. "How do you want it?" he asked heavily.

"Have you got a pen on you?"

"Yes."

Cellini trained a pocket flash on the sheet of paper in Ned Lyams' nervous hand. "Date it today and write it to the Turk— since he's still your client." He laughed harshly. "The Turk hires you to find out who killed Morton Miles!"

Lyams waited with poised pen. "Sure—we know it's ironical and stuff. What else do you want on this report?"

"Where it says *Re* write *Murder of Morton Miles.* On the next line under Result you know what to write."

"I don't know a thing. This is your party.

Cellini gave a soft laugh and dictated: "The Lyams Agency reports that Ned Lyams is the murderer."

"And circumstances?" came Lyams' flat voice.

"Circumstances: justifiable homicide during attempted blackmail. Is that all?"

"Except the fee."

"We mustn't forget that," said Cellini. "Put in what you'd normally charge."

Cellini watched Ned Lyams trace the numerals. "Two G's! You get fancy prices, Ned. O.K. Now sign it." There was a perceptible instant of hesitation and Cellini repeated: "Sign it!" Lyams put his signature to the bottom of the report. Cellini took it and carefully folded it into his wallet. "I just hope for your sake I never have to use it."

Lyams started the car. "I'll drive you home."

"No, thanks," said Cellini. "I'm going back to see if Haenigson has found what the murderer was looking for. And while we're on the subject, Ned, you needn't wait for me to come out because I can leave this block by any one of three ways and you won't know which. And don't bother waiting for me at my apartment because Duck-Eye is probably there. Besides, I'll be very careful from now on."

"I told you I'm not a killer. You don't have to be afraid."

Cellini merely slammed the car door behind him and stepped off the curb to return to the late Jesse Lee Ward's home. There was a too-sudden grinding of gears and Cellini instinctively hurled himself back to the curb as the throbbing La Salle leaped forward with throttle open. Fenders grazed him.

Cellini stared after the disappearing tail-lights. He laughed aloud. You had to admire Ned Lyams! He was certainly persistent!

11

Scrap

WHEN AT TEN the following morning Cellini Smith's slumbers were assassinated by the off-key clank of a cracked dinner bell and the explosive coughing of a broken exhaust, he was none too happy. He lay there with eyes shut trying not to hear the raucous baritone that surmounted the noise in a paean of joy. Like a relentless triphammer, over and over, the voice drove the wedge of words into his consciousness: "Tires! Papers! Rags! All kinds metals and good junk! Tires!..."

He climbed out of bed and crossed to the window where he saw the two-ton Model-T truck of a junk dealer crawling up the street in fits and starts. He stuck two fingers into his cheeks and, after several tries, managed to emit a shrill whistle. The clanking ceased and the truck started maneuvering around.

He went into the bathroom. His eyes were red-rimmed, his stomach squeamish, and his tongue felt like a pine cone from the many cigarettes he had smoked the night before. He scrubbed his teeth, then used all manner of mouthwashes that were calculated to their precise efficacy by long and dismal experience. Besides the liquor, he was trying to take the taste of Detective-sergeant Ira Haenigson out of his mouth.

What Ira Haenigson probably resented more than the murder was the fact that Ned Lyams had alibied him. After Lyams' rude departure and Cellini's return to the house, the Homicide man had reminded him more than once that were it not for Ned he'd be in the soup.

A gargle in Cellini's mouth was suspended as he again contemplated turning Lyams in for the murder of Morton Miles. It was murder fathered by blackmail, but Miles' own hands were none too clean. It was the old story of cheating cheaters—and Morton Miles was left holding the sack. He felt no benevolence for Lyams, but in jail he could do him no good. The Hangover's pugs, grifters, and torpedoes whom the grapevine had summoned to Ward's house within an hour after the killing, would still want to know who had killed Jesse Lee Ward. Especially would Earl Nikken want to know. Lyams might be of some help there. All in all, it might be more sensible to let things slide while he tried his hand at finding Ward's killer.

He heard his apartment door slam and he called: "I'll be right out."

Ward's killer! He'd actually seen him. It was gall and wormwood that he got away. Worse, he didn't know what the killer had been searching for. But neither did the cops—if that were any consolation. The department experts had currycombed the house till four in the morning with no result.

He capped the antiseptic solutions and returned to the living-room.

The junk dealer was waiting. He was an Italian named Pasquale, he wore blue denim, and he sported a handlebar mustache. He was staring at the Capehart with cupidity. "You got *Rigoletto?*" he demanded without preface.

"No."

"No?" There was scorn in the word. "Well, I haven't all day. What you got to sell?"

"You buy all kinds of metals?"

"Yes—all kind. *Pagliacci?*"

"No *Pagliacci.*" Cellini shook his pajamas off and began to dress. "I haven't any metal to sell but I'd like some information about it."

"Mister," snorted Pasquale, "I got no time to fool crackpots."

"Have a drink."

The mustache wagged quick acceptance and Pasquale headed for the bottles. "What you want to know?" he asked a bit more amiably.

"What do you pay for metal?"

"Three and half cent for pound brass. Copper same. Nine for German silver and—"

"How about scrap iron?"

"No buy. Weigh too much."

"Who does buy it?"

"Big wholesale yards. Don't forget once I own one maybe," he added dreamily.

"I see. Well you're in the business so maybe you could tell me if there's any crookedness or racketeering among the various big dealers who handle scrap iron."

"Maybe," said the Italian cautiously.

"Don't you know?"

"I know lotsa things but don't tell because I make living. I got two cousin in Bologna so I don't tell what I think about Il Duce. Anybody ask I say Il Duce is wonderful."

"Fine," said Cellini. "Are there any big wholesale junk yards near San Pedro that deal in scrap iron?"

"Sure, plenty. Boone yard right near end of Western."

"Thanks."

"You sure about *Rigoletto?*" Pasquaie asked wistfully.

Cellini said that he didn't have it but that he'd play him some Wagner and the junk dealer fled as from a plague.

Cellini finished dressing and wondered why it had never occurred to Ira Haenigson to ask where Olive Fain had been during the time of her husband's murder.

Olive Fain

CELLINI BREAKFASTED AND read a newspaper. Der Fuehrer had just pulled another double-cross so Jesse Lee Ward fared no better than the second page. However, the reporters had not failed to connect him with the Morton Miles case and in the absence of facts and morgue clippings on Ward they gave space to many implausible speculations. The double crime had also provoked an editorial that began with: *The cesspool that is the fight racket in this state....*

He put the paper aside, had more coffee, and drove to his office. There were two more bills in the morning's mail and these were dropped, unopened, on top of the growing pile in the wire basket.

Duck-Eye Ryan said that there was no news and asked Cellini if he knew that Jesse Lee Ward was killed. Cellini replied that he'd heard the rumor, told Duck-Eye to lock the office, and the two of them went down to the car. Across the street, the Hangover appeared dark and quiet.

They drove for South Hope Street. Now, more than ever, Cellini felt that Morton Miles had probably rooked the Turk in the scrap-iron deal. If it had been on the level, Miles would not have feared Ned Lyams sufficiently to try to kill him. This Seiicha Sawamura Company, in fact, was a suspect outfit. And then there was the extreme possibility that the *City of Kobe* hadn't an ounce of scrap iron in her holds.

They reached their destination and Cellini cut the motor. He got a cold chisel from the rear baggage compartment and sat behind the wheel again. For five minutes they observed the automobile and pedestrian traffic. When they felt assured that no one watched the building they left the car and casually sauntered through the doorway.

Cellini and Duck-Eye walked up the flight of dust-laden stairs. As before, the door to the Sawamura Export Company was locked and all was quiet within. Cellini said: "Start singing. Not good but loud."

Duck-Eye Ryan obediently launched into a ribald barroom lyric as Cellini rapped smartly on the corrugated glass with the blunt end of the chisel. A small section of glass shattered.

"All right," said Cellini. "Stop singing. The breaking glass was sweeter." He gingerly reached through the break, felt for the inside latch, and opened the door.

It was a dirty and musty little room. Cellini walked to the window and found that it gave on a deserted parking lot in the rear of the building. He pulled the shade down and turned on the ceiling light. Somebody was paying electric bills.

The furnishings consisted of one desk, several chairs, and a large wall cabinet. On the desk was phone, blotter, and sundry items of stationery. Cellini tentatively tried the door to the cabinet and the desk drawers and found them all locked. He brought the cold chisel into play again and pried open the doors on the cabinet.

The bulk of the space in the cabinet was taken by boxes of envelopes and letterheads for the Sawamura Corporation. There remained a bottle of ink, several boxes of paper clips, bundles of pencils, and a very un-Japanese magazine that claimed to have extra spicy stories and art photographs. Duck-Eye Ryan pounced on the latter with glee and began to thumb it.

Cellini turned his attention to the desk and pried a drawer open. It was empty. He inserted the cold chisel into the crack of the top drawer, pressed up, and forced the lock. Inside were several stock certificates of the Sawamura Export Company, the papers of incorporation in Delaware, and a receipt for a check placed in escrow at the Seamen's National.

Cellini began reading through the papers of incorporation when suddenly he stopped. A satisfied smile settled on his face. There, among the Japanese names, was the more familiar name of Earl Nikken—as secretary of the corporation.

CELLINI AND DUCK-EYE Ryan circled back till they picked up Western and then headed south for the San Pedro docks. Ten minutes before they reached the harbor they sighted a huge sign, above a two-acre tract full of junk, that said: *Francis Boone—Junk Wholesaler.*

Cellini stopped, told Duck-Eye to remain in the car, and went into the offices of the Boone junk yard.

Francis Boone was short but square and wide after barn-door style. To Cellini's request for information he graciously replied he'd help as much as he could.

"Good," replied Cellini. "Could you tell me what scrap iron sells for?"

"It would depend on the kind of scrap and the size and weight of the individual pieces and what the traffic would bear, but I'd say it sells for about eight bucks a ton now."

"That's pretty cheap, isn't it?"

"It used to sell for less," said Boone, "before a lot of it went over to Japan. What are you," he queried shrewdly, "a talent scout for San Quentin?"

"Private. Who imports most of the scrap iron into Japan?"

"Mitsui. The Mitsui people have their finger in most anything in Japan—and most especially when it relates to exports or imports. However, many other companies—more than I've ever heard of—go in for it."

"In other words a company called the Seiicha Sawamura could operate pretty much on the quiet."

"Sure it could."

"I see. Tell me this, Mr. Boone. You say that scrap brings approximately eight dollars a ton. In view of that, how does it pay to ship it? How can the cargo have any value since the bulk of scrap is so tremendous?"

"They get a lot in."

"How."

"They do it with compressors. These are giant hydraulic presses and they squeeze the scrap into small compact masses. I'll show you one out in the yard. That's how they get so much scrap into one shipload. You'd be surprised at the power of these compressors. Once a particularly annoying Chinaman, who kept organizing picket lines against shipments to Japan, was thrown into one of these compressors and he was cut down to size. Nothing could be proved because there wasn't even any dew left when the presser got through with him."

Cellini said: "I see. Serious business, eh?"

"Uh-huh," replied Boone. "Quite serious. I don't think they'll ever crack Joe Miller's joke book with their tricks."

"Go on. Tell me more."

The junk dealer began to talk quickly and to the point. He told Cellini of the vast network of small junk dealers who patrolled the streets of the country in automobiles, horse carts, and hand-wagons. Some were specialists, most of them purchased and bartered anything that represented value. Their vehicles were filled with rags and papers and automobile tires, with batteries, bottles, cans, machine parts, wire, and useless furniture, with hats and shoes and iron pipe, and all kinds and shapes and sizes of metals.

Out in the yard Cellini was shown a giant machine into which men were feeding rusty junk. The metal came out at the other end clean and shredded and this was fed into a hydraulic compressor which stamped it into bales weighing nearly two hundred pounds. Nearby, another machine processed cans to remove the tin plate and then the cans were stamped into bales. Heavy, motor-driven shears clipped iron piping and steel rails into lengths that could be more readily handled.

Tremendous, wholesale junk yards such as these existed on the outskirts of every large city. To them, the junk dealers carried and resold, for a slight margin of profit, their daily collections. To them came the jobbers and exporters and local manufacturers to look over the mountains of bottles or papers or metals. Smashed glass was resold to be manufactured into new glass. Rags and cardboard cartons were eventually processed into new forms. Velvets were shipped to Japan to be converted into powder puffs, metal into bullets, old shoes into fertilizer, silk stockings to be rewound into men's hosiery.

Done on a large scale, Francis Boone assured Cellini, there was much money to be made in trading in scrap. The prodigality of the living standard made these huge wastes possible. Junk, in fact, was the oldest commerce in the world.

"Mind you," added Francis Boone puckishly, "I said the oldest *commerce* in the world—not the oldest profession."

CELLINI SMITH AND Duck-Eye Ryan reached the harbor a short while later. Trucks rumbled to and from the wharves, dock laborers, longshoremen, and sailors moved about their business, and tourists and travelers hurried to catch out-bound steamers.

The third person Cellini asked was an aged, myopic seaman. He said: "The *City of Kobe?* Hell, I don't know what anyone wants with that old tub but you'll find her berthed 'bout a half-mile south." They found the ship as directed. She was moored alongside a dilapidated dock, The dock was deserted save for a longshoreman who smoked a pipe and contemplated the *City of Kobe* with a detached but inquisitive air.

Even to Cellini, who knew nothing of the sea, the ship was a shabby one. She was a steel-hull steam boat of an obsolescent type. The mooring lines were frayed and encrusted with weed. Her hull was dirty and badly in need of paint.

With amusement Cellini noted that the ship rode as though

loaded to capacity—with her Plimsoll mark down to the water's edge. He wasn't sure how it was done but he knew that Plimsoll marks could be faked, that water could be pumped into the holds, that the ballast tanks could be filled with fuel oil. Whatever the method, he was sure of one thing—that the ship was a phoney. It carried no scrap.

As they appraised the ship, the longshoreman transferred his attention to them. "You don't think you're going aboard that hulk, do you, boys?" he called.

Duck-Eye Ryan seemed to swell in size. He vaguely felt the time had come to assert himself. "Who says so?"

Cellini nodded approvingly. "That's right, Duck-Eye. And if you don't get a chance to beat him up I'll throw you a mouse to squeeze later."

"I'm not saying so," reassured the longshoreman. He pointed on deck. "They are."

Two men stood at the head of the gangway gazing down at them with unfriendly eyes. Cellini Smith and Duck-Eye Ryan began walking up. As they neared them, they could see the three stripes of the chief mate on the sleeves of one. He was heavy-set and surly. The other, a second engineer, had two stripes. He was thick-necked and powerful and in his hand was an efficient spanner.

"You've gone far enough," called the mate. "Stop there. What do you want?"

Cellini said: "We want to talk to you."

"What about?"

"We're going to find out what your ship's carrying."

"No you're not," was the reply. "Put one foot on my deck and we'll crack your skulls open."

"O.K., Duck-Eye," said Cellini. "You've got two mice up there waiting."

Duck-Eye, followed by Cellini, started up the plank very slowly until he was within ten feet of the deck. Then he suddenly sprang forward and dashed for the engineer with amazing agility. Cellini was two steps behind.

The engineer stood bewildered for an instant, as he watched the charging mammoth, then began to bring up the spanner just as Duck-Eye grabbed and held the arm suspended in mid-air. The huge engineer shook himself and twisted his arm, but it wouldn't yield. Then, effortlessly, as if he were handling a child, Duck-Eye began to bend the arm backward. All this without a word on either side.

The momentarily disconcerted mate sprang for Duck-Eye. Cellini had expected it. He leaped in his path, landed in a low crouch, and planted a heavy fist three inches below his belt. The mate doubled up on the deck with a single, high-pitched moan of agony.

Slowly, with a happy grin, Duck-Eye bent the arm backward, forcing the mate to his knees on the deck. He twisted the wrist sideways and the spanner slipped from the paralyzed fingers. He jerked the large engineer forward again, raised him aloft with both hands, and then dropped him in a heap on top of the chief mate.

There was an appreciative shout from the longshoreman on the dock. The engineer untangled himself from the chief mate and lumbered to his feet dazedly. Duck-Eye started for him again.

Cellini said: "O.K. Relax."

Holding his mid-section with both hands, the mate crawled to the lee rail and retched over the side.

"That was because you boys go in for lethal weapons," Cellini informed him.

The mate breathed deeply and felt his stomach. The engineer worked his arm back and forth. He cast a sad, almost accusing glance toward the spanner on the deck but neither of them evidenced any intention to continue fighting.

"I'm quitting this goddamned job," the mate finally said. "There's a limit. I'm digging in on land."

Cellini asked: "Why'd you want to stop us from coming aboard and looking around?"

"Look where you damned well please. I'm quitting this stuff. I'm turning landlubber."

"He asked you sumpthin'," Duck-Eye said.

"I know," replied the mate, "and I'll answer. With a lady-finger for an engineer I'll answer anything. It's because the skipper told me no visitors. I follow orders."

Cellini beamed happily. "Nobody was allowed aboard to check! That can mean only one thing. The cargo you're supposed to carry doesn't exist."

The mate said: "I'm quitting. I'm going to sling the anchor over my back and walk down the road with it. Then right where the first guy asks me what's that I'm toting on my back—that's where I'm going to settle down and live."

"Who gave the captain those orders to keep visitors off here?" asked Cellini.

"I don't know. But the only guy that gives the skipper orders is the owner—that fighter that was killed a couple days ago."

"Morton Miles?"

"Yeah."

"Have you had any instructions since then?"

"No."

"Good enough," said Cellini. "If you don't mind, we'll take a look around. You two boys stay right with us." As an after-thought, he added: "Better make it in front of us."

CELLINI SCANNED THE deck. The hatches were battened down and covered with tarpaulin as if the cargo were already stowed below. The decks were clear and all rope stowed in the lockers and a lifeboat that Cellini peered into was duly provisioned with hardtack and water. The *City of Kobe* seemed ready for departure. No other crew members were visible and the mate told Cellini that the skeleton crew kept on pay was on shore leave. He and the second were gangway-watch.

Duck-Eye Ryan poked the chastened engineer in the small of his back and they filed down 'tween decks toward the forward holds. They passed through the dark and narrow companions that were lightened only by the pencil flash that Cellini produced. They reached the number one hold and the mate slid open the massive, steel, fireproof door. Cellini looked inside, then began to swear slowly and carefully for several minutes, savoring the sound of each word.

The hold was jammed full, from port to starboard, from deck to deckhead, with baled scrap iron. The tons of cleaned, shredded, and compressed bales of the metal lay side by side and lashed one on top the other—ready for their appointment in Japan.

They shut the door and took another companionway. The number two hold had the same full complement of bales of scrap. They went aft. Three and four holds were likewise loaded to capacity.

Cellini's angry befuddlement simmered down to helpless uncertainty. "There's no sense to it," he muttered.

"What?" asked the mate.

"Never mind. Where'd this cargo come from?"

"Don't know."

"When was it taken on?"

"Don't know that either. She was loaded down to her mark already when I was hired."

Cellini led the way toward one of the cargo ports amidships. He said: "Things just don't connect. I don't know why."

Duck-Eye Ryan asked hopefully: "Can I make 'em talk?"

"Go ahead and ask," snapped the mate. "You won't get any fight out of me. I'm through. I'm turning in my ticket. I'm going to become a lousy landlubber and learn how to swim."

"If I only knew the right thing to ask," mused Cellini. "Where was this cargo supposed to go?"

"Kobe or Osaki in Japan. Wasn't decided yet."

"What's going to happen to the cargo now?"

"Don't know," replied the mate, "and I'm quitting before I find out. Somebody'll probably try to buy the ship from the Miles estate and try to sail her over."

"How's your belly?"

"I'm never gonna try to hit your fist with it again, mister. I can tell you that much."

"Take it easy." Cellini beckoned to Duck-Eye Ryan and they quit the ship. The longshoreman was still on the dock, smoking his pipe, and they approached him.

"Nice set-to," remarked the longshoreman. "Find out anything to make it worth your while?"

Cellini said: "Suppose you let me do the asking."

"Why should I?"

"Here's why." Cellini selected a fiver from his wallet and tendered it to the longshoreman. He accepted the bill and regarded it thoughtfully.

"What seems to be wrong with that money?" asked Cellini.

"Nothing," said the longshoreman. "Absolutely nothing. It looks perfect. All you want is to ask me a couple of questions for all this and I was just thinking how it bears out Thorstein Veblen's theory of conspicuous waste."

The Terrible Turk

"Ah, hah," said Cellini. "I.W.W.! Right?"

The longshoreman nodded. "Right. What do you want to know for all this money?"

Cellini said: "There's no work around this dock. It's as dead as Veblen's theories. What are you doing around here?"

"I'm interested in that ship."

"Why?" pursued Cellini.

"I couldn't say. That's the reason I'm interested."

"Don't try to go abstruse on me. Who stopped this ship from sailing?"

"Unions, individuals, Chinese and liberal organizations—anyone with a little sense."

"All right," said Cellini. "That's all."

"I didn't give you five bucks' worth of anything, mister," the longshoreman said. "But since you seem plenty interested and dumb I'll ask you a question. Lots of ships get out with scrap and why doesn't this one? And if this is one of those unlucky ones that have been stopped for good, then why keep her crewed and full of cargo and food and fuel while she's idle? And that tail shaft and those plates? Besides, who's paying those bills? That's bad economy. A production force kept on with nothing being produced. Now suppose you play that one on your piccolo, mister."

Duck-Eye Ryan said, "Huh?" but the longshoreman had already turned away to smoke his pipe.

12

Dead Man's Bride

CELLINI SMITH WAS morose and uncommunicative on the journey back from San Pedro. He was worried. The case was untidy. Everything had pointed toward a simple confidence game in scrap. But then it developed that the Sawamura Company had actually put up the money in escrow and that the scrap had actually been bought for shipment. In the face of those facts it was reasonable for Lyams to have found everything aboveboard in his investigations.

What then was the meaning of Earl Nikken as secretary of the Sawamura Corporation? Didn't that belie the facts? Would a man like Earl Nikken operate from behind a dummy Japanese corporation to buy scrap iron from his closest intimate? What was technically legitimate, was psychologically false. And where stood Jesse Lee Ward in this odd relationship? Had he been caught in the middle in a squeeze play, only to pay with his life? Bearing this in mind, Earl Nikken's phone call ordering Ward back from Palm Springs took on added significance.

Cellini still worried and kneaded these questions in his mind when he reached the Professional Building. Duck-Eye Ryan announced that he was hungry and set off for an evil-smelling beanery two blocks away. Cellini crossed the street to the Hangover and nearly collided with Olive Fain as she came out.

Cellini was taken with her. The black mourning made her no object of pity but rather enhanced her desirability. It set off the texture and translucence of that marvelous skin.

He said: "If you're here I imagine Earl Nikken's inside, but I'd like to speak to you first."

"Please don't think I'll ever admire you for being reckless, Mr. Smith. I dislike fools."

"Black becomes you, Elektra. Meet me in my office across the way in fifteen minutes."

As she passed on he could not tell whether or not she agreed. He entered the club.

It was still early afternoon and customers were scarce. Like a council of regency, Earl Nikken sat at his table surrounded by several of the Hangover's fighting fraternity. Cellini made for them.

The gaze they turned on him was suspicious and their manner belligerent. Of them all, only Chicago Earl was friendly, if somewhat patronizing. They asked about his progress and they quizzed him on Ward and Miles and demanded results. They were tired of waiting. The cops weren't doing anything. They just showed up every other hour and hauled a couple of them down to the D.A.'s office for questioning. It was becoming tiresome. When would he get busy?

They didn't seem to worry much about Jesse Lee Ward's murder. He was one of the boys and it was tough luck. Lots of people get killed. The Kongo Kid was killed by a rabbit punch only last week. But with Morton Miles it was different. In their mind, Morton Miles was assassinated while Jesse Lee Ward was rubbed out. It was a delicate distinction, as between the passing of a monarch and the death of a mere vassal. Ward's murder interested them only insofar as it could shed light upon Miles'.

As the barrage let up, Cellini began to talk with Earl Nikken and the bruisers drifted off to the bar. Nikken lit a cigarette and said: "Well?"

"I'll skip the preliminaries, Mr. Nikken. How does Ward's murder affect my status? Am I still working for you?"

"Yes. I always go through with my deals. Get the person who killed Miles and Ward and I'll raise the ante to two G's."

"Fine. But you seem to be sure that Miles and Ward were killed by the same person."

"It's obvious."

"O.K. Do you mind telling me what you know of Olive Fain?"

Earl Nikken said: "I think she's one of the most wonderful women I've ever met. Jesse was a very lucky man to be her husband—if only for a day."

"There's no question of that, is there? I mean that they were actually married."

EARL NIKKEN'S JAW squared and he became taut so that the tendons on his neck stood out. For the first time Cellini saw something beyond the pleasant, retired business man—something indicative of the powerful racketeer he once was.

Before Nikken could speak, Cellini said: "It's all in the day's work. Forget it. What I really want to know is why you don't deal them straight to me if you're really so anxious to clear up the murders?"

Earl Nikken relaxed. When he spoke it was in his normal, polite tone. "What progress have the police made?"

Cellini shrugged. "I don't know but I can guess. They thought Ward had ventilated Miles and now they're busy explaining to the D.A. that it was all a mistake and they're looking for somebody else. But why don't you help me out and answer my question?"

"What's the trouble now?"

"I'm beefing about you, Mr. Nikken. Ward said he came back from Palm Springs because of a call from Morton Miles. Miles never phoned Ward in Palm Springs. You were the only one to phone him."

The elderly racketeer gave no hint of surprise. "That was only a technical lie, Mr. Smith. What actually happened was that I phoned Jesse in Morton Miles' name because Morton was busy. The police accepted that explanation this morning and there's no reason why you shouldn't."

Cellini took a deep breath and plunged. "O.K. There's another lie that wasn't so technical. You told me you had nothing to do with the scrap-iron dealings. This morning I discovered that you're secretary of the Seiicha Sawamura Corporation—the outfit that placed the order."

Earl Nikken fixed his gaze on the top of Cellini's head for a few moments before replying. When it came, his voice was surprisingly mild. "You asked me whether I'd backed Morton in his venture—or words to that effect—and I said I hadn't. I just happened to own stock in the corporation that placed the order with him."

"Splitting hairs with a meat ax," mocked Cellini.

"On the contrary. Being accurate."

"O.K." Cellini was disgusted and dissatisfied and he took no pains to conceal it. "Everybody makes a long speech about helping me and then they dummy up. I take just so much of that sort of thing but then I quit. First the Turk gives me that line and now you. The only difference is a cigarette instead of a water pipe."

Earl Nikken smiled tolerantly. He said: "I'll be glad to help you with the Turk."

"How?" asked Cellini.

"I could lend you Gutty and the Gimp if you want to visit him again. They'll make him answer your questions."

"What are they?" asked Cellini. "A couple strong-arm boys you used to know?"

"More or less. Both the Gimp and Gutty used to work for me. I've pensioned Gutty off by letting him think he's my bodyguard."

"That's very nice of you, Mr. Nikken," said Cellini suspiciously. "But why so suddenly helpful?"

"Morton was a friend of mine and Jesse Ward was. You said I don't help you and here's proof I do. If you don't want it, though, I won't mind."

"Sure," said Cellini slowly. "I'll take your help if it kills me— and it might at that. Does the Turk know your torpedoes?"

"Yes."

"Good. It might impress him if he thinks you're in back of me. When can I have them?"

"Any time. Name the place and the Gimp and Gutty will be there waiting for you."

Cellini said: "At my office across the way. They can make it around six or a little after so's I'll be sure to get the Turk in."

Earl Nikken nodded. As Cellini left he felt vaguely disquieted. Earl Nikken had been too calm. He had taken too great pains not to ask why he'd disregarded his warning of the previous day to leave Jesse Lee Ward and Olive Fain alone.

OLIVE FAIN WAS waiting in the hallway when Cellini crossed the street to his office. He unlocked the door and they entered. She stretched out on the settee with a happy sigh.

"Tired?" he asked.

"Yes," she said, "I've spent hours up at the D.A.'s office being questioned and cross-questioned. Then I came down to see Earl. I've been on my feet all day. Now don't you start questions."

Cellini sat down behind the desk. "What shall I call you? Miss Fain or Mrs. Ward?"

"You may call me Olive," she replied, "but please don't say you can learn to like olives after a while."

"I thought we were better enemies than that."

"I'm sorry. I really have a higher opinion of you."

"Besides," continued Cellini smoothly, "making verbal passes at women whose husbands were killed only the night before isn't in the books—not even the Hollywood books."

"Thank you, Mr. Smith. I'm glad that isn't why you asked me up here."

"Did you care for your husband a great deal, Olive?" he asked.

"Ah. The man with the one-track mind. Of course I cared for him. I married Jesse. I loved him."

"Yet each man kills the thing he loves," he murmured.

Olive Fain smiled. "And by each let this be heard, Mr. Smith. Some do it with a bitter look and some with a flattering word and so forth. But that's not applicable in my case. Firstly, I'm not a man. I'm a woman—"

"I've noticed. I'm a detective."

"—and while men may react to love with murder, women rarely do. Those pictures on the wall seem to indicate you're interested in anthropology. Read your Briffault on the mating instinct. He'll tell you that women are cruel to their mates to protect their young—the mating instinct. It's not a matter of love. And the second reason why your Wilde quotation is meaningless in my case is because I lied when I said I loved Jesse."

"Of course. We both knew that."

"And," she continued, "don't give me that suave Gable lift of your eyebrows, Mr. Smith, because if I didn't love Jesse it doesn't follow that I hated him. It was neither."

"Call me Cellini," he said. "You want me to believe you married the man, stayed with him, and your attitude is impersonal!"

"Partly true. I married him but, as you know, I didn't stay with him."

"Why?"

"Never ask a woman that. The dispensation of her favors is her own prerogative. But, to return, Jesse's death affects me as yours would."

"I can well believe that. If you didn't kill your husband, who did?"

"I don't know. May I have a cigarette, please?"

CELLINI WALKED OVER, gave her a cigarette, lit one for himself, sat on the edge of the settee. He gazed down at her face, her eyes, and lips without speaking. Finally, he said: "I suppose you think I'll try to kiss you."

She shook her head. "No. I think you're the type who always tries to do the unexpected."

He gave a shrug and returned to the desk. "What's the explanation you gave the police when they asked you where you spent your wedding night?"

"I told them that Jesse had confessed he'd been married before and had secured a Mexican divorce. And since Mexican divorces aren't supposed to be legal I decided to leave him till he got one in Reno."

He whistled with admiration. "You think quickly, Olive. I'm beginning to like you. I asked Earl Nikken if you had really been married and he nearly blew a fuse. Why?"

"I don't know."

"Can't you guess?"

"No. Unless, it's that he's touchy about women and marriage because his wife's suing him for divorce. Her name is Valena Nikken, she doesn't live with him and since I know your next question, she's staying at the Carlotta Apartments."

"Thank you. Why tell me?"

"The more you meddle with Earl the sooner you'll get your neck broken."

"Nice girl."

Heavy footfalls sounded in the hall outside and Ned Lyams stumbled in. He was red-eyed, unshaven, and semi-drunk. He carried a half-empty bottle of bourbon in his hand. He caught sight of Olive Fain and said: "Excuse me. I wanted the men's room." He turned to leave.

"Sit down," said Cellini.

The private operative mumbled something, sank into a chair, and began to suckle the bottle. Olive Fain stood up.

"Don't mind him," said Cellini.

"I was going anyway."

"Very well, but there's one more thing I'd like to know. I

can make a pretty accurate guess but you tell me why Valena Nikken is suing Earl for divorce."

"It's one of those alienation of affection things."

"And who's the woman who took Earl Nikken away from his wife?"

Olive Fain said: "Me."

NED LYAMS KEPT up his wheedling for a good ten minutes. "Why don't you talk? I told you I'm sorry I busted in on you and your girl. She's a tasty dish."

Cellini told him to keep quiet and let him think. Presently he picked up the receiver and dialed Joe Lucca. When he had his connection he said: "Joe, do you know a couple of local boys called Gutty and the Gimp?"

"Uh-huh. Strong arm stuff."

"What else?"

"Nothing. They do independent work—the highest bidder. If you've got anything to do with them watch the Gimp. He used to be Earl Nikken's ace trigger-boy back in the old days. Out here he picks up loose change by running a poker game. And he's pretty bad. If he thought there was any oil under his mother's grave he'd let them drill right through it. It wouldn't worry him one bit."

"O.K."

"I'm glad you called, Cellini. I was going to give you a ring."

"Why?"

"I just thought I'd give you a friendly tip, Cellini, for old times sake. Stay away from the Three Nuns tonight."

"What are you talking about?"

"The Three Nuns. Keep away."

"Sure, Joe, but I think you're cracking. There'll be a lot of places I won't be tonight. That might as well be one of them because I've never even heard of it."

Lucca replied that he had spoken his piece. Cellini said, "Take it easy," and cradled the receiver.

Ned Lyams mumbled, "I'm sorry I busted in on you and your woman," and took another swig.

"She's not my woman. What have you been doing all day?"

"I've been worried sick. All night, too. I've been waiting for you to sic the shams on me. Cellini, give me back that report I signed on Miles' murder. You know you held me up last night."

"It's put away in a safe place."

"If I were a killer, Cellini, I'd go after you. You're lucky I'm not."

Cellini stared at him, frankly amused.

"Sure," said Lyams sadly, "I know what you're thinking. But that was a big mistake. I didn't see you step in front of the car."

"I understand, Ned. Just forget it. Only try to avoid those big mistakes in the future because if something happens to me, I've arranged for that report to go to the police."

"That's not fair, Cellini. I worried about you all night. Suppose you go to sleep smoking a cigarette and you burn to death. What happens to me?"

"I told you not to worry about it."

"Damn you, Cellini. I said it was justifiable homicide."

"And I said if I can stick Ward's murderer for both jobs I'd do it. I thought you were going to help me on this job instead of worrying what I'd do about you. Why don't you go home to bed and sober up."

"I don't wanna sober up. Besides I got to go someplace

tonight. Some mugg stopped me on the street and said I'd find out something very interesting if I went to a joint called the Three Nuns tonight."

Cellini sat up straight. "The Three Nuns? Did you recognize who stopped you?"

"No, but he smelled like he was ripe for a third term."

"Are you going?"

"I don't know. Maybe. I can drink and worry there like anyplace else."

"Where is it?"

"The Three Nuns? Don't know but I'll find out. It's a hangout for small-fry gangsters. I heard about it. I'm sorry I busted in on you and your woman, Cellini. She's zoftig. I feel like crying."

"Ned, try and understand me. I'm going now, but you lie down there on the couch and try to sleep your jag off. After a while my side-kick, Duck-Eye Ryan, will be here. Tell him not to go away. Tell him I'm going down to see the Turk around six and that I want him to come with me. Tell him to stay here and don't give him a drink."

"Sure. You're all right, Cellini. You won't turn me in."

"Don't forget. I'm going out to do some work now."

"More scrap iron," muttered Ned Lyams. "I like you and I'll make you the Feuhrer of junk. It'll be a divine mission. Your job'll be to make all the junk dealers in the country conscious of their tradition, heritage, and racial superiority and I'll be your minister of culture and enlightenment. Then when we collect all the junk from everyplace we'll give the world twenty-four hours to get out."

"One fool makes a hundred," Cellini quoted from his name-sake's biography. "Now don't forget to tell Duck-Eye to stay here because I want him to go with me to the Turk." He dragged Lyams over to the couch and pushed him down on it.

"I won't forget," promised Ned Lyams. "And I won't forget to go to the Three Nuns because the guy who told me to go there said I'd find out who killed Jesse Ward and I want to find that out because then maybe both murders can be stuck on…" His words trailed off, his head sagged, and his breathing took on the regularity of sleep. Cellini made a thorough search of Ned Lyam's pockets and clothing and when he found nothing of especial interest he left the office.

13

Discarded Lady

MAX CUSHMAN KEPT Cellini Smith waiting in his ante-room for fifteen minutes. Cellini spent the time making little boats out of a stack of Cushman's business cards and wondering who it was that told Lyams that Ward's murder would be solved that night. At the end of the fifteen minutes the ash-blond secretary began angrily to collect the boats and said that Mr. Smith could go in now.

Jesse Lee Ward's attorney still exhibited the dyspepsia and surliness usually attributed to successful lawyers. When Cellini asked what he thought of his client's murder he replied, "Here today, gone tomorrow," and when Cellini persisted he informed him that he ought to know better than to start pumping an attorney.

In the succeeding twenty minutes Cellini garnered little information. Max Cushman said that he didn't know where Ward had come from and that he had handled only special jobs for him so that he didn't know much of his affairs. He informed Cellini that he had also been Morton Miles' attorney as the affairs of Ward and Miles usually overlapped. As Cellini rose to leave he asked if by any chance he was also Nikken's attorney.

"No," replied Max Cushman.

"Ever hear of him?"

"Chicago during prohibition days, wasn't he?" said Max Cushman. "He lives out here trying to keep quiet but his wife's got different ideas. She's suing for divorce and she's not taking one of those quickies from Reno or Mexico either."

"That's the one," said Cellini eagerly. "Tell me about his wife—"

"I don't even know the woman," said Max Cushman irritably. "I've just read of her divorce proceedings. She's also prosecuting a suit for alienation of affections against some girl or other. She put the alienation suit in just before the new law."

"That's interesting. Against Olive Fain?"

"That's the name. Though I happened to hear this morning that Valena Nikken is dropping the alienation suit against this Olive Fain. And for God's sake don't ask me why because I don't know why."

"Can't you guess?"

"No. I've nothing to do with it."

Cellini thanked him and left for the Carlotta Apartments.

THE CARLOTTA WAS exclusive and overpriced and did not strive to hide the fact. Valena Nikken, Cellini decided, either still received money from Earl, despite the divorce proceedings, or she had an income of her own. He pressed a button that touched off a series of chimes on the inside.

Valena Nikken admitted him. She was well over forty and did not accept it gracefully. She was a colorless blonde and her features had neither blemishes nor especial attributes. She was a negative but highly emotional type.

Cellini sat down on a sofa. Valena Nikken seated herself next to him and listened intently as he introduced himself and explained his presence.

"Anything," she said when he was finished. "I'll tell you anything you want to know." Her speech was jerky and nervous.

"That's such a rare attitude"—he smiled—"that it almost makes me suspicious."

There was no counter-smile—just an intent stare—and he asked: "Is it true that you're suing Earl Nikken for divorce and Olive Fain for alienation of affections?"

Valena Nikken said: "Yes. Or rather yes and no as I'm suing for divorce but dropping the alienation proceedings."

"Why are you dropping them?"

"Because I doubt if I can win it. I take after my husband, Mr. Smith. I play only to win."

"Will Mr. Nikken contest the divorce?" asked Cellini.

"I imagine he'll follow the course that will make for the fewest headlines—the least notoriety."

"May I ask why you are divorcing Mr. Nikken?"

"Yes," said Valena Nikken. "Everybody will know soon so why shouldn't you? Two years ago he met Olive Fain and purchased her as his mistress. He fell insanely in love with her."

"At least that's an apology for his throwing you over," murmured Cellini.

"You're wrong, Mr. Smith. If only he did not love her I wouldn't mind. I could hope he'd come back to me."

"You care for him, don't you?"

She said, "Yes," hollowly.

He asked: "Well, why not just remain separated, as now, and mark time in place of embarrassing him with a lot of publicity?"

"I know it may get him in trouble, Mr. Smith. With his name in print, civic organizations will start denouncing him and objecting to his presence out here."

"Then why do it—if you care for him?"

"It's the only way I can fight." She leaned close to him and he could see a fine, blond down on her upper lip. "Mr. Smith, I married Earl Nikken twenty-three years ago. I loved him then and I love him today. I stayed by him for those twenty-three years, starving half the time and the other half evading the police. He was just a bum—a chewing-gum-machine-pilfering bum in Chicago. Neither of us belonged in that crowd, if only because we both went to school. I stayed by him all that time and now he throws me over for a trollop—a beautiful trollop who admits to his face she doesn't love him."

"Olive Fain seemed to be a very intelligent and talented woman when I talked to her," Cellini said.

"Of course she is, Mr. Smith. That's why I'm insanely jealous of her. If I knew I could get Earl back ultimately it would be easier for me. But I know in my heart that she's better than I am. She's better than I am in bed or in conversation at the dinner table. Why should Earl come back to me?"

"Have you and Mr. Nikken any children?" asked Cellini.

"No. Earl's career was too uncertain for us to risk it. I was a beautiful woman once, Mr. Smith. Do you believe it?"

"Yes, of course," said Cellini politely.

Her face sagged into a poignant smile. "You're a very kind liar, Mr. Smith. Thank you. But I truly was. Today even my hair is dead."

She swallowed heavily. Cellini Smith squirmed uncomfortably and inched away from her. But she leaned forward and gazed into his face with the same relentless, discomfiting stare.

"Cigarette, Mrs. Nikken?"

"Don't you think I'm sufficiently nervous without smoking, or do you think it would calm me?"

"Mrs. Nikken," he said, "if this liaison exists between Olive

Fain and your husband, then why did Jesse Lee Ward marry her?"

"Because Jesse Lee Ward also was insane about her. Most men are. Her kind has it easy."

"You're fighting big odds," Cellini said for want of better.

VALENA NIKKEN LEANED still further forward. Cellini felt her hot breath on his face. She said; "The divorce is my method of fighting it, Mr. Smith. I keep telling myself that I may scare him into taking me back—and I know it's quite impossible even as I say it."

"It's very possible though," lied Cellini.

"No. He'll never take me back. He doesn't want me any more. No man wants me. If I could get another man I would fight him that way—with more subtle weapons—but I'm washed up, Mr. Smith."

"Do you know that Olive Fain's husband, Jesse Lee Ward, was killed last night?"

"Yes, I've heard. I didn't kill him."

"What do you intend doing when you get your divorce, Mrs. Nikken?"

"What I'm doing now. Nothing. I'm a very tired old woman. I will just sit here."

They fell silent.

"I won't give him up for some trollop!" she suddenly cried. "I've known him since he was an ordinary, cheap, gun-carrying hoodlum and I won't—" She broke off.

Her eyes were clear and hard and tearless but her fingers clawed a small, lace handkerchief in her hands until it tore. "I'll have that cigarette now," she whispered.

Cellini supplied it and lit one for himself. They smoked for a while and when she presently spoke again her voice was calmer. "Forgive me, Mr. Smith. I know I'm boring you. It's just that thing eating my insides."

Cellini shrugged. "Spill it. I don't mind. That's what I'm here for. Did your husband see Morton Miles and Jesse Lee Ward frequently, Mrs. Nikken?"

"Occasionally, while we lived together. Though he didn't see anyone frequently. He tried to live a quiet life."

"Both those men were killed. You know nothing of them?"

"Nothing that could help."

"What about Jesse Lee Ward?"

"He was very handsome and very stupid to marry Olive Fain," she responded.

"What else? Who might have killed him?"

"I don't know. Many people are capable of murder. *She* would be capable of anything—as I would. But I don't know."

Cellini shifted uncomfortably again. "Does Mr. Nikken pay for this layout?"

"Yes. He sends me a lot of money the first of each month. He's very kind and very considerate. Very wonderful and very horrible, Mr. Smith."

"You said before that Olive Fain didn't love your husband, Mrs. Nikken."

"No. She's even told him so. To his face! That's the mockery. She just *likes* him. As if a man like my husband could only be liked!"

"Well," said Cellini, "thank you for talking to me. I hope things turn out well for you. At least you have a beautiful place here."

The wisps of her mustache trembled nervously. She said; "Mr. Smith, suppose you were forty-eight and the man you loved threw you out. And suppose you had nothing to look forward to but dying in an apartment-hotel like this with expensive chinaware and velour drapes—everything but a little warmth. Would you care for it? Tell me."

"I guess not."

"No. Of course not." She stared squarely into his face in her disconcerting manner. "Twenty-three years of it, Mr. Smith. Afraid of the law and knowing only hoods and thugs and game-cocks from poolrooms with flash apartments. The kind that don't care two cents for human life but select their tailor with exquisite care. And now when we have something to live for he throw's me over. Damn those velour drapes anyway!"

She suddenly leaped to her feet and sprang for the heavy drapes. It took all her weight and strength to bring them down into a heap at her feet. She stood still for a long moment, panting, then passed a hand across her face. Cellini barely heard her voice as she spoke. "Tired, Mr. Smith. Very, very tired."

Cellini rose and fled.

14

Gutty and the Gimp

IT WAS FIFTEEN minutes shy of six when Cellini Smith left the Carlotta Apartments. He was not far from his office when he remembered he'd neglected to ask Valena Nikken precisely why she had dropped that suit for alienation against Olive Fain. It was certainly not because she had undergone a change of heart toward her husband's mistress.

But it was too late and harrowing a prospect to return. Gutty and the Gimp, the two torpedoes, were due at his office shortly and then he'd see the Turk. He maneuvered the car into a space at the curb and went upstairs.

The office was unlocked and empty. He went out and looked into the hall toilet but found no trace of Duck-Eye Ryan or Ned Lyams and he returned to the office. He sat down behind the desk, then suddenly frowned as he was struck by something amiss.

The signs were few: A drawer not fully shut or a bottle of ink slightly out of position—but there was no question that the room had had a thorough going over.

Cellini adjusted the ink bottle and waited. Ten minutes later he heard footfalls in the hall and Ira Haenigson entered.

The Detective-sergeant of Homicide sank heavily into a chair. "I was just going home, Smith, but I thought I'd drop in and see how you're doing."

"Will you be sympathetic or tough this time?"

"Sweet like the driven snow."

"O.K., but don't be long. I'm expecting visitors."

"I can't get away from it, Smith, but it's peculiar how you happened to find both the bodies."

"Why do you always gun for me, Haenigson? How about Ned Lyams for a change? What is he—Caesar's wife?"

"I know Ned and I know how far he'd go but I don't know you."

"O.K.," said Cellini, "But you also know I was with Ned Lyams last night so why not drop it. Maybe you want to be a good detective and check my rod."

"You're pretty lucky you had a guy like Ned to alibi you. Are you sure you didn't leave him for a half-hour or something?"

"Sure I'm sure. Ask him."

"I did. Might as well take a peek at your rod though."

Cellini said: "I've only got one." He took a Smith & Wesson from a drawer and pushed it across the desk.

The detective-sergeant barely glanced at it. "O.K. Wrong caliber. As if you didn't know. Smith"—Haenigson's voice was chummy—"who ventilated Ward last night?"

Cellini returned the gun to the drawer and said: "At midnight tonight a gypsy crone will answer that question for me with the help of sundry herbs, potions, and amulets."

"I'm serious, Smith."

"You're just trying to take advantage of my innocence, Haenigson. You want to find out everything I know and then toss me aside like a useless glove. Suppose you give out for a change. Who do you pick as the murderer?"

"I don't know. It can't be Ward. If only I could prove it was you it'd be a good way out."

Cellini said: "Take the needle out of your arm. I heard you talked to Earl Nikken this morning."

"Yes. I wish I knew where he figured in this. I had to go easy with him because he's got a lot of ins at H.Q."

"What's Nikken's alibi for last night?"

Haenigson shrugged. "What's the difference? His kind gets them a dime a dozen. The best. So you got nothing new to tell me?"

"No. I told you the murderer was crawling around Ward's living-room floor looking for something. Have you found it?"

Haenigson shook his head. "Maybe you found it. I ought to put Boggs to check you."

"I thought of that," said Cellini. "I was looking for one of your bright boys to shadow me today."

"No use. You're hep."

"Haenigson, if you thought I held out something I found at Ward's house, maybe you sent Boggs around here this afternoon to case my office unofficially."

"No."

"O.K. Then forget it because I know who did it."

"It wouldn't have been a bad idea though, I could have picked that lock on your door with a charlotte russe."

CELLINI HAULED FORTH a bottle and two glasses secreted in a bottom drawer of the desk. They drank and Haenigson observed that it was nice of the man who searched the office to leave the whiskey alone.

Cellini asked: "What have you been doing outside of cadging drinks, Haenigson?"

"This and that," replied the Homicide man vaguely. "Earl Nikken—know him well?"

"Like a brother," said Cellini.

"All right, but something funny's going on. He's the one who called Ward back from Palm Springs and I found out that Ward's wife and Earl Nikken do light housekeeping together. Do you think that's true?"

Cellini refilled the detective-sergeant's glass. "I couldn't say, Haenigson. Does all this look like a woman's job?"

Ira Haenigson shook his head decisively. "Nope. It's some baby who knows this town and knows what's going on. I wish I knew who," he added yearningly. "The reporters are getting wise too. They're beginning to spell my name wrong again."

"Your captain putting on the pressure?"

"Yeah. I always get the tough jobs. If I couldn't depend on you for a couple of drinks every once in a while I'd try to pin it on you."

Cellini said: "I'll remember that."

"I was kidding," said Haenigson. "You're all right. I'd pin it on you only if I thought you were a little guilty." He rose. At the door he turned for his parting shot: "Sure, you're all right, Smith. Like an overgrown rattlesnake. That's how all right you are." He slammed the door behind him.

Cellini pulled cigarettes from his pocket, draped two long legs over the desk top, and leaned back in the chair. He wondered how much punishment the Terrible Turk would take before he'd crack and he guessed where Duck-Eye Ryan and Ned Lyams might be. He thought of Valena Nikken and that burning hatred which would think nothing of murder. He wished he knew what Jesse Ward's murderer was searching for on the floor and behind sofa pillows and again he told himself that if he had sense he'd let Ward's killer alone and turn

Lyams in for the Morton Miles job. Business was business—and there was no reason why he shouldn't mind his own. What did it matter if Joe Lucca invited him to keep away from some underworld hangout and someone else urged Ned Lyams to be sure and go?

TEN MINUTES LATER the door opened and Gutty and the Gimp made their entrance. Gutty was beefy, round-shouldered, and loose-limbed. A furrow from each corner of his bluish lips to his nostrils endowed him with a permanent sneer. The Gimp was unpleasant, small, almost dainty. A perfume or, at least, some sort of toilet water clung to him. He had just a few strands of hair that were strategically plastered over his skull and the cane he carried was heavy-topped and brass-tipped. A pair the Turk would certainly respect, thought Cellini.

They introduced themselves and formally shook damp hands with Cellini.

Cellini said: "Nice of Nikken to lend me you boys. He must want to see this thing cleared up as badly as I do."

"Bury the bull," said the Gimp politely. "Glad to do it. It's pretty tough to tackle the Turk alone and a couple of helpers don't harm."

"Sure," said Cellini. "You were trigger man for Earl Nikken back in Chi, weren't you, Gimp?"

"Uh-huh. But no more of that stuff now. Earl's retired. Let's get going."

"Joe Lucca told me you ran a poker game, Gimp."

"Just afternoons and some nights. It don't mean much."

"How is it," asked Cellini, "that a guy like you goes in for a two-bit racket like that?"

The Gimp shrugged. "You know how it is, Smith. A dollar here, a dollar there. It all adds up at the end of the year. Why don't we blow?"

"I'm waiting for a couple of friends of mine," said Cellini.

"Let's get it over with. I'm busy after."

Gutty added: "Me too."

Cellini stood up. "O.K." He passed by them. On closer examination the cane seemed to be an even nastier item. He preceded them downstairs and when they reached the sidewalk led the way to his roadster. "Pile in," he said.

"We'll go in our car," the Gimp demurred. "It's larger."

Gutty nodded agreement.

Cellini said nothing. Unexpectedly, the Gimp said, "O.K.," they wedged themselves into the Plymouth roadster, and Cellini made for the bowling alley.

THE THREE MEN stepped through the wide doors and casually scanned the place. The alleys, bar, billiard and pool tables were crowded and noisy. The Siberian Adonis and a two-hundred-pounder whose ring name was the Manhattan Muscovite were swapping tall stories of their brawn at the bar. The boy with the gun and the close-cropped hair was not in sight. They circumspectly walked by the wrestlers at the bar and pushed through the door at the end of it. Cellini noted with satisfaction that the din of the bowling balls and flying pins were small and distant. Those tapestries had some use. A perfect place to discuss matters.

The Terrible Turk was alone. His abnormal length was sprawled, as usual, over the cushions and a bottle, half-filled with some white wine, stood on the floor beside him. He observed their entry without movement and waited for the closing of the door before he said: "So you finally come back for more, Smith."

"I came back to give more," corrected Cellini. "These are two friends of mine—Gutty and the Gimp."

"I know them. Since when they your friends?"

"I used the term only in its technical sense. They're doing me a favor."

"I told you last time Ned Lyams takes care of my business with you."

"Sure, and there's a couple of things you didn't tell me. Do you know that Jesse Lee Ward was killed last night?"

"I heard all about it, Smith," said the Terrible Turk darkly. "I got my ears to the ground but don't start pinning Ward's murder on me, too, because I never even met him and you can check on it with the boys at the Hangover. I didn't plug Miles and I didn't plug Ward and I'm getting puking sick of private dicks. I been talking to friends of mine at the police department and I found out my own peeper was messing around Ward's home last night. I give him no instructions to do that and you been hanging on my tail for the Miles killing ever since he was counted out. That sort of thing just ain't done, Smith—not with me." The ex-wrestler sounded hurt.

"I'm just a little devil," replied Cellini.

"You're a little ———— ——— —— ——————," said the Turk deliberately, "and you're not little."

Cellini said mockingly: "You're not in a spot to get tough, Turk. You make long speeches about cooperating but every time you're asked a question you fly off the handle. How do you tie that up? Why're you so scared of a visit from the cops?

What gave you the idea to get Ned Lyams to check on Morton Miles in the first place? What's your alibi for last night? What about a lot of other things?"

"Smith, all I say is I don't have to tie up nothing for you. If I was a killer you'd be the first guy I'd pick on."

Cellini said: "I'm waiting for you to tell me something else, Turk."

"What?"

"I'm waiting to hear you ask me to go or stay away from the Three Nuns tonight."

"You know that hangout?" the Gimp asked of Cellini.

The Terrible Turk said: "I don't give a hootinhell what you do, Smith."

Cellini advanced a few steps to be nearer the Turk. "Listen," he urged, "let's you and I cut this out. I've got around five or six questions I want to ask and you tell me the truth without getting tough and we'll stay friends. I won't bother you again after that. If you don't shake on that I'll have to beat up on you, Turk, so talk. Talk now because if you don't I've got a couple of artists here who'll make you talk."

THE TERRIBLE TURK drank from the white wine and then set the bottle on the floor again. "You're pretty sure of yourself, ain't you, Smith?"

Cellini beckoned to Gutty and the Gimp. They circled around some cushions to his side. He said: "O.K., boys. Get busy."

"Busy?" asked Gutty with a stupid expression on his face.

Cellini said: Yes. Start working on him."

"Oh!" A compact, vicious sap materialized in his hand. He

said: "You mean like this, Smith, don't you?" His hand lashed out and he whipped the sap in a side-swiping blow over Cellini's face.

A long red slit appeared on Cellini's right cheek and blood began to bubble from it. The blow threw him backward against the Gimp. The Gimp jammed his brass-tipped cane into the small of Cellini's back and shoved him forward again at Gutty. Gutty aimed carefully and drove his left fist into the center of Cellini's temple and knocked him down. The Terrible Turk began to laugh.

Very slowly, Cellini stood up. His face was bleeding concrete as understanding penetrated.

The sap came around again in a careless arc. Cellini ducked under it and delivered a smashing blow to Gutty's chest that threw him against the ottoman. Gutty righted himself immediately, took a firmer grasp on the black-jack, and eyed Cellini with somewhat greater caution as he considered his next move.

The Terrible Turk still lolled on his cushions. "And *you* were going to give me a work-over," he roared. His next few words were incoherent as spasms of uncontrolled laughter shook him.

Cellini wiped the cut with the back of his hand and streaked his face with blood. His ears strained for the sound of any movement from the Gimp behind him, and his eyes measured the distance to the door as he said: "It sure was nice of Earl Nikken to lend me his playmates."

"Very nice!" roared the Turk. "I'm sendin' him a thank-you card."

Gutty, with the sap poised, began inching forward and the Gimp began moving in from behind. Suddenly they stopped as the door opened and Duck-Eye Ryan and Ned Lyams, their arms twined around each other's shoulders, strolled in. A happy smile spread over Duck-Eye's broad, moon of a face. "It's a fight," he informed Lyams confidentially. They were both drunk.

Gutty made for them, then stopped short as he realized the massiveness of Duck-Eye Ryan.

Ned Lyams stayed behind Duck-Eye. "That's right," he said belligerently. "Run along, small change, before we spend you."

Gutty didn't move. Cellini whirled to face the Gimp and the Turk. There was now a heavy automatic in the Gimp's hand.

The moment of dark silence was broken by the Turk. He said sharply: "Pack it, Gimp. No gun-play here."

Cellini backed off toward the door. As he passed Gutty he touched the gash and said: "I always pay off my debts, Gutty. Remember that."

"All right, Smith," said the Turk, "beat it. I'm letting you off easy. You, Lyams, stick around. I got a couple things to settle with you."

Ned Lyams told the Turk what he could do.

As Cellini opened the door and backed out with Lyams and Duck-Eye Ryan, the three men in the room burst into ear-splitting bellows of laughter.

DUCK-EYE RYAN, CELLINI Smith, and Ned Lyams left the washroom. Cellini had scrubbed his face clean and he pressed a handkerchief to the cut to staunch the flowing blood.

Ned Lyams said: "I can't stand the sight of your blood. I need a drink."

They went to the bar and ordered scotches. The bartender brought the three drinks and frowned as he noted Cellini's cheek. "Who done that?" he demanded darkly. "I'll fix his can for him. There's no rough stuff allowed in here."

Cellini sank his drink with one gulp and hurled the glass against the door at the end of the bar. "That's who done it," he said calmly. "Your boss—the Turk."

The bartender's eyes grew wide. He moved off and became busy at the other end of the bar. He did not return and they left without paying for the drinks. They crossed to a nearby drug store where the cut was smeared with mercurochrome and taped. Then they returned to the Plymouth roadster.

A quivering, maddening anger possessed Cellini's insides. He drove swiftly, with utter disregard for traffic-lights. Ned Lyams and Duck-Eye Ryan, but little sobered, sang some old ragtime tune.

Ned Lyams had long since ceased to worry over his fate. He was just out to have one hell of a good time whether he was picked up and booked for murder the following day or not. He finally stopped singing and asked: "Where we going, Cellini? To the Three Nuns?"

"Forget about the Three Nuns. We're not going there tonight."

"Don't be mad at me, Cellini. You're mad because Duck-Eye and me didn't wait in the office. We just went down for one little drink because Duck-Eye was a nice guy. Aren't you, Duck-Eye?"

"Forget it," said Cellini.

"Then you're mad 'cause I searched your office for that report. Don't be mad, Cellini. It wasn't there."

"Forget it."

"I won't," insisted Ned Lyams. "I'm never gonna forget it. I failed you twice today, Cellini. First I busted in on you and your woman and then me and Duck-Eye didn't wait to go with you to the Turk like you said. Sock me, Cellini."

"Forget it. We've got to find Earl Nikken now."

"The hell with him," said Lyams. "Let's go to the Three Nuns. The guy told me I'd find out who killed Ward there and you said maybe you'd stick both jobs on him. Remember?"

Cellini made no reply. Presently he reached the Hangover and parked the car.

They entered the night club, sat down at a vacant table, and ordered drinks. The band was playing and the Sioux City Slasher was exhorting everybody to dance with magnificent disregard for the fact that the booths and tables covered every inch of floor space. The *Reserved* card was on Earl Nikken's table. He was nowhere in sight. Hump returned with the three drinks.

"Where's Earl Nikken?" asked Cellini.

"He ain't here," replied the waiter.

"Do you know where he is?"

"No."

"Where does he live?"

Hump looked blank.

"I'm working for him, Hump. I've got something important to tell him."

"O.K. It's in Hollywoodland 8273 Maple."

Ned Lyams wagged a finger at Hump. "Now tell *me* something. Where's the Three Nuns?"

Hump said: "Personally, I'm a Catholic and I don't like that kind a talk." He stalked off.

Cellini finished his drink and stood up. "You two stay here. I'll be back."

"I failed you twice today," said Ned Lyams tearfully. "I'm going with you."

"What I've got to say to Earl Nikken I'll say alone. I'll be back." He walked out.

EARL NIKKEN'S HOME was large and fronted on a quiet street and the vast acreage that spread out in the back of it was completely surrounded by an eight-foot-high anchor fence. There were no cars on the driveway and the house was dark. After Cellini had pressed the buzzer for some minutes a Filipino house boy came to the door and said that Mr. Nikken was not at home and that he didn't know when he would be.

"Tell him Cellini Smith dropped in. Tell him that Mr. Smith got his gift and that he just wanted to return the compliment. "

He returned to the car and drove back to the Hangover. The dull, unremitting throb from the blow on his temple irked him, but he felt less angry. His hands trembled less and the knot in his stomach was beginning to uncoil. He had had neither lunch nor dinner that day and he thought he could eat something. After all, it was his fault. He should have expected something like that. But there was still a score to settle and dinner could wait.

He arrived at the Hangover. Kate Kelly was still keeping Morton Miles' memory green by singing *My Man* again. Duck-Eye Ryan and Ned Lyams were higher than before. They were feeding drinks to some woman loaded down with imitation jewelry and a moth-ravaged caracul. She was sweating profusely but was determined not to doff the fur.

Cellini passed by their table and sat down at the bar. He ordered a drink and immediately a second. His stomach was empty and the liquor hit him hard. But he had no thought for food. The single idea in his mind was to repay his debt to Gutty.

Denver Ed, Tim Moore, and the Slasher were leaning against the bar. Their nod of greeting to Cellini was not friendly.

Denver Ed said: "Well, if it ain't the guy who was gonna find out who killed Morton Miles!"

"Somebody bopped him on the puss," Moore contributed. "Maybe we ought to hire a dick to find out who did it."

"Don't rush him, boys," said the Slasher with magnificent sarcasm. "He's waitin' for the old-age pensions."

Cellini said calmly: "If one of you crumbs would help me once in a while, instead of shooting your mouth off, I might get something done."

"The gentleman calls for help! And what kind of help?"

"Where can I find a torpedo called Gutty?"

"He don't come here," said the Slasher. "We kick his kind out of here. Your kind too."

"Where does he hang out nights?"

"He probably hangs out with his kind at the Three Nuns."

Cellini's eyelids flickered. "You don't say. And where's that?"

"That's on First, off Main. Opposite the Mission house."

"Thanks."

The three fighters came up close, surrounding Cellini. Tim Moore snapped Cellini's tie out of the jacket and fingered the end. The Slasher said: "Now that you had our help, Smith, what are you going to do about it?"

Cellini finished the drink and braced his elbows against the bar. He said: "Leave it alone, Moore, or I'll kick your stomach through that wall."

Moore dropped the tie. "What'll you do about it?" repeated the Slasher.

"Your conception of time is pretty odd," said Cellini. "This is only the third day since the murder."

Denver Ed clapped his hands together with mock admiration. "My! He talks like Gene Tunney."

Kate Kelly, her song completed, spotted them and came over. "God," she exclaimed. "Talk, talk, talk all the time. Miles would've made things jump if one of you was killed. Why don't you let up on him and maybe he'll do his job?"

The menacing circle of fighters around Cellini didn't budge. The Slasher said: "We're getting not to like Smith. He's getting too smart for his own good. We tell him who fogged Miles but he don't believe us. He's tryin' to find out what me and the boys had to do with that scrap-iron shipment."

Kate Kelly's eyes clouded. "You're barking up the wrong tree, Smith. Go and pin it on that infidel Turk and leave Morton's memory alone. He was making scrap-iron deals a long time without your help."

Moore, Ed, and the Slasher pressed closer, till Cellini could feel their stale breath. But he no longer cared. A glimmer of light slowly began to penetrate his liquor-fogged brain. He called for another scotch but didn't drink it. He kept the glass in his hand. He said: "That's swell. I'm leaving now, boys. The first one that tries to stop me gets this glass smack in his kisser."

The circle opened. Cellini walked past them and waved to Duck-Eye Ryan and Ned Lyams.

Lyams came unsteadily to Cellini's side. "Don't let's go," he pleaded.

"We're going to the Three Nuns. That's what you wanted."

"Not any more, Cellini. I got to work on her some more. She's married. I've always had more luck with married dames, Cellini."

"Come on," said Cellini. "We can drink there. We've got a couple of things to say to Gutty. Besides, we found out all we can here, Ned." His face relented a little. "I think we can begin reeling in the lines."

The detective in Ned Lyams struggled to the surface. "What you find out?"

"You may not think much of it but it means a lot. I found out that Morton Miles has been dealing in scrap iron for a long time now and I found out that the boys around here know all about it—and won't tell."

15

The Three Nuns

IT WAS A nondescript, walk-down honky-tonk at the wrong end of town. Cellini Smith, Duck-Eye Ryan, and Ned Lyams negotiated the hazardous steps with inebriate care.

They found a small, twelve-table place with a grimy, unswept floor. Wall space was disfigured with the work of amateurs who felt impelled from time to time to add their own concepts to the dominant theme of Woman. The dirt was encrusted and augmented by time. It all seemed strangely like an evil fungus that still grew. The bar to the right, however, was not spurious. It was solid, carved mahogany, probably the relic of some happier establishment, and ran right up to the band stand and small, once-waxed area for dancing.

At the moment, three of the musicians were eating and the fourth, an undersized, scared-looking man, was pecking out a tune on an upright. In the rear were lavatories, kitchen, and a door that was apparently a rear exit. A few couples sat at tables and five or six men were bending elbows over the bar. Gutty was not among them.

A waiter with greasy apron, dirty fingernails, and the name Leo took the order for scotches.

"This is a dump," said Ned Lyams. "There's nothing doing here. Let's go back to my married dame. She said she'd wait."

Cellini shook his head. The scotches arrived. "We'll see. It's early yet. Drink your scotch and try to sober up."

They drank and applauded the pianist. Duck-Eye Ryan stared vacuously at nothing. Ned Lyams wondered what the difference was between a Scot and Scotchman.

"The same," said Cellini. "Only Scotchmen prefer to be called Scots. It's classier. Now don't bother me."

Ned Lyams immediately ordered three scots and sodas. "What's worrying you?" he asked.

"Earl Nikken," replied Cellini. "I can't figure him out. I wonder whether he was just doing the Turk a favor, whether he's tied up with the Turk, or whether he was just warning me—just trying to get rid of a lot of embarrassing questions."

"Keep talking. I'll drink."

"And his wife, Valena Nikken," pursued Cellini. "Do you know what a puss-peerer is, Ned?"

Ned Lyams said he didn't.

"A puss-peerer is someone who brings his pan right up close to yours and keeps staring at you all the time. That's what she is—a puss-peerer. It makes you nervous as hell."

"I know the type."

"She's a woman scorned, Ned, and she's the kind that's capable of anything."

"Maybe we can blame Miles on her," Lyams said hopefully.

"That puss-peerer is very lucky she's married to Earl otherwise he'd get her ventilated and drop her in some ditch. This way he doesn't want the publicity."

"She murdered him," said Lyams with drunken finality.

Cellini gargled a mouthful of scotch, then swallowed it. "That's to kill the germs," he explained.

Ned Lyams tried to balance his glass on a mustard jar. "Don't do that or you'll break the glass," called the bartender. Cellini chose a twenty-five cent piece from his pocket and gave it to Duck-Eye Ryan. Duck-Eye placed it on top of two fingers and pressed down with his thumb. The twenty-five cent piece doubled into right angles. Cellini tossed the twisted coin on the bar. The bartender had a whispered consultation with Leo, then ignored them.

Ned Lyams was lost in admiration. Cellini said: "My Newfoundland can also bite the caps off beer bottles with his teeth." They had Leo fetch a beer bottle and Duck-Eye dutifully bit the cap off.

After a while Lyams said: "You know something about the puss-peerer. What is it?"

"Nothing. She makes my spine crawl. I don't like that type of positive personality. She hates Olive Fain. That's another thing I've got against her."

"And you don't hate Olive Fain, Cellini?"

"No—even though she and Earl Nikken hold hands. After all," asked Cellini sadly, "who am I to cast stones?"

"Sex is the only thing in which you have fun without laughing," propounded Ned Lyams apropos of nothing.

Cellini gave a salute of appreciation. "That's pretty good."

"Think nothing of it," replied Lyams grandly. "Think nothing of it."

Cellini said: "I won't."

The small, carrot-haired piano player stopped playing and went through the door marked: *Gents.* "He swishes," observed Ned Lyams with the proper inflection. "I'll just bet he swishes."

CELLINI WONDERED WHETHER to turn Lyams in for murder. He drank some more and decided Lyams was a swell guy. He said: "Let's do some deep thinking."

"How deep?" asked Lyams.

Cellini spread his hands. "About this much, I'd say. A little more. I'd like to know who had the bright idea to tell you you'd find out who killed Ward by coming here. I'd like to know more about Ward's history and his nice profile and if he was killed because he was going to spill what he knew."

Duck-Eye Ryan reached for his glass and missed by a foot. He tried again and spilled it over the table. "Why is this place called the Three Nuns?" asked Lyams.

Cellini said: "Because three nuns stopped here once."

Lyams considered it, then asked: "Why did they stop here?"

"Because it was called the Three Nuns."

"I see. What do you think Jesse Lee Ward could have spilled?"

"Maybe why Olive Fain married Jesse Ward, maybe about a few of those scrap-iron deals that Miles had before the one with the Turk—or maybe he was ready to come out with something that the murderer was looking for. I don't know."

The effeminate pianist returned and sat down to play again. "Like he learned in six hard lessons. That's how he plays," observed Cellini.

"Look at him," sighed Lyams. "Isn't he lovely?"

"Stunning."

Ned Lyams said: "I bet if I spit in his face he'd say 'Excuse me, I think it's raining.' Let's get back to my married dame. Nothing'll happen here."

The door opened and a party of six walked in and sat down at a table near the band stand. They were Gutty, the Gimp, two women and two men. The Gimp's girl was young, drunk, pretty, and vaguely familiar to Cellini. Gutty had the other girl in tow. She was blowsy and dumpy and had legs like warped bowling pins and a splotched, shallow skin. The two men looked hard and tough and a shoulder holster bulged under the jacket of one.

The Gimp waved a breezy hello to Cellini and Lyams. Gutty ignored them.

Lyams said: "Ah, women!"

"So nothing's going to happen here, is it?" asked Cellini.

"My mistake," said Ned Lyams as he examined the two girls with a professional eye. "That young frill with the Gimp could be worse, but that other one ought to sue the city for building the sidewalk too close to her behind."

Cellini said: "The young one's very familiar. I've seen her some place. So nothing's going to happen here?"

"I said excuse me. The female touch was missing. I thought you and Gutty would dive for each other."

"Sit tight," said Cellini. "I'll take care of him at the right time. Remember you're supposed to find out who killed Ward." He nagged Leo. "We've got to eat something and sober up." The waiter came to the table. "We'll have three more scotches and something to eat."

"And keep those fingernails out of the eats," added Lyams.

Leo smiled as if he'd been complimented. "And what'll you gents have?"

Cellini said: "We want frogs' legs. Without your crummy meat-hooks, like my friend told you."

"We got no frogs' legs," stated the waiter.

"Frogs' legs," repeated Cellini, "and be sure they're big."

"Very big," supplemented Lyams.

"I said we got no frogs' legs."

Ned Lyams said: "We're getting frogs' legs or we're going into that cockroach kitchen of yours and find 'em."

Leo gave an, "Is zat so?" and backed off. He went to the bar and talked with three of the men lounging there, then, with fists bunched, they all headed for Cellini's table.

Duck-Eye said, "Jeez," and stood up with Cellini and Lyams. They kicked their chairs away to have room. Cellini wrapped his hand around one of the glasses and, with a smart blow, broke the top off on the edge of the table. It left an ugly, jagged edge. Leo and the bouncers paused.

There was a sharp whistle from the Gimp who shook his head at Leo. The waiter shrugged phlegmatically and the three bouncers returned to the bar.

Cellini muttered, "I'll be damned," as they sat down. Aloud, he called, "Thanks," to the Gimp.

AS IF TO say he'd do anything for a friend, the Gimp waved and the young, very familiar girl with him took notice of Cellini and smiled. He politely returned the smile and she blew him a kiss. She was very drunk.

"Now I remember her," said Cellini. "She's the baby of the slipping shoulder strap I once saw with the Turk. So there's nothing doing here! I wonder why the Gimp did it."

"That's the only kind of shoulder straps they should make," said Ned Lyams with a bleary smile. "The kind that slip."

Cellini said: "Your mind's always on women—thank God."

"The flesh is weak, Cellini."

Leo arrived with the drinks and went away again. "We're drinking too much," said Cellini with the glass at his lips.

The girl of the slipping shoulder strap gave a yell of good cheer and began singing in a distressing voice. The Gimp curtly told her to shut up and she asked the pianist to play *Give Me*

Something To Remember You By. The mousey pianist played it three times.

Several more couples came in. Duck-Eye suddenly remembered that Gutty had hit Cellini. Cellini and Lyams grabbed him and held tight till he subsided.

The Gimp roared at the pianist: "You ain't playing that with the right feeling. You need a couple of drinks."

The pianist nervously told the Gimp that he never drank and the Gimp replied that he never would if he didn't start then. A whiskey was fetched. The two strong-arm men leaned over the piano and watched the unhappy player drain it to the last oily drop.

Cellini said: "Something stinks besides the food. Let's see how mad we can get them without their going for us."

"All right," grumbled Lyams. "But I'd still like to find out why this dump's called the Three Nuns."

The Gimp kept plying the piano player with drinks and he continued to down them, not daring to refuse. With each additional drink *Give Me Something To Remember You By* became a greater horror. The dumpy girl with Gutty finally told him to switch to *Love For Sale* and he began to play that.

Cellini called, "No sale," to the dumpy girl.

Gutty's face turned livid and he leaped up. The two strong-arm boys froze, awaiting instructions. The Gimp pulled Gutty down and did some earnest whispering.

With simulated ferocity, Cellini called: "Let them come, Gimp. I can beat them with spit balls—and you thrown in."

One of the newer arrivals hurried out of the joint.

"Forget it," said the Gimp and ordered three drinks sent to Cellini's table.

"I wonder what's holding them back," said Cellini in a worried tone. "A few hours ago they beat up on me. Now they're sweet as a maiden's bathwater."

Leo arrived with the complimentary drinks. Ned Lyams asked him: "Why is this dive called the Three Nuns?"

With a bored air, the waiter produced a card. It read: *Just so donkeys should wonder.*

"Joke," muttered Ned Lyams darkly.

"Anyway, thanks for the drinks," Cellini called to the Gimp.

The young girl of the slipping shoulder strap noticed him again. She smiled, rose, and weaved an unsteady course till she reached Cellini, then dropped into his lap. The Gimp followed.

The girl threw an arm around Cellini's neck. "I still think you're cute. My name is Belle Polk. What's your's?"

"Cellini Smith, Belle."

Belle Polk pulled his head down and kissed him full on the lips. Cellini wiped the lipstick off with the back of his hand. She said: "Your mustache tickles."

"So does yours," responded Cellini.

"Oh hell," cried the girl. "You spoiled it all. You should have said you haven't got a mustache. I know an answer for that one." Again she pulled his head down and kissed him.

Lyams said: "I'm keeping score."

"Maybe the man don't want to be bothered," the Gimp suggested again.

"How old is she?" asked Cellini.

The Gimp didn't like the question and his forced cordiality vanished. "I wouldn't know, Smith, but I can tell you I'm old enough to take care of you."

Cellini said: "Watch it, Goebbels. One day you'll be caught

with some San Quentin quail and they'll put you where the sun doesn't shine."

The Gimp made no reply. None too gently he grabbed Belle Polk by the arm and hauled her to her feet. The two returned to their table.

Cellini said: "I'm beginning to feel better. That's more like the Gimp."

Belle Polk began to yell for music. They discovered that the pianist had taken advantage of the distraction to sneak out the back door. One of the strong-arm men went after him.

"There's *plenty* doing here," muttered Cellini.

"F'rinstance?" asked Ned Lyams.

"F'rinstance what is that little oscillator, Belle Polk, drinking?"

"Cuba libres—and too many of them."

"Well then," said Cellini, "f'rinstance when Miss Belle Polk kissed me I could taste no rum and the last time I attended a W.C.T.U. meeting I was told that rum was the essential ingredient of cuba libres."

"How can you taste it?" asked Lyams dubiously. "You're drinking yourself."

"Scotch. I would have noticed the rum if she'd been drinking any. It's not as bitter. She's as sober as a bishop."

"Then," said Ned Lyams, "maybe we should start drinking our scotch and sodas without soda."

Cellini called for three scotches without soda and the remains of the meal were carried away. The strong-arm man brought back the frightened little pianist at gun's point. He shoved the player on the stool, jammed the revolver into his ribs, and said: "Play!"

The pianist's eyes rolled with fright and sweat dripped down his face as he punished the instrument and swallowed the drinks that were supplied him. More people wandered in. Most of them seemed well acquainted with the place and Cellini recognized several as petty gangsters, grifters, and small-time confidence men.

Cellini said: "I can't figure it out but if something isn't going on you can eat my hat."

"With mayonaise?" asked Lyams.

The little pianist, by now thoroughly sick and drunk, began yelling, "No, no," as another drink was forced on him. With a gun jabbed against his ribs, he finally put the glass to his lips, took a sip, and fainted dead away. Leo dragged him outside by the coat collar. Everybody laughed and somebody cried: "Gimp, you're a card!"

The other three musicians, good union men all, finished their leisurely meal and mounted the band stand. They picked up drumsticks, saxophone, and guitar and began playing *Give Me Something To Remember You By* with two minute rests. Gutty began to dance with the dumpy girl.

"A tomato," remarked Lyams.

"I got an idea," mumbled Cellini. He stumbled over to a pay phone on the far wall, dialed the Hangover and asked for Earl Nikken. He wasn't there and Cellini dialed Nikken's home. He drew another blank and returned to the table. "I think Nikken have taken a powder," he said.

"Can't you get your mind off business for two minutes?" muttered Lyams. "And stop feeding your drinks to Duck-Eye. We're having a good time."

16

Something to Remember You By

AGAIN THE DOOR opened and in walked Joe Lucca with a girl and four men. Lucca was his usual, affable, well-dressed self. He chose a table in front of the band stand on the side directly opposite the Gimp's party. The Gimp and Gutty growled annoyance and turned their backs on Lucca's party.

Ned Lyams wet his lips as he stared at the girl with Joe Lucca. She was the tall, model type, with willowy figure, small ankles, high insteps, and very long legs. He undressed her with his eyes and then, reluctantly, stalling for time, dressed her again. He heaved a deep sigh and said: "No home should be without one. I'm smitten with that girl on stilts. Who is she?"

"She'd be nice on the mantelpiece," agreed Cellini absently. "I don't know her but the man is one of our more prominent nobodies. His name's Lucca and he told me not to come here. Those four babies with him must be from his gorilla farm."

"I know Joe," said Lyams. "I been around. I want to meet her, though. She's as purty as red shoes."

Joe Lucca caught sight of Cellini and walked over.

"Hello, Joe. Why'd you ask me to stay away from here?"

"Forget it. You're here now. Do you need any more alibis?"

Cellini nodded. "Always. I suspect I'm still a suspect. The shams drop in to squeeze me once a day."

"I heard one of my friends took a one-way trip last night," said Lucca.

"You knew Jesse Ward?" asked Cellini.

"Uh-huh. From away back."

"You'll have to tell me about him sometime."

"Name the day," promised Lucca.

"That girl on stilts, Joe," said Ned Lyams suddenly. "Who is she?"

"Like her?" parried Joe Lucca. "She's as purty as red shoes."

"Want to meet her?"

Cellini said: "No."

Lyams said: "Yes."

Joe Lucca smiled. "Maybe later. Take it easy on the drinks, boys."

"That's right," said Cellini. "I forgot." He shouted to Leo for another trio of scotches without soda.

Ned Lyams fumbled for the highest compliment he could think of, then said: "She's swell enough to be a cigarette ad. Why didn't you let me meet her?"

"We're aloof from sex tonight," said Cellini primly. "We're just neutral observers. I wonder whether Joe wanted me here tonight or didn't want me here tonight. I wonder how well he knew Jesse Lee Ward. I wonder."

Ned Lyams suddenly delivered a surprised yelp. "That gorilla with the dirty neck in Lucca's party! He's the one who told me I'd find out who killed Ward if I came here tonight!"

"My God," said Cellini disgustedly. "He's been here for ten minutes, you lousy detective."

"Be tolerant, Cellini. That's the sign of a great man. You can't blame me for noticing a certain other party with long legs first."

The Girl On Stilts asked the band to play *Eagle Eyed Finkel Of The Moscow Daily News*. Belle Polk and the dumpy girl told the musicians they'd better keep on playing *Give Me Some-*

thing To Remember You By. Two of the musicians played the one number and the third started on the other. One of Lucca's gorillas bunched his fingers and said: "Make it *Eagle Eyed Finkel* boys—if you know what's good for you."

The two themes clashed for a few seconds until, one by one, the frightened players stopped. Belle Polk shouted at Joe Lucca: "Ain't you got no respect for a lady?"

Lucca appraised Belle Polk coolly and then smiled with approval. He gave a gallant bow and said: "Excuse me. I didn't know it was for you. Go ahead with her number, boys."

The relieved musicians started playing again. Belle Polk simpered a coy, "Thanks, mister." With the air of a victor, the Gimp tossed several bills on the band stand. Not to be outdone, Joe Lucca jammed a fistful of bills into the bell of the saxophone and returned to face the disapproving glare of the Girl On Stilts.

A BALD-HEADED, MIDDLE-AGED man at the bar stumbled over to Cellini's table and sat down. Tears welled from his eyes in a steady stream. Cellini bought him a beer, asked him why and he said, "I'm a bum."

Cellini said: "Sure."

The bald-headed man insisted. "I am. I'm a bum because I got no education. I never had any. I never learned shorthand. You can't go through life unless you know shorthand. I might have been a writer but how can you be a writer if you don't know shorthand?"

Cellini said that he couldn't say and the bald-headed man returned to the bar. "Why is Belle Polk pretending she's drunk if she isn't?" asked Cellini.

Ned Lyams said that he wasn't interested in Belle Polk. Although, he admitted, he admired the bells on her, she was like nothing at all compared to the Girl On Stilts.

Joe Lucca and Belle Polk were making eyes at each other. In a sudden splurge of generosity, the Gimp ordered drinks set up for the house. Lucca countered by setting the house up with two drinks.

"Trouble," observed Cellini sagely, "and lots of it. We're headed for a peck of trouble."

Ned Lyams tried to say "Pick a peck of pickled peppers" to prove he was sober but failed.

Cellini snorted over some secret thought. "So the crumbs at the Hangover know all about scrap iron! So there's no connection between the Miles and Ward murders!"

Cellini morosely pondered his problem as he toyed with his glass but did not drink. Here was one of those underworld dives that flourish in any large city. It was in no way unique, yet, for some reason, Joe Lucca had warned him not to show up and somebody else had told Lyams to come—if he wanted to discover Jesse Ward's murderer. It was significant that Miles' murder was not mentioned. Or that a similar message had not come to him, Cellini, who had an equal, if not greater, stake in ferreting out Ward's killer. And if the message delivered to Ned Lyams were the least bit valid, someone else was sure to show up. Nobody present was likely to know who had killed Jesse Lee Ward. Would it be Olive Fain, the Terrible Turk, Earl Nikken out of hiding, or his intense, puss-peering wife, Valena?

Cellini's clouded brain refused to think further. He gave Duck-Eye Ryan a twenty-five cent piece and asked him to bend it. Duck-Eye twisted the coin and Cellini tossed it at Gutty.

The man at the bar who wanted to know shorthand cried copiously into the free drinks. He suddenly shouted, "I'm a bum," and lurched over to the Gimp's table. One of the gorillas straight-armed him backward and another splashed a glass of whiskey in his face.

"Why?" asked Cellini. "Why are they so damn tough with everybody but us?"

Ned Lyams muttered: "As purty as red shoes."

Cellini said: "I gotta find out why Earl Nikken let Jesse Lee Ward marry his mistress."

THE GIRL ON Stilts was forgotten as Lucca started on a campaign to impress Belle Polk. He yelled: "Close those doors and let's make a night of it! Three set-ups on me!"

There was a cheer for him. Leo bolted the front door and began to dispense drinks. Everybody became drunker and gayer and noisier and the band played its single number louder.

The Girl On Stilts came halfway to their table but hurried back to her own when she saw that Joe Lucca continued his play for Belle Polk.

Joe Lucca stood up and spread his arms. Belle Polk stumbled into them and they began to dance. The Gimp's face distorted with jealous fury. He uttered an oath and stood up. Gutty and the two strong-arm boys also stood up. Joe Lucca's four gorillas rose to face them. Silence burst on the place. Duck-Eye Ryan was suddenly wide awake. Lucca and Belle stopped dancing.

"You ———— Leave my girl alone." The Gimp spat out each word as if every letter were rotted.

"Watch your lip," said Lucca too calmly.

"I said let her alone!"

"I take what I like, Gimp."

The Gimp's hand went for his back pocket with a practiced movement. There was a flash of arms among the gorillas as they reached under coats. In a second Joe Lucca was the only man among them without a gun in his hand. Neither faction uttered a word. They just stood motionless, glaring at each other with steely hatred over their guns.

Belle Polk clutched the Gimp's lapels. "God, I didn't mean to start all this," she cried. "Please pack the rods."

The Gimp smashed her across the mouth with his left hand and said: "Don't bother me now." She fell down. He kept his gun leveled at Lucca's stomach.

Cellini Smith, Duck-Eye Ryan, and Ned Lyams were standing at their table. Cellini's eyes, as they watched the two factions of gunmen, were calculating. All three of them had sobered.

"Well?" asked Joe Lucca almost politely. "I've got four rods to your four, Gimp. Do you still feel tough?"

"You ————," said the Gimp. "I'm gonna fix you so you don't tail any dame of mine again, you ————."

Cellini's fingers took a firm grip on the edge of the table and the toe of his right foot groped for Duck-Eye Ryan's ankles. Everyone began to press away from the eight guns leveled against each other.

Cellini watched the knuckles of the gunmen whiten and the trigger fingers quiver. He had seen those twitching, yellow-white fingers before and while he didn't know exactly when to expect it, he knew as surely as he knew his name that the fusillade was imminent.

His foot wedged between Duck-Eye Ryan's ankles and a sudden twist brought him crashing to the floor and simultaneously he up-ended the table and dropped for cover behind it. There was a surge of movement and then a deafening blast as the triggers of eight guns were depressed at once.

Each of the next sixty seconds hurtled down into a hell of screams, snarls of rage, racing feet, and shattering glass, to be succeeded by a void of silence even more terrifying.

As the acrid pall of powder-smoke began to lift, men and women cautiously reconnoitered from behind chairs, tables, the bar. Cellini and Duck-Eye quit the shelter of the table. Whether any of the gunmen had been killed or wounded could not be determined as the Gimp and Lucca gangs had fled with their women through the rear door. Two bouncers now blocked that door and repulsed the others who tried to flee. "No you don't," said one of them. "We need witnesses."

Someone who shouted that he was a policeman was pounding and kicking on the front door. Cellini looked about for casualties. He could find only one.

Ned Lyams lay dead on the floor with a bullet in his right lung and another that had smashed through the face and lodged in the brain.

Duck-Eye Ryan pointed at something. "Kee-rist," he said. Cellini bent down to look. Two deflected bullets had passed through the table which had shielded them.

It was not more than forty minutes later that Ira Haenigson and his crew of Homicide men barged in. A thousand times and in a thousand different ways it was explained that Ned Lyams had been caught in a gang feud and accidentally killed. Questions were asked and over and over again Cellini Smith swore that with eight guns shooting wildly, anybody might have been hit.

When at five in the morning Cellini Smith and Duck-Eye Ryan were finally permitted to leave the Three Nuns they drove to an all-night drugstore and ordered coffee. Cellini vainly searched the telephone directory for Belle Polk's name. Then he called the Sheraton Manor and asked Nina Saunders to turn her Young Woman's Aid Society inside out to track down the girl. Despite the hour, she was gracious and promised to meet him at the Hangover at three that afternoon.

Cellini returned to Duck-Eye and his coffee. "I've got to find Belle Polk," he said.

"Huh?" asked Duck-Eye Ryan.

"Never mind. You wouldn't know."

Duck-Eye Ryan had one of his rare moments of loquacity. He said: "I been thinking, Cellini. Those two slugs the table stopped. They was goin' straight for—"

"Smart boy," approved Cellini. "I didn't think you'd catch on it was all one big gag to kill Ned Lyams—and me, if there was lead to spare."

"Kee-rist," said Duck-Eye Ryan for the second time that day.

17

The Vanishing Earl

IT WAS TWO o'clock of a cheerless, Friday afternoon when Cellini Smith awoke with wooly mouth and the pulsing, inevitable headache.

For some minutes he regarded venomously Duck-Eye Ryan's muscle-bound torso on the cot. At the preposterous hour of seven that morning Duck-Eye had awakened him, tugging at his pajamas, and giving out with: "I got it! Cellini, I figgered who got Ned Lyams rubbed out!"

But Smith drew some comfort from the, well-spiced opinion he had delivered anent Mr. Ryan's lineage, along with the injunction: "Go back to bed because I figured it out too. Only it doesn't prove that the same hand killed Jesse Lee Ward."

He treaded his way carefully into the bathroom, dropped his pajamas, and took every ounce of pressure the spray-nozzle could give him. It dispelled some of the fuzziness and helped him think. He thought of Ira Haenigson and how dubious he had been of Ned Lyams's "accidental" death. The detective-sergeant had sworn at, wheedled, and threatened the reluctant witnesses. They, very sensibly, remembered their families or themselves and said they were not sure exactly what happened.

Then, as the department men scoured the Three Nuns and extracted precious bullets from the woodwork, Ira Haenigson applied himself exclusively to Cellini. Indeed it was nice to have Cellini here—gave it that homey touch. In fact a corpse wouldn't look natural without Cellini holding its hands. But, just to while away the time, would he volunteer a few words of explanation? But to tell the detective-sergeant that he too had been a target of those bullets would have been as futile as trying to get him to believe now that Ned Lyams had killed Morton Miles!

THERE WERE NO messages or mail at his office. Cellini sat behind his desk, stabbing at the blotter with pen points. Ned Lyams killed Morton Miles in self-defense. It was a simple exercise in homicide. But what connective link was there between that and the subsequent murder of Jesse Lee Ward—and then the assassination of Lyams himself?

Did the motive stem from scrap iron? If it did, then the solution was not far off as the few words dropped by Kate Kelly and the Slasher had suddenly snapped the disordered fragments of scrap iron into place. Or did the motive stem from Earl Nikken's penchant for Olive Fain, from that curious marriage with Ward, and from Valena Nikken? But the crux of it all was still Jesse Lee Ward's murder. What had the killer been searching for in Ward's house? He must get Lucca to tell him of Ward's background.

Without a sound or any preliminary knock, Valena Nikken entered.

She sat down beside the desk and her eyes searched his face. She was strained, strangely pathetic—on the outer edge of hysteria. Without preface, she said: "I want to talk to you, Mr. Smith."

"Yes?" he asked politely.

"I'm looking for my husband. He's disappeared."

18

For a Small Fee

WITHOUT PEFACE SHE said: "I want to talk to you, Mr. Smith."

"Yes?" he asked politely.

"I'm looking for my husband. He's disappeared."

"I haven't got him."

"I'm in deadly earnest, Mr. Smith."

"He's not here. I think he's hiding out."

"Then I want to know where he is."

"Why, Mrs. Nikken?"

"To plead, threaten—it's none of your concern. I went to his home this morning but he was gone. Do you know where he is?"

Cellini said: "This is an office, Mrs. Nikken, and I'm in business."

"Oh, of course. You want money. What's your price to tell me where my husband is?"

"A hundred dollars."

"Well, money means nothing to me. I'll pay. And now—where is he, Mr. Smith?"

"I'll get in touch with you, Mrs. Nikken. I'll probably phone you tonight and tell you. Before you leave may I ask you a few questions?"

"Yes, you may."

"Ned Lyams was killed last night," he said bluntly.

Her dull, steady gaze on his face did not waver.

"I hadn't heard. I don't read the papers. I don't even know the man or what you're driving at."

Cellini said: "Forget it. About Jesse Lee Ward—is there anything you can add to what you told me about him last time?"

"No."

"Was he in love with his wife, Olive Fain?"

"Yes."

"I don't understand it. I happened to find out that they didn't spend their wedding night together."

"Of course not," said Valeria Nikken. "If Jesse Ward had insisted on that prerogative, Earl would have had him sewn into a burlap sack and dropped into a sewer. Earl is intensely keen about some things—and that slut is one of them."

"If all that's so, why did Ward marry her in the first instance?"

"First, he loved Olive Fain. Then, he was not rich. When Earl offered him five thousand dollars to marry her—and leave her alone—he snapped at the offer. And, finally, Jesse Lee Ward no doubt hoped that after a while Olive Fain would really become his wife."

For the first time she laughed.

"Rather sordid details, aren't they, Mr. Smith?"

"Uh-huh," he said vaguely. "Then that call Earl Nikken made to Ward in Palm Springs must have been his offer of five G's to Jesse Ward if he came back immediately and married Olive Fain. It ties up nicely. Tell me, Mrs. Nikken, just why did your husband want Olive Fain married off? What advantage did he hope to gain by that maneuver?"

"I was suing him for divorce and her for alienation," she

said. "Because Ward married her I had to drop the alienation proceedings."

"He wanted to save Olive Fain embarrassment?"

"That was the purpose."

"I see. It was very clever of your husband."

"No. It was clever of his attorneys. My husband's methods are infinitely more direct."

Cellini touched the tape that still adorned his cheek. He said: "Yes. I remember."

"Is that all, Mr. Smith?"

"Yes. Unless you've heard of a girl called Belle Polk."

"I haven't."

"Do you think your husband knows her?"

"Perhaps. I said I've never heard of her. "Good-bye Mr. Smith. I'll wait for your call." She walked out slowly, precisely, as if propelled by strings in the hands of a puppeteer.

Cellini waited a few minutes, then began to make telephone calls. But either the boys didn't know or didn't care to tell him where Earl Nikken was hiding out. Earl was not the kind of man about whom you gave free information. He shoved the phone back and took his revolver from the desk. He checked the loading, rested the hammer on an empty chamber, then dropped it into his pocket. It was near three o'clock as he went downstairs.

19

Jail-Bait

THE HANGOVER WAS calm. The first, unreasoning excitement over Morton Miles' death was now a cumulative, almost morbid, determination to do something. As of old, the fighters were gathered to discuss their art, curse the fight managers and sports writers, or re-fight some insignificant bout of a week ago in El Centro or Pomona. Only to an eye well acquainted with them and their profession was there any evidence of the disciplined anger and desire for revenge that needed only focus and direction. Morton Miles had been a friend and ruler. Death magnified him into a martyr demanding vengeance.

The fighters ignored Cellini. The headlines of the morning—large type that talked of an operative caught in the cross-fire of two gangs—meant little to them.

Morton Miles had been killed three days ago.

Nina Saunders was waiting, all her repressed impulses for adventure clothed in becoming sports combination and knitted tarn. "I've been here five minutes," she chided.

"Couldn't you find any men to pick up?"

"You're a brute."

"Belle Polk. Let's hear."

"Well, it wasn't easy," Nina Saunders said. "I had to check through all the files of the society for this Belle Polk. About a year and a half ago she applied to us for financial aid but never returned to fill out the questionaire. In those cases we always assume that the person got a job so we never followed it up."

"Get her address?"

"Yes, but she may have moved. It's Apartment 3-A, 18 South Marivale. It may be a rooming house."

"Live alone?"

"Our files mention no family or husband."

"O.K."

Nina Saunders gave an exaggerated sigh.

"Don't you see what I mean, Cellini? You rouse me at dawn, I go through a great deal of trouble, I get you confidential information, then you don't even say 'thank you'. And you resent it when I adore you for it!"

"I'm a boor," said Cellini.

"You are. Cellini, are you sure you've been busy or don't you want to come and visit me?"

"I—" He stopped short as Ira Haenigson's comfortable though uncomforting figure loomed over their table.

"Sure, I'll sit down," said the Homicide man. He seemed tired. "The newsboy outside told me you were in here, Smith."

Cellini performed introductions and Nina Saunders insisted that she was most charmed to meet the officer. Haenigson lapped it up. Unconsciously, he patted down his thinning hair. He said: "So this is the young lady you phoned to alibi you the night Miles was killed. Eh, Smith?"

Nina Saunders blushed as she recollected the conversation. "Mr. Haenigson, do you know about—"

"Ma'am," he hastened to reassure her, "I only know Smith tried to get you to alibi him. Nothing else. I don't blame someone like you for not wanting to get mixed up in a murder."

"You're very kind," was her relieved murmur.

"Not at all. Did you just happen to drop around to visit Smith this afternoon?" he asked too casually.

"Yes. That's not a crime, is it, Mr. Haenigson?"

"It's all according to the way you look at it, ma'am," replied the detective-sergeant. "You spend your time assisting at the Young Women's Aid, don't you, Miss Saunders?"

"Why yes. Have you been checking on me?"

CELLINI THOUGHT IT time to interrupt. He said: "Haenigson is being subtle, Nina. He's probably found out that a Miss Belle Polk was involved in something last night and he figures I asked you for data on her."

The Homicide man smiled sweetly at him.

"Well, you're right, Haenigson," continued Cellini. "Miss

"I'll kill you!" the Turk screamed

Saunders came here to tell me she couldn't find a thing on Belle Polk in her files."

Ira Haenigson said: "You're slick, Smith. Too—excuse me, ma'am—damned slick." He turned to Nina Saunders. "Is what Smith said right?"

"That I found nothing on Belle Polk? Absolutely."

Haenigson looked dubious. "Are you sure Smith didn't put the words into your mouth? After all, yours is a pretty big outfit and the chances are you'd have a card on her."

Nina Saunders said professionally: "Mr. Haenigson, do you realize that here in Hollywood there is a floating population of twenty-five thousand unattached girls? Only a few of them are absorbed as waitresses, car-hops, and so on. If we include Los Angeles the number becomes much greater and they all move about so rapidly that it's impossible to keep track of even those that apply for assistance."

Haenigson shrugged. "That's all right. We've got other ways to track her. My men are working on it now."

"I'm sure you'll find her. You people are so clever."

"Thanks."

"You have such fascinating work," said Nina Saunders. "Moulage, microphotography, the Keeler polygraph, and all that. You know—science versus crime. How you must admire your great trail-blazers—Bertillon, Dr. Alphonse Poller and men like that."

Cellini Smith guffawed.

Ira Haenigson grew red with embarrassment. "Well, ma'am," he said, "I guess you know more about that sort of thing than I do. When I go out on a job I just sort of poke around. If I'm lucky, I stumble on something. If I'm not lucky, I call it suicide."

"You're modest, Mr. Haenigson."

"All right, Nina," said Cellini. "Stop flirting with him. He's here to bother me, not listen to you."

She pouted. "Mr. Haenigson, am I flirting with you?"

"Yes."

Cellini said to Haenigson: "Well, you old moulage expert? You're here for something. What is it?"

"What's happened to Earl Nikken?" asked Haenigson flatly.

"I don't know. Why?"

"I wanted to pay him a visit this morning and ask him a couple more questions about Jesse Lee Ward and he wasn't home. He's disappeared. Where is he, Smith?"

"I said I didn't know."

"Sure you did. You said a lot of other things to me, too, at the Three Nuns. Was Joe Lucca there last night?"

"I don't think so. I don't remember."

"Well, his prints were there," said Haenigson. "The set of prints we collected at that joint look like a *Who's Who in the Rogue's Gallery.*"

Cellini said: "That doesn't necessarily mean that Joe left them there last night. He might have been at the Three Nuns earlier or the night before."

"Lucca can alibi himself, Smith. He'll think of something better than that so leave it to him. And if I were you I wouldn't let him know I was talking about him."

"I know when to mind my own business," said Cellini.

"Don't forget it. Why didn't you tell me about Belle Polk at the Three Nuns?"

"She slipped my mind," said Cellini with innocence. "You found out by yourself though, Haenigson, so what are you beefing about?"

The Homicide man stood up. "I'll be darned if I know why I like you, Smith."

"Come off it," said Cellini. "Do you think Earl Nikken's mixed up in this?"

"Can't say. But if he's really taken a powder it looks kind of bad."

"Must you leave, Mr. Haenigson?" asked Nina Saunders.

"Yep. I've got to go find this Belle Polk chop-chop before

she skips town." He then promised to take Nina Saunders to a line-up some morning, said goodbye, and left.

Cellini waited for just five minutes by his watch, then left Nina Saunders, and went out to his car. For another five minutes he circled side streets until he was sure that nobody followed him. And only then did he drive for Belle Polk's address on South Marivale.

CELLINI SMITH PRESSED the buzzer. A cautious slit appeared in the door. When Belle Polk was satisfied that he was alone, she said: "O.K."

He shut the door and followed her into the bed-living-room. Belle Polk had just come out of the shower. She wore a dirty, faded wrapper and mules. The wrapper hung loosely and she wore nothing underneath. The only other item she wore was a wide-meshed snood to keep her hair in form. Her lower lip was purple from the blow the Gimp had given her last night at the Three Nuns. She was very sober. As Cellini looked at the young girl he could see nothing of the barfly but only a clean, shiny-faced, and almost likable kid. The room was in disorder with half-packed baggage on floor, table, and chairs.

She stood in the center of the room, her hands aggressively on her hips. "Well, what of it? It was smart of you to find me, mister. When you get enough of looking at me maybe you'll say what you want."

He indicated the luggage. "Powder?"

"I'm movin'. What do you want?"

"To ask you why you're moving right now, Belle, and a few other things."

"What other things?"

"I want to ask you about last night at the Three Nuns."

She sat down at a vanity and opened a make-up kit. "Why talk to me, mister? There were lots of other girls there."

"Who were they?"

"I don't know. I never met them before."

"That's all right too, Belle, because I think you were the only one in on the gag—"

"The gag?" Mascara, eyebrow pencil, lipstick brush, rouge, and powder she applied with facile fingers. Under her practiced hand the shiny-faced kid disappeared and a hard young girl who knew all the answers took her place.

Cellini said: "Yes. The gag. We'll get along much better if you play ball with me."

"Dust, mister. You're picking on the wrong girlie."

"Give out, Belle. Talk."

Slowly she stood up from the vanity. The wrapper slipped from her shoulders to the carpet. Her eyes took in Cellini from head to toe. They were calm and calculating.

"And get dressed," he added.

She walked toward him, naked.

"Well?" asked Cellini.

She said: "Well I don't like your questions and I could fix your can for you and start screaming right now."

"I thought you said I was cute."

She came close to Cellini and twined her two arms around him. "You are cute, but I'm not interested in that right now. I just want to light out of this town. I want to go far and I want to go fast and that takes dough. Plenty of cabbage, mister."

Cellini was annoyed. "Get dressed. What gave you the idea you could pull something like this with me?"

"You gave me the idea," she replied, "when you called me jail-bait last night. I'm only seventeen, mister, and if I start screaming it'll go bad with you. The walls are awfully thin here."

"Oh, hell. What are you up to, Belle?"

"I want some sugar."

"And if you don't get it you'll scream?"

Her arms pressed even tighter around his back. "Yes."

"Are you sure you mean it, Belle?"

"Yes."

Cellini said: "All right, Belle. Steady now. Here it comes."

With one hand on her stomach he shoved her backwards as he brought up the other in a smart blow to the jaw. Her head snapped back and he caught her as she sagged and carried her to the bed.

He felt pulse and heart beat, then gathered her clothing from chair and hanger and started to dress her.

BELLE POLK BEGAN to stir as Cellini was sliding on her stockings. He said: "Hold still till I get these seams straight." He forced the 3-D shoes on her feet with difficulty and then went to her luggage. In the bottom of a valise he found what he wanted. It was a small lady's flask of hammered silver and half full of some blended rye. He returned to the bed, slopped some of the whiskey on his hand, and then rubbed her face and lips with it. In a little while she sat up.

She was not angry—just disappointed. She'd been hit harder for lesser reasons. She felt her chin and examined it in a mirror. She said, "I picked on the wrong guy, I guess," and walked into the bathroom.

"Leave the door open, Belle."

She bent over the basin, washed the alcohol from her face and returned. "You shouldn't a done that, mister. I wouldn't have screamed. I have to beat it from this town."

Cellini picked up her purse from the table and opened it. He found inside a roll of ten fifty-dollar bills. "I didn't think you would scream," he replied, "but I couldn't take chances."

She reached under her dress, rearranged her garter-belt, and then began to apply rouge and powder anew. "What do you want? I'm in a hurry."

"Afraid the shams will get a line on you, Belle? That half a G in your purse. How'd you get it?"

"It's mine. I saved it up."

"How?"

"I car-hopped in a drive-in."

"No you didn't," said Cellini. "You couldn't make five bucks at that racket. You got that dough for taking part in the act last night to rub out Ned Lyams."

"Ned Lyams the guy who was killed?" she asked ingenuously. "Yes."

She shook her head sadly. "Tough break."

"He had it coming," said Cellini. "Why don't you tell me?"

"About the act, mister? What gives you the idea it was one? Does this Lyams think so?"

"Ned Lyams was a private dick, Belle, and there's going to be trouble."

She gave an involuntary start. "I got to get out of this town," she said.

"Sure you do, Belle. Now why don't you admit that scene between you, the Gimp and Joe Lucca was all a plant to get the bullets popping?"

"I don't get your drift, mister."

"For God's sake," said Cellini impatiently. "I know you're pretty young, Belle, but try and act your age. You were dead sober last night. You were drinking cuba libres without rum. What about it?"

"I shouldn't have kissed you. Sure I was sober, mister. I wasn't feeling well so I didn't drink. But I didn't want to spoil the Gimp's good time so I made believe I was sloppy."

"Joe and the Gimp are good friends," stated Cellini.

"They weren't last night."

"Last night someone told Ned Lyams to show up at the Three Nuns. When he was there you gave Gimp the go-by for Joe Lucca so that their gorillas could train their rods on Lyams as if by accident."

"You're a hop-head, mister," she said calmly.

"How is it Ned Lyams got two slugs and neither Lucca's nor the Gimp's boys got any?"

"Maybe this Lyams had a magnet in his pocket."

CELLINI HEARD THE sound of a car outside. He strayed casually to the window and looked down in time to see a black sedan pull into the curb. He turned back. Belle Polk was buffing her scarlet fingernails. He said quickly and persuasively: "I always keep my promises, Belle, and I'm willing to make a deal with you. I've got some information about the cops that concerns you and I'm willing to trade with you if you'll answer just a few questions for me. I'll never let on where I got the answers."

"Is that information about the shams on the level?"

"Yes. On my word."

She searched his face intently, then abruptly said: "A deal. Shoot."

"Ned Lyams wasn't killed accidentally?" he asked.

"No, he wasn't."

"Are Joe Lucca and the Gimp gunning for each other?"

"No," she replied. "They just put that on last night."

"Was that five hundred bucks your cut for taking part in the act, Belle?"

"Yes."

"Are they good friends of Earl Nikken?"

"Never heard of him."

"And now, Belle, who got Joe and the Gimp to do all this? Who gave them their orders? They did that job for *somebody.* If you know you've got to tell me, Belle."

"I don't know."

Cellini said: "I believe it."

"O.K.," she snapped, "trade. What about me and the shams?"

"Oh, I nearly forgot, Belle. The news is they've finally gotten a line on you and where you live and they're coming to pick you up."

"God! When?"

The buzzer to the apartment sounded. Cellini said: "They're here right now, Belle."

Her face fell in shocked disbelief.

"It's the truth, Belle. See? I keep my word."

She went to the door as the buzzing persisted and opened it. Ira Haenigson and his assistant, Boggs, strode in.

"You ——," she muttered.

"So you didn't know where Belle Polk lived?" asked the Homicide man sourly.

"I only found out a little while ago," Cellini replied.

"Is that so? You knew I wanted her. Why didn't you get in touch with me?"

"I was afraid she'd fly the coop so I came to save her for you. Take her, Haenigson, she's all yours."

Belle Polk's face was white through the rouge. Her voice was pitched low and quivered with fury. "Don't let him go. He can't get away with it. That lousy —— tried to attack me."

Haenigson pulled at the lobe of one ear and shook his head regretfully. "Sorry, sister. No dice. Much as I'd like to hang something on that guy, you've got to remember to scream and not have so many clothes on when you pull that stunt."

Cellini saluted and moved for the door. He was grinning. Belle Polk whirled on him and reached for his eyes and face with her long, lacquered fingernails.

"You ——!" she screamed hoarsely. "You lousy double-cross-ing ——!"

20

M.D. Affidavit

CELLINI SMITH DINED early. If he wanted to pump Joe Lucca on what he knew of Jesse Lee Ward and Ned Lyams' assassination there was not too much time left. Ira Haenigson would listen to Belle Polk's denials for perhaps an hour—an hour and a half at the outside—before he would become bored and jug her. His next move would undoubtedly be to visit Joe or have him brought in. Lucca might then be out of circulation for several days, or longer. Ward was still the crux of the problem—the link between the solved murder of Miles and the assassination of Lyams. And Lucca had known Ward for some time.

Cellini flooded his stomach with a quick cup of coffee and left the restaurant. Fifteen minutes later he reached the inconspicuous apartment building where Joe Lucca lived.

Cellini used the knocker, Lucca called, "Come in," and he entered through the unlatched door.

Joe Lucca lay on his bed wearing nothing save a towel around his middle. There were three others in the room. Lucca said: "Hello, Cellini. Meet Dr. Malcomb and Dr. Sloane." He indicated a woman seated at a desk wearing nurse's white. "I don't know her name but meet her too."

Cellini returned the polite murmurs, then asked: "Am I in the way, Joe?"

"No, no. I'm glad you came. I need a witness. Put it any place."

Cellini sat down. "I come to tell you that the shams will be picking you up. Got your prints at the Three Nuns, of course."

Lucca said: "I know." He waved to the two doctors. "Let's get on."

Dr. Sloane was over fifty, of professional cut. He had a bluff basso and the overbearing personality that patients confuse with competence. Dr. Malcomb was a few years younger, more pleasant, and more talkative. Medical ethics was his favorite topic—almost suspiciously so. The nurse, an eagle-beaked, elderly woman, sat with fingers poised over a portable typewriter.

Efficiently, the two doctors continued to thump, measure, and examine Lucca. As they ascertained the racketeer's temperature, pulse rate, or blood pressure they dictated the findings to the nurse who typed them out.

Cellini laughed. "It's a new one but it's a good idea."

"Figured it out myself," said Lucca. "Anyway, it was nice of you to come up and tell me."

"It was nice of you to miss me last night," returned Cellini.

Joe Lucca indicated the doctors with a nod of his head. "We'll talk about it later."

"Sure, but the bulls will be around later. Would you mind taking up the time with a sort of non-inflammatory discussion of Jesse Lee Ward?"

"O.K."

"He's my answer to a lot of things in this mess, Joe, and I've got to get a line on him. You told me last night you knew Ward. For how long?"

"A long time," said Lucca. "I met him when he first pulled into New York. He used to do the Broadway spots and he'd put the bite on me every couple of weeks."

"Let's hear," cued Cellini. "Where'd he come from?"

"Jesse Ward was a tank-town Romeo. Lindenville, in Ohio, I think. It's just like any other jerk-water town and all the boys do there is float around looking for jobs and drinking needled beer at the saloon. After a while they'd pick out some girl that had a couple of shreds of reputation left and settle down and marry her—but not Ferdinand Ward. Jesse was too good for that, if you know what I mean."

The doctors began to measure a scar on Lucca's left abdomen. "Probably a knife wound," hazarded Doctor Sloane, "and at least five years old."

The nurse said, "Yes, Doctor," and began typing.

"That's right, Doc," said Lucca. "Don't miss a trick. About Jesse Ward," he continued, "he peeked in the mirror one day and saw he had a build and how all-fired handsome he was and so he blew and went to New York."

"When was this?" asked Cellini.

Joe Lucca paused as Dr. Malcomb poked an orange-stick into his mouth and peered down his throat with the aid of a reflector. He gave several *aaahs* and the doctor dictated the results to the nurse. "About five years ago," he finally went on.

"What happened when Ward didn't find any reception committee waiting at Grand Central?"

"You can guess. He found that the Lou Tellegen era of profiles and matinee idols had just closed and that New York wasn't going for his type any more. They were getting close to the soil—going social-minded."

"I remember," said Cellini. "Every second play had a strike in it."

DR. SLOANE SAT Lucca on the edge of the bed and tapped his knees with a small mallet. "Patellar reflex normal," he observed.

"Patellar normal," repeated the nurse.

Lucca said: "Jesse Lee Ward had a pretty good voice, too—like everything else about him—but that was just about the time the crooners began to get the needle."

Cellini remarked that that was one good thing.

"Another thing that Ward had was nice long fingernails. He was so proud of them he never auditioned for ditch digging or any jobs like that. As time went on he did cop a couple of chorusboy jobs but not enough for grits and the kind of clothing he liked. Too many of his type. Besides, the depression kept getting deeper and they weren't doing many six-sixty musical shows. That was just about the time when somebody said that if Max Gordon would produce another smash-hit musical he'd go broke."

The telephone's jingle interrupted. It was Dr. Malcomb's office calling. "Yes, of course," said the doctor into the phone. He looked at his watch. "About an hour. Yes." He replaced the receiver and said: "Some woman's waiting. She wants me to bandage her arm or something in splints so that her boy friend should feel sorry for her. Where could they get the idea I'd undertake anything so unethical?"

He shoved a pillow under Joe Lucca's head. "And now open both eyes wide, please, and try not to blink."

"How'd he take to women?" asked Cellini.

"God's gift to them," said Lucca. "He was the great lover."

"Then if he missed out on a dame he'd be pretty miffed, wouldn't he?"

"Like what kind of dame?"

"Like Mrs. Jesse Lee Ward."

Joe Lucca kept staring up at the ceiling as Sloane and Malcomb examined and tested his eyes but his thumb pointed down at the floor. He said deliberately: "So Ward slowly drifted around to the dance halls—the taxi joints—and worked them for meals and the chance to get around, if you know what I mean. Then when he could no longer sink the hook in guys like me he started borrowing dough from the women and after that he worked them strictly for tips and any extras."

Dr. Sloane bent over to sound Lucca's ribs. Cellini asked: "Did Ward try blackmail?"

"I don't think so."

"Yellow?"

"I suppose so but he didn't even need to because he began to be sure of himself and hang out at more fashionable cocktail bars. You know the kind. The places were lousy with wealthy middle-aged wives in for the afternoon from Westchester and the North Shore of Long Island."

"What have you against Jersey?" asked Cellini.

"Jersey, too," said Lucca. "They'd buy him his eats, drinks, and pay him to dance. He kept this up till one time he spent the whole afternoon dancing and drinking at one of these bars with some twist. The owner of this particular bar was some small-time torpedo and what Ward didn't know was that this girl was one of the owner's dolls."

"Beat up on him bad?" asked Cellini.

"Pretty bad. They got Jesse into a side room and two tough babies went to work on him. To top it they got a penknife and cut off those fingernails he was so damned proud of right down to the moon. That's what really decided Ward to quit that game. Not the beating."

"Enlarged heart," remarked Dr. Sloane.

"That's nothing to worry about," said Dr. Malcomb.

"Not for you, perhaps," snapped Sloane. "He's the one that has it."

"I've never seen it to fail," stated Dr. Malcomb witheringly. "My colleagues resent me because I'm a Mayo man."

JOE LUCCA CALMED them, told them to get on with the examination, and said: "So Jesse Ward decided to quit the penny-ante field. He wasn't a dumb boy and he figured out a racket with a new angle. He asked me about it at the time and I told him it would work if he kept his nose clean."

"Like everything else," added Cellini.

"Well, he put on his dinner jacket and went out late that afternoon to one of the better cocktail lounges. He picked out his woman and got into conversation with her. He was good at that. She was well-dressed and wore an expensive Persian lamb coat. She accepted his invitation to dine at some club— one of those small, classy places the city is full of. At the door they gave their things to a hat-check girl. He naturally took both the checks and they went inside. In a minute he excused himself to make a telephone call. He returned to the hatcheck girl, got the two coats, and beat it from the club.

"I steered him to a couple of fences because he promised to start paying back what he owed me. Ward got only eighty-five bucks for that Persian lamb but it was clear profit."

The nurse began to read back the report on Joe Lucca's condition while the physicians made a careful double check. They paid particular attention to listing the precise location of every scar, bruise, abrasion or foreign mark on his body.

"When did the shams catch up with him?" prompted Cellini.

"A peculiar thing happened to Jesse Lee Ward," Lucca continued. "He kept up that racket for some time, pulling it once or twice a week, and he was able to get along pretty well. It was safe. It doesn't sound too good for any woman to say she was invited to dinner by some man whose name she doesn't even know and say he stole her fur coat. At that, he was pretty careful. He kept on the move and New York's a large place."

"You're wrong there," said Cellini.

"He didn't know it then. He kept doing it till one day he picked up a girl at a hotel bar. She wore an expensive fur like the others but pinned right on the inside lining of that coat was a police badge."

The doctors and nurse completed the double-checking of the report. The three signed and dated it and Cellini put his witnessing signature on the original and the carbon. The nurse dialed for the time and recorded it on the report. Lucca handed the nurse a ten-dollar bill and gave each of the doctors a hundred-dollar check. They said good-bye and left.

CELLINI SCANNED THE report. Joe Lucca's health and physical condition were listed to the minutest details. "In case you fall down the stairs, isn't it?"

Lucca said: "I'm mighty sick and tired of getting beat up by a couple of career cops every three months."

"What did Ward do when he spotted the police badge?"

"He sold the coat."

"That was a mistake," said Cellini.

"Of course it was. He was panicky. The dame went to town. She knew what he looked like, his habits, his likes, dislikes, and the kind of places he would hang out at. As you said, New York's a small place and she picked him up three weeks later. He spent two years in college."

Joe Lucca took the towel off, picked out fresh underwear, and, after some hesitation, selected a tan tweed and a pair of brown, perforated sport shoes. He began to dress.

Cellini asked: "And then?"

"And then he came out here. He knew me and he knew Morton Miles from the old days. Funny thing, those two really liked each other. He was a good mixer and inside a year he had his finger in most of the better rackets out here. He did a lot of Miles' undercover work and he had the sense to stay away from publicity. He got along swell—swell until a couple of days ago."

"Did he work for the Turk?"

"I doubt it," said Lucca. "I don't even think they ever met."

"That's a nice suit," said Cellini. "Now that we're alone will you tell me a couple of things?"

"Ask them."

"Where's Earl Nikken?"

"I don't know."

"You don't know or you won't tell me?"

"I don't know."

"Are the boys still gunning for me?"

"I made it a special point to tell you to stay away from the Three Nuns last night," Lucca said.

"I appreciate it," said Cellini. "Only you might have thought that that was the surest way to get me there."

"You're still alive, Cellini, so stop beefing."

"Where's Earl Nikken?"

"Has he disappeared?"

"You know he has."

"Well, I couldn't say where he is." Joe Lucca's gaze was blank, his voice unaccented. Cellini nodded surrender. Lucca was not the sort of man who could be bluffed or threatened. He picked two revolvers out of a secretary and placed them on the bed.

"I thought you knew you could trust me, Joe."

"About certain things I don't trust myself," replied Lucca. From his wallet he extracted a permit for small firearms and laid it next to the guns. Then he sat down to wait.

Cellini said: "You're not much help." He went to the phone and dialed for Olive Fain.

After a while she responded and said: "This *is* a surprise, Mr. Smith. Have you succumbed to my allure?"

"Where's Earl Nikken?" asked Cellini abruptly.

"You've wounded my vanity," she parried. "I had imagined you wanted to see me."

"I just want to talk to him for a few minutes. That's all. Then he can go back into hiding."

"I'm sorry, Cellini. I don't know where Earl is. You must have an exaggerated idea of my claim on him."

"All right. I'd like to see you tonight, Olive."

"Second best?"

"No. You're in a different department. You're first in yours."

There was a faint pause before she asked: "Where?"

"Some place quiet," he said. "How about my office? You've been there."

"All right. Not for about an hour, though. Around eight."

Cellini replaced the receiver. The racketeer watched him

through squinting eyes, then said: "You're out of your class, Cellini."

"I couldn't back down now if I wanted to. The boys didn't miss me by much last night. Sure they're not gunning for me any more?"

Lucca shook his head. "Not mine, anyway."

"That's something."

"Of course, it doesn't mean they won't start tomorrow."

"Ned Lyams was murdered, wasn't he?" asked Cellini. "That was no accident."

"Of course," said Lucca impatiently. "Use your head."

"Joe, I know that you and the Gimp and Gutty had about as much to do with it as the rods that held the bullets. Somebody wanted Ned Lyams out of the way. Who dished out those orders?"

"You know better than to ask that, Cellini."

Cellini's smile was friendly but his voice was earnest. "You and the Gimp put on a little murder play at the Three Nuns. I don't think either of you were very interested. You did it as a favor or you were paid for it. Now who asked you to do it?"

Joe Lucca remembered that he had a third revolver in a bureau drawer. He secured it and put it beside the first two. He said: "I had my order and I did it." Then, "You know better than to pump me," he added in a tone of reproach.

"Sure," said Cellini. "If I thought it would do any good I'd go to town. Anything else you want to say to me?"

"No—unless it's to tell you not to bite off more than you can chew."

"Anything to say about Earl Nikken, or the Turk, or whether rubbing me out in addition to Lyams last night was the Gimp's own bright idea, or about who gave you those orders, or what they consisted of?"

"No."

"Any other places you want to tell me to stay away from?"

"Not for the present."

The buzzer sounded. Lucca said, "It's them," went to the door, and admitted Ira Haenigson and Boggs.

THE HOMICIDE MAN stopped short as he caught sight of Cellini and frowned. "I thought I asked you not to tell Lucca I was coming for him, Smith," he said irritably.

"Joe knew."

"It's a shame," said Haenigson, "a big shame." When no one asked what was a shame he continued: "It's too bad I've got to take a nice guy like you down a peg or two, Smith. But that's what I'll do. You'll never get any more cooperation from the police in this town—and I'll see to it you don't even get a job. You might as well pull in your dick's shingle, Smith."

"I thought I was the prima donna here, copper," interrupted Joe Lucca.

Boggs moved next to Lucca and said: "Close it."

"What'd Belle Polk have to say when you arrested her?" asked Cellini.

Haenigson lost his interest in the conversation and strolled over to the bed. He gazed down at the three guns and the permit without touching them. He said: "That's thoughtful foresight, Lucca, but I don't think we want any of these. If you don't mind we'll search the place anyway. There may be a couple more around we'd want."

"Have you got a warrant?"

Boggs turned quickly toward Haenigson and said: "He wants a warrant." As he turned, he raised his arm to smooth his hair and his elbow smashed accidentally into Joe Lucca's mouth. "He says he wants a warrant," Boggs repeated mildly.

Lucca felt his jaw and mouth and worked at a loose tooth. He said: "If this tooth comes out it's going to cost you money."

Ira Haenigson rubbed the palms of his hands together. "Well, well! What makes you think so?"

"Don't worry. If you go to work on me I can prove it."

"Cellini Smith won't talk. Oh, no," said Haenigson. "Smith won't do anything because I'm getting angry at him."

Boggs worried his knuckles and eyed Joe Lucca speculatively, as a butcher might a side of beef.

"Cellini Smith will do anything he damned well pleases," Cellini Smith said.

Lucca walked to the desk, picked up a carbon copy of the doctor's report, and handed it to the detective-sergeant. He said: "If it comes out it'll cost you money because there's no mention of any loose tooth in here."

HAENIGSON READ THROUGH the report slowly and when he was done he blinked in disbelief. He beckoned to Boggs and they both read it over again carefully.

"And those aren't chiropractors," Lucca went on blandly. "They're well-known doctors and their word'll go far on a stand. They have the original of that report and if you still want to chance taking me down to headquarters and beating me up go ahead. I've got a mouthpiece there right now waiting for me to be brought in so you won't be able to hide me. I've taken too many third degrees from you boys when you were scared to go after the big fish. I'm just tired of it and if you try so much as mussing my hair I'll make a stink that'll—"

Ira Haenigson leaped for the telephone. He fumbled about for several minutes until he was finally connected with Dr. Sloane. His voice was tempered by a grudging admiration for Lucca's tactic. "So two reputable physicians are afraid the police'll get a little exercise on a gangster," he said ironically. "Can't you boys find an honest citizen to treat?... I don't get you.... I see.... Thanks for the suggestion." He cradled the receiver and smiled sourly. "The doc reminded me of Mussolini's invention—castor oil. He says he doesn't want to be quoted but that it wouldn't affect the report. He says maybe I could also find some rubber hose down at the station which wouldn't leave any mark. Now what do you suppose he meant by that, Boggs?"

"Rubber hose!" said Boggs. *Tsk, tsk.* What'll they think of next?!"

The Homicide man whirled on Lucca. "Maybe you had your voice examined so you can't answer any questions."

"Fire away."

"O.K.," Haenigson snapped to Boggs. The young policeman began a methodical search of the apartment and Haenigson turned back to Lucca. "Were you at the Three Nuns?"

Joe Lucca said: "Yes."

"You know damned well I meant last night."

"No, I wasn't there last night. And to save time, I'll let you know I was up here last night. I was having a little party and I've got a dozen people to prove it. If you found my prints at the Three Nuns that must be from some other—"

Cellini yawned loudly. "Well, good luck, boys. I've got a date with a gorgeous frill so you can think of me during the next hour or two. Take it easy."

21

Gutty Again

AS OLIVE FAIN stepped into Cellini Smith's office, the lone light of the desk lamp gave her black-clothed figure and pale-white face a banshee quality. He said: "I've heard a lot of terrible things about you from Valeria Nikken. Seeing you, I don't believe them."

She sat down on the edge of the couch. "We know each other too well for that sort of thing, Cellini. You believe every word of it."

He made no denial. He rose from behind the desk, carrying cigarettes, matches, and ashtray and sat down next to her. The desk light was barely sufficient to silhouette their faces as they smoked. After a while he said: "Thank you for coming."

"I surprised myself," she replied, "but I wanted so badly to talk to somebody tonight—if only to be pestered by your endless questions. I was feeling blue."

"Thinking of the future, Olive?"

"What?" she asked sharply.

"When you won't be one of the most beautiful women I've ever seen? When you'll be on the beach and the Earl Nikkens won't want to support you and your whims?"

"I like Earl," she said simply.

"What of it? That word covers a multitude of things. For that matter, I like you."

"I also like nice things, Cellini. And God how I loathe poverty."

"Fine! Now you've come out fearlessly against poverty. Pretty soon you'll be against debt and disease."

"I've never thought much of love in a cottage, Cellini. Even as a girl I wondered whether those cottages had hot and cold running water, if they had unit heat and electric light. I don't think it's bad or even unmoral to want those things."

"Where is he?" he asked abruptly.

"Earl? I don't know."

"Why is he hiding?"

"You know that, so why ask me?"

Cellini said: "I can guess. He's either involved or afraid he'll be involved in the deaths of Ward and Lyams."

"Exactly."

"But you know where he is, don't you, Olive?"

"Well, if you must have it so, I do," she admitted.

"Why don't you tell me?" he cajoled. "I'm not a cop and he wants this cleared up as much as I do. He's paying me. I just want to ask him three or four questions. The whole thing won't take more than five or ten minutes."

"What do you want to ask him?" she countered.

"Among other things, what, if anything, he had to do with the murder of Ned Lyams."

"So the poor man was murdered."

"Of course. Even the police suspect it. Perhaps that's why they want to talk to Nikken. Gang assassinations are familiar things to him."

"So that's why he's hiding. I'm sorry," she said with finality, "but I can't let you see him."

"Olive, he can't hide out forever. He's one of my major weak links and unless I can get at him I don't think I can clean up this mess."

"No."

Suddenly he surrendered. "All right. I'll get at him in my own way. Do you know where the Gimp's running his poker game now?"

"Please, Cellini. I may know Earl but I don't get daily reports on his friends."

"How about the Terrible Turk?"

"All I know of him is that he's supposed to be very ugly, very tall, and a former wrestling champion."

"O.K." He put his hand over hers. "Olive, why did you marry Jesse Lee Ward?"

"Because Earl asked me to."

"On account of the divorce suit, of course. Then why did Ward marry you?"

"There's nothing to compel me to answer your questions," she drawled.

"No. If there were you wouldn't say a word."

"Jesse married me because Earl gave him a large sum of money to do so on the strict proviso that we live apart. In addition, and I say this in all modesty, he cared for me a great deal and imagined that there was the chance I actually would become his wife."

"Was there that chance?"

"There wasn't," she said. "Now that we've let our hair down, I'll admit I'm sorry Jesse died—was killed—but I never liked him. I wear this mourning to avoid embarrassing questions." Her voice became distant. "I always found his protestations of love very amusing. He was so obviously in love with himself."

"What about Earl Nikken?"

"What about him? He at least is a man."

"Where is he? I've got to ask him one or two questions."

"I can't tell you."

CELLINI SHRUGGED GOODNATUREDLY. "Very well, Olive, I'll forget about it." He gazed at her in the dim, imperfect light. She met his eyes with a hint of amusement and shook her head almost imperceptibly as if to say that he was veering from the strict confines of business. He slowly leaned forward—as if to give her ample warning—then kissed her full, half-parted lips. She did not return, but neither did she repulse it.

He said: "What do you know of the scrap-iron deal between Miles, Ward, Nikken, and the Turk?"

She withdrew her hand from his.

"Nothing."

"It's important, Olive. To what extent was Earl Nikken mixed up in it?"

"I don't know. All I can remember is that once, in my presence, he had a few words with a Japanese on scrap iron."

"Well," asked Cellini with tense interest, "what did they discuss?"

"I wasn't sitting near them. I just caught a few meaningless words."

"Try to remember, Olive."

"Don't badger me, Cellini. I said I can't remember."

"And the name of that Japanese? Was it Seiicha Sawamura?"

"I don't know. I wasn't introduced."

"O.K." He said it as if he had come to some inner decision. He placed two cigarettes between his lips, lighted them, and gave her one. He tried his crooked, winning smile and said:

"It's very difficult to become tough with you."

She asked: "Why?—though I suspect your reason."

"Your suspicion is legit. If you wore a mask over your pan I'd manage to become very nasty and get some information out of you that'd probably crack this case. But—and I say it in no predatory spirit—your beauty is too disconcerting."

She said lightly: "Your faculty for alternating between gutter slang and quite passable English is amazing."

"Seriously, Olive, you *are* very disconcerting. Probably your only blemish is perfection. Perfection is tiresome. One side of your face is a boringly perfect as the other. Some mole, some deviation in your lines, would make you human."

She laughed. "That's by way of being an abnormality."

"No. All I ask for is something to convince me you're human and approachable. For example, I'd like to see cleansing cream on your face—or your hair done up in curlers."

She laughed again. "I know what you're getting at."

"You mean I'm trying to find out where Earl Nikken is?"

"Yes."

"That's partly true, Olive, but I also meant what I said."

"Cellini, you've tried seduction, argument, charm, and even veiled threats but I still can't tell you."

"Earl Nikken would do anything in the world for you, wouldn't he?"

"Yes," she replied, "but I don't ask him to. That may be the very reason why he'd do anything."

Cellini's voice became surer and more persuasive as he began working toward a definite objective. He said: "I haven't much money for nice things or even your minimum requirements of unit heat and electric light. In fact, I haven't any money."

For the first time he could glean a hint of tenderness in her voice as she spoke. "For all your knockabout experience, you're a fool, Cellini. I wonder what you take me for. I do live well by the grace of Earl Nikken but do you imagine I'd accept anything from him if I didn't like him? Do you think I'd be sitting here, fencing with you, if I didn't want to? A word from me and Earl would see to it you never bothered me again." She laughed with warmth. "God, what a fool you are."

"I was wondering," he said. "I'm glad."

"Of what?"

By way of reply he slipped an arm around her waist. She gave to the pressure of his arm and his free hand felt for her neck and chin. He tilted her head back and kissed her fiercely. His hand dropped to her knee and their lips meshed again. Her two arms twined around his neck. Suddenly, rudely, he shook her arms off and moved away to the end of the couch. He did not look at her. He lit a cigarette.

"Cellini—why?"

"I don't get you."

"Why?"

"I was wondering."

"What?"

"What those kisses would cost me."

"Cellini! What do you mean?"

His eyes smarted from the smoke of his cigarette. He dropped it and ground at it viciously with the heel of his shoe. He still stared ahead of him. "I was trying to figure what you charge Earl Nikken and I was wondering if I'd get the same rate. Will I?"

"You're mad," she said. "Mad."

"Tell me," he demanded harshly. "I haven't had much experience with women. Will you charge me pro rata or a flat rate?" He dug into his pocket and found some crumpled bills. He tossed them into her lap. "There's a couple of bucks. Will that do or—"

There was a strangled gasp and a hand smashed across Cellini's mouth. She leaped from the couch and ran out. When he no longer heard the headlong flight of her steps he lit another cigarette.

CELLINI WAITED. HE still sat at the end of the couch but now a profusion of cigarette butts littered the threadbare linoleum at his feet. When a half-hour had passed he stood up. He switched on the ceiling light and trained the desk lamp on the unshaded street window. He took the revolver out of his pocket and broke and checked it. Before returning it he revolved the chamber so that a cartridge faced the hammer. Then he went out and secreted himself behind an elbow in the dark hallway, pressed his back against the wall, and waited.

He thought of the chance remark, the small telling word that Olive Fain had let fall. It induced an entirely new interpretation to Jesse Ward's murder. In effect it named his killer. Had he thought of it himself it might even have been unnecessary to see Earl Nikken. Tomorrow, he thought, he would crack the case. There was still the large problem of motive but that would follow, had to follow naturally now that there could be no further doubt of the murderer of Jesse Lee Ward, the person for whom Lucca and the Gimp had assassinated Ned Lyams.

Suddenly Cellini stiffened and his every nerve prickled as he distinguished careful and measured footsteps ascending the pitch-dark stairs. He waited until he judged that the visitors were a few feet from him. His right hand tightened on the revolver butt and his left switched on the hall light.

He said: "Stop where you are and put your hands behind your necks."

The two men emitted grunts that could have meant surprise or malignance but did as they were bid. They were Earl Nikken and his guard, Gutty. They watched Cellini with cool, baleful eyes. Cellini stepped closer to them.

Earl Nikken said: "It will be the first time in my life, Smith— the first time I watch a man die and laugh at him."

"Me, too," parrotted Gutty.

Cellini lashed out with the barrel of his gun and struck Gutty on the side of the face. The gunman gave a mingled cry and oath and his arms began to drop.

"Not yet," said Earl Nikken in a dry, emotionless voice.

Cellini swept them with the revolver and said: "You better add 'not never'."

Gutty retwined his fingers behind his neck. Flecks of blood appeared in a corner of his mouth as if a tooth had been broken in its socket.

"Why?" asked Earl Nikken. "Why not me?"

"That's just returning it to Gutty for playing his sap on me at the Turk's. He should be glad I don't take interest."

Earl Nikken stared at him with inexpressible hate. His eyes not wavering from them, Cellini backed up a few steps and threw open his office door. "Go into the room without removing your hands from your neck. I'm an old billiard drinker so don't try anything. Go straight ahead to the opposite wall and stop there."

Earl Nikken mumbled something low and indistinct to Gutty and they passed through the door. Cellini followed them. With rapid strides Nikken went to the left end of the office and Gutty to the extreme right before Cellini apprehended the maneuver.

Cellini shut the door and pressed his back against it as if to stay as far from the two men as possible. Out of the corners of his eyes he watched every breath of Earl Nikken's on his left and Gutty's on his right. He said: "This won't help you. Stand together."

"Tell me when," Gutty said to Earl Nikken. An ugly purple welt stood out on his left cheek. Blood gathered and oozed from it slowly but steadily and coursed under his jaw to his neck.

Earl Nikken's luminous eyes gazed at Cellini with detached curiosity as if he were observing the final, playful antics of some steer in a slaughter house. He said: "That's your second big mistake, Smith—not keeping us together."

"And the first?" asked Cellini.

"The first, of course, was your behavior with Olive." His voice became chilling. "Smith, you have the distinction of being the only man who's ever made Olive Fain cry."

Cellini said: "Start walking together and I shoot for the first man who drops his arms."

"No," replied Earl Nikken. "We stay where we are. We both have rods on us and we can both go for them fast. You haven't a chance in the world, Smith."

CELLINI KEPT SHIFTING his eyes from one end of the room to the other. Earl Nikken was not speaking idly.

At the first instance of carelessness on his part, Nikken and Gutty would draw fast. The ruse was simple. They had spread to opposite sides of the room so that it was impossible for Cellini, standing where he was, to cover both of them at once. In action, he could shoot for only one before the other used his back as a target.

Cellini said: "Don't try it. I'll get at least one of you before you can pull your heaters on me."

Earl Nikken gave him that same curious gaze of cold loathing. "Believe me, Smith, when I say that I don't care if you get both of us provided we get you. You should never have let us separate. Now you're going to pay for it."

"Good enough."

Gutty looked to Earl Nikken, waiting for the sign. The side of his face and neck was a red and purple mass of coagulated blood. Cellini came to a decision. He abruptly turned his back on Gutty and covered Earl Nikken.

"Don't try it, Gutty," snapped Cellini. "My finger is pretty heavy on this trigger and if you put a slug in me I let go for your boss's belly. You wouldn't know, but that's called a reflex action." There was no sound from the gunman. Cellini walked forward till he reached Earl Nikken and jammed the barrel into his stomach. "Don't try it," he repeated.

Gutty apparently made a questioning sign behind Cellini's back for Earl Nikken said: "No. Wait a second."

"Good," approved Cellini. "Just keep cooling off and we can talk this over."

"I'm not cooling off, Smith. Gutty's right in back of you now and I want you to know exactly when and why you're getting it. I want you to know I'm talking to a dead man."

Cellini felt the barrel of Gutty's gun find the small of his back. "You're committing suicide."

"Perhaps," Earl Nikken said dispassionately, "but then I'd do anything for Olive Fain. You may understand that."

"That's exactly it," said Cellini. "I didn't expect you to go as far as this. I expected you to come here and slap me around. But I thought you'd quit killing."

"I have, Smith, but I still believe in selective violence. Everybody has something he values above life."

Cellini said: "You'd be very foolish to kill me and to be killed in turn on account of what I said or did to Olive. I beg her pardon and I beg——"

"It's too late for that."

"——your pardon. I think she's a wonderful woman."

A frigid smile of disgust played on Earl Nikken's lips. "Crawl, Smith. You haven't much time left."

The pressure of bored metal against Cellini's back was portentous. "If you cooled down and considered the thing," he said, "you'd realize I'm speaking the truth. You went into hiding, Nikken, and I had to see you. You ought to know that. Olive was the only person who could tell me where you were and she wouldn't. I broke her down purposely knowing that she'd turn to you and you'd show up gunning for me."

"Damn you, Smith, don't try to talk your way out. I don't let anybody hurt Olive." Nikken's voice was hoarse and showed, for the first time, a trace of emotion.

"Don't be a milkhead," said Cellini tensely. "If I didn't know you were coming I wouldn't have been waiting outside in the hall for you. I'm not trying to talk my way out of anything. Maybe you've got a gun in my back but don't forget this rod in your belly."

Doubt began to show on Earl Nikken's face. "She was crying, Smith," he said harshly.

"Hell!" exclaimed Cellini. "I said I beg your pardon. I want that dough you promised if I cracked this case and I had to talk to you. Don't think I didn't try other ways of getting at you first. Plenty!"

EARL NIKKEN'S HANDS dropped from behind his neck. The gun stopped pressing against Cellini's back. Nikken walked over to the couch and sat down. He stared at the floor, saying nothing. Gutty waited a moment, then went out to the hall toilet.

Cellini pulled up a chair close to Nikken and sat down. "Where's your hideout?" he asked.

"A court in the Valley. The Apex. All right, Smith, ask your questions."

"There won't be many," said Cellini. "First, why are you laying low?"

"I want to keep out of this whole mess. I couldn't afford the publicity. Smith, you made her cry. God, how she must hate you—or like you."

"I'm sorry," said Cellini impatiently. "How often do you want me to repeat it? Will you tell me now where you came in on the scrap-iron deal? Why you're an officer in a Japanese concern?"

"No."

"Why the hell not?" demanded Cellini angrily. "You've hired me for that purpose. I'm your dick and all you've done by way of cooperation so far was beat up on me or go gunning for me."

"Friends of mine are involved in it. I can't tell you."

"What friends? The pugs at your place—the Hangover?"

"If you're interested, the boys there are talking of ganging up on you."

"I'd guessed as much," said Cellini. "Do you still want me to work for you on this job?"

"Yes."

Gutty returned. The caked blood was washed off his face, leaving the raw welt where the gun had struck, but he was spitting a thick red into a handkerchief. Cellini asked: "Why did you turn this baby and the Gimp on me when they came with me to the Turk?"

"That was just a hint for you to keep out of my business."

"I thought so. It was a pretty strong hint. Where's the Gimp got his game now?"

Earl Nikken shrugged and indicated his bodyguard. Gutty said: "He's workin' it at the Hotel Montclair."

"Thanks. Tell him to answer my questions when I see him. Now this is the important question, Nikken. It's the reason why I had to go to all this trouble to see you. The way you'll reply will be all-important to me and to you. Tell me this: Did you know beforehand that Ned Lyams would be killed last night at the Three Nuns?"

"It's foolish to ask that," said Earl Nikken. "My reply is obvious."

"Sure. I know *what* you'll say but I want to hear the *way* you say it. That's the only way I can guess if you're lying. It's the only reason for this meeting and it's more important than I can say. Did you know beforehand?"

"No."

Through half-closed eyes Cellini studied Nikken, tried to remember some tremor, some faint reservation in his voice as he had made his monosyllabic reply. Abruptly, Cellini turned on Gutty and peppered him with questions about the Three Nuns. If it was true that Nikken hadn't known about it, then who was Gutty working for when he played his part in the Lyams killing? Who gave the orders? Who knew about it beforehand? In reply, Gutty simply passed the buck by saying that he didn't know what it was all about but that he was just following orders from the Gimp.

Earl Nikken stood up and walked for the doorway. Without turning, he said: "Keep my hide-out quiet."

Cellini said, "Of course," and they left.

When Cellini heard the door downstairs bang shut, he picked up the phone, and dialed Valeria Nikken. When she replied he said: "Earl's staying at an auto court in the Valley called the Apex."

Valena Nikken gave a sharp intake of breath. "Thank you, Mr. Smith."

He said: "Say it with a check—for a hundred bucks."

22

Lawyer-Gambler-Thief

CELLINI LAZED IN bed, occupied with waking-dreams. Morton Miles was killed Sunday night. Today was Thursday and if he cracked the case before tomorrow it would mean two thousand dollars for four days work. He wondered how the bruisers at the Hangover were doing and he was reminded of Earl Nikken's chance remark that they were thinking of ganging up on him. He decided to give them something else to worry about.

It was after eleven when he got out of bed. He showered and dressed, quit the apartment, and drove for the nearest drug store. Here he had a twenty-cent counter breakfast. He then stepped next door to a Western Union office and after some thought dispatched two telegrams. He left both unsigned.

The first, to the Hangover, read:

DON'T LIKE FIGHTERS WHO MAKE DIRTY ACCUSA-
TIONS ABOUT TURK STOP QUIT OR WE SEND SOME
VASSAR GIRLS OVER TO SLAP YOU AROUND

And the second, to the Turk, brief and obscure:

IT IS MANY MILES TO HELL

Cellini decided that this might sublimate their ganging-up

energies on each other rather than on him and went to his office.

Duck-Eye Ryan was already there. In fact, he proudly informed Cellini, he was keeping real office hours that day as he had come in at ten in the morning. Cellini congratulated him and went through the mail. The first envelope contained a hundred-dollar check from Valena Nikken with no accompanying note. The rest were bills.

Cellini said: "What's new, Duck-Eye?"

Duck-Eye Ryan consulted some meaningless hieroglyphics he had scrawled on a sheet of paper. "That frill from the Sheraton Manor that's been chasin' after you called."

"Nina Saunders?"

"Yeah. She asked you should call her back."

"Anything else?"

"Oh, yeah. Earl Nikken called too."

"What?"

"That's right. He told me to tell you you ain't getting no money from him because you give his hide-out away to his wife."

Cellini sat heavily into a chair. He was suddenly tired. He picked up the check from Valena Nikken and stared at it sickly. On account of it he had lost his chance at real money—a chance to pay some bills, buy clothes, eat and drink when he wanted to. He crumpled the check in his hand but then smoothed it and carefully put it away in his wallet. He thought of seeing Earl Nikken but then dismissed the idea. Earl Nikken meant what he said. If he had decided not to pay, nothing would change his mind.

Cellini sat for a long time as anger and disgust tore him.

Presently, he shrugged wearily and reached for the phone and dialed Nina Saunders. "What is it?" he asked.

Nina Saunders said: "Oh, Cellini, I spent the morning with that most delightful shin friend of yours. It was thrilling."

"You mean sham, don't you?"

"That's the word. Mr. Haenigson. He was very sweet."

"What'd he want?"

"Frankly, I don't know, Cellini. It was all very mysterious. He asked me all about the night we went out together when that Morton Miles was murdered. He's a big, gruff darling, Cellini. He said my name would never be involved."

"I'm crazy about him myself," said Cellini. "What kind of questions did he ask?"

"Mostly about you, Cellini darling. He wanted to know who your friends are, what kind of people you went around with, and all that. I thought I'd better call and tell you. It's all so fascinating. What do you think he wanted?"

"He knows I've got a birthday this year and he's trying to figure out what to give me. Good-bye."

He cradled the receiver, then abruptly stood up and strode out of the office. He went down to his roadster, and drove toward the office of Max Cushman, attorney-at-law.

THE ATTORNEY OF the late Miles and Ward was friendlier than usual—almost suspiciously so. He said, "Good-afternoon," offered a cigarette.

"Anything new turn up on Jesse Lee Ward?" asked Cellini wearily.

"Nothing that could help you. Have you made any progress?"

"I know who pulled the murders but I've yet to understand

exactly why. With a little luck I'll find out today. Who gets Ward's bank account and anything else he had?"

"I don't know," replied Max Cushman. "His wife, I presume, but she seems very uninterested in the whole thing. I couldn't find any relatives and I don't know who his regular attorney was—if any—so I've taken care of burial details and so forth."

"When I found Ward's body I was scared to search it because I knew the cops'd yell bloody murder. What was on him when he got killed?"

"Nothing that seemed important."

"Was there any letter on Jesse Ward from someone asking to meet him at the Three Nuns the following night?"

"No. I don't think so. The police went through him first, of course, and they may be holding something back but I don't think so. They sent all the things Ward had on him, down to the burial parlor."

"And where is that?" asked Cellini.

"Down at Undertakers Row at Washington Boulevard. The Apostles are doing the burial."

"The Apostles?"

"That's what the trade calls them," the lawyer explained. "The place is owned by two brothers—Peter and Paul Englebrecht."

"Now, tell me this. If a woman called Olive Fain was being sued for alienation of affection by another woman would the suit be nullified if Olive Fain got married?"

"No," said the lawyer. "Especially not if Olive Fain married *after* suit was brought against her. However, her advantage in marrying would be great because she could claim on the witness stand that it was silly to accuse her of alienating the affections of one man while she was engaged to be married to another. In other words, the marriage wouldn't throw out the suit, but it would certainly make it hopeless for the plaintiff to win it. Now if you've nothing more to discuss about my clients—my ex-clients—let's terminate this meeting. I'm busy."

"What's up?"

The lawyer leaned forward on his swivel chair and gazed earnestly at Cellini. "All right, Mr. Smith. This office has long ears and I know pretty much everything that goes on downtown. Today I happened to hear that Ira Haenigson is going after you."

Cellini's voice was unnaturally low and menacingly quiet. "Do you mean he's trying to revoke my private operative's license?"

"Bluntly—yes."

Cellini lit a cigarette. "And bluntly—why?" he asked calmly.

"That detective-sergeant, Haenigson, was even in here this morning to ask about you. I haven't the facts but you seem to have stepped on his toes. You seem to have made two of their important witnesses valueless by warning them of the police beforehand. I think their names were Lucca and a girl named Belle Polk."

A joyless and bitter smile played on Cellini's lips. "Ira Haenigson! He goes around patting you on the back to find a soft place to stick the knife!"

"He said," the attorney continued, "that your kind is a discredit to your profession. I told Haenigson that it was hitting below the belt to take a man's living away from him."

"It doesn't matter."

"Why?"

"I found out this morning I'm not being paid on this job even if I tie it up."

"That's too bad."

"Did you ever draw up the corporation papers for the Seiicha Sawamura Corporation?"

Max Cushman gazed at him in astonishment. "You mean to say," he marveled, "that you're continuing the case without getting paid for it? You, above all people?"

"Will you answer my question, please?"

"No. The first time I heard of the Sawamura Company was when Jesse mentioned it that morning after Miles was killed. But I can't understand, Mr. Smith, why you're still interested if—"

"Who wouldn't be?" exploded Cellini. His voice was harsh and strident. "Pay or no pay do you imagine I could quit now? After all the pushing around I've taken? Listening to bushels of lies and pecks of truth? After all the chasing, crawling, and running around I've done the last four days? Wasting time on bums, hoods, phones, tramps? I've been tailed, I've had pot shots taken at me, I've taken beatings. Too much has happened, Cushman. Too much excitement. I'm seeing it through. I couldn't quit now if I wanted—and I don't want to. Somebody's playing too rough and maybe I won't get paid for it but I certainly intend paying off."

THE ANGER CELLINI had against Earl Nikken and Ira Haenigson resolved into a restless determination to see the thing through. He parked the roadster and entered the handsome, stuccoed building fronted by a large neon sign that spelled: *Engelbrecht Mortuary*.

He found himself in a dimly lit anteroom that possessed a superfluity of heavy portieres and tarnished candelabra. A tall, thin, cadaverous man approached him. He wore a black swallow-tail and was completely bald. Following him was his twin edition, excepting for thick-lensed spectacles from which a black ribbon curled around his neck.

In a deep, resonant voice, the man said: "A good day, sir. May we be of help?"

"Yes," replied Cellini.

"Ah, indeed. I am Peter Engelbrecht and he"—he turned to the one behind him—"is my brother Paul."

"That's nice. You had a stiff brought in here Tuesday or yesterday. Jesse Lee Ward is the name. I want to see about him."

"Ah," said Peter. "Perhaps in this time of sorrow you would first like to step into our chapel."

Cellini said: "I'm not sorry about anything. Have you all the stuff that was on Jesse Ward when he died?"

"Yes, indeedy. The police returned it and we are holding it for disposal by Mr. Cushman."

"I'd like to look through it."

"Ah, yes," contributed Paul. "The effects of the dear departed always have a sentimental value. Perhaps you would like to view the body. He looks beautiful—as if in peaceful slumber."

"And perhaps you would like us to supply you with a coach for the funeral this afternoon," added Peter.

Paul sighed. "It will take place at five o'clock—the most beautiful hour. The sun will set on the world and symbolically on Mr. Ward's corporeal existence."

Cellini said: "Now look, boys. Check the euphemisms. I won't want a coach and I don't want to look at the body. I just want to check through what Ward had on him when he was fogged."

The brothers exchanged nervous whispers and then Paul went to an over-carved, massive desk in one corner. Peter said in his soft unctuous voice: "We have done all we could for your departed friend, and we want you to feel assured that the mark of the bullet has been eliminated. We have employed all the arts of the mortuoso and he now looks as if had passed away in bed with the utmost serenity. A soft-nose bullet in the fore-head is unfortunate."

Paul approached with a large manila envelope which he handed to Cellini. Cellini opened the envelope and looked inside as he said absently: "A slug in the kisser is always safer in case the guy's sporting a bullet-proof vest."

The brothers looked covertly at each other and sadly shook their heads. Grief weakens the strongest minds. Paul said: "But you need have no fear. We have employed pink wax judiciously and he looks beautiful now. If you would but step into our parlor…"

Cellini said: "Don't bother me." He emptied the envelope onto a leather easy-chair. He had little hope. Anything that the police had returned could not be very important—except for the slim chance that they had overlooked something. He returned a key ring, handkerchiefs, cigarettes and matches, expensive wrist watch curved to fit the wrist, and a fountain pen to the envelope. There remained a slim, tooled-leather wallet and three letters.

"I do hope you'll attend the funeral this afternoon," Peter said.

"No."

"Passages from First Corinthians will be read," Paul said temptingly.

"No." Cellini looked into the wallet. There were eight bills of varying denominations.

"It is curious," Paul Englebrecht mused with a professional air, "how few visitors there are when death results from violence. Not even Mr. Ward's wife has come to see him. But with Mr. Morton Miles the case was exceptional. His was a beautiful funeral. More orchids than I've ever seen, though"—his voice became secretive—"I suspect that several of the mourners had been *drinking*."

"That's right," said Cellini. "Max Cushman sent you Miles' stiff too."

"His body, sir. Yes, he did."

The rest of the wallet exhibited nothing of interest. Cellini said: "What does Cushman get out of it? Will you give him a free funeral for steering all this trade your way?"

The brothers were shocked. "It is just the freemasonry among professional men," Peter said stiffly.

"All right." Cellini opened the first two letters. One was a clothing bill of impressive amount and the other a sentimental but guarded letter from a girl in New York. "Who pays your bills for Ward?" he asked.

The brothers unbent again. "You are kind to think of it, sir, but Mr. Cushman, his attorney, took care of all that."

Cellini opened the third letter. It was addressed to Ned Lyams and originated from the Bureau of Marine Inspection and Navigation, Department of Commerce at San Pedro. It read:

Dear Mr. Lyams:

In response to your query of the 12th, we submit the following particulars explaining this Bureau's refusal to grant the CITY OF KOBE clearance papers on the grounds of unseaworthiness.

Our inspection revealed that present boiler plates were inadequate to secure the proper pressure and that extreme crystallization of the tail shaft made a replacement imperative before she could sail.

The letter amplified these items and concluded by stating that, to their knowledge, the replacements had not been made or new clearance papers applied for.

Cellini slipped the letter back into its envelope. He said: "I'll take this along."

The brothers looked doubtful.

"I was the departed's dearest friend," Cellini said sadly.

Peter and Paul clucked in sympathy. "Of course. We understand. Forgive us. We will call Mr. Cushman for his permission."

"Forget it," said Cellini quickly. "Is that all there was on Ward's body?"

"Yes, sir."

Cellini turned to go.

"Are you sure," asked Paul Englebrecht wistfully, "that you do not desire to step into the parlor to view the body? He looks beautiful."

Cellini's patience was becoming strained. "Why shouldn't Ward look good?" he snapped. "He spent the last two months in Palm Springs!"

IT WAS NEARLY four in the afternoon when Cellini Smith drove off from the Englebrecht Mortuary. His feelings were mixed. He was bitter over Earl Nikken's welsh on his promise of two G's to uncover Ward's and Miles' killers. The letter, though, was some solace. It was lucky the police hadn't thought enough of the thing to hold on to it.

Morton Miles and Jesse Lee Ward had loaded the *City of Kobe* with scrap, secured a crew, gone through all the forms—but had never had any intention of sailing her to Japan. They hadn't bothered to repair the freighter, expecting no one to think of checking her. But why the first application for clearance papers? Ned Lyams had written the Bureau of Marine Inspection and had discovered all this but had not revealed it to his client, the Terrible Turk, or even confessed it to Cellini after his murder of Morton Miles. He had saved that item for blackmail. Now there was no longer any question that the deal had been worked as a racket. The question remaining was how it had operated. If only he could connect Earl Nikken's officership in a Japanese concern he'd have the answer.

Cellini cut into the curb across the street from the Hotel Montclair and killed the motor. He waited for the traffic lights, then crossed and entered the lobby. The hotel was small, ancient, moderately priced, catering to a transient clientele.

Cellini flagged a bellhop and dropped a half dollar into his hand. He said: "I play poker."

"Two-fourteen," was the boy's bored reply. "But you're too early."

Cellini walked up a flight of stairs and at the end of the uncarpeted hallway he found the room. He knocked and entered. The Gimp was sitting alone by the window but a table was set up and ready for the evening's play.

"Gutty tell you to be palsy-walsy with me," Cellini said without preamble.

"You're here talking to me, ain't you?" replied the Gimp.

"I'll ask a couple of things you can answer," said Cellini. "Why'd the boys try to pot me?"

"You were in the way—you still are."

"Why?" asked Cellini. "What do I know? Who thought I was in the way?"

"Nothing doing."

Cellini sat silently for several minutes as an idea hit him. Even as he thought of it he knew it had to be true, that it was that fragmentary piece of information that changed the scrap-iron dealings from question to fact. When he spoke he tried to appear casual and to conceal the excitement he felt. "Gimp," he said, "I found out something the other day. There's a ship called the *City of Kobe* down at San Pedro harbor and it's loaded to the Plimsoll mark with scrap. It couldn't sail because of strikes and picketers. At least, that was supposed to be the reason. What I found out was that while the longshoremen were striking and the Chinese and everybody else were picketing, you and Gutty and a lot of the boys from the Hangover were down at San Pedro. I found out that you and the boys were suddenly social conscious. I found out that you joined the picketers, that you did everything to make trouble so that the ship couldn't sail in time."

"I never carried no picket signs," said the Gimp with a slight tone of resentment.

"Maybe not—but you did everything else you could to prevent the sailing."

The Gimp shrugged. It was a shrug of admission.

Cellini Smith leaned back in his chair and grinned. He had the solution. The case was finished.

23

Dog Eat Dog

CELLINI SMITH QUIT the Montclair and drove for a steak house. Only five in the afternoon and he was already hungry. When he reached the dining place he gave his order for a blood-rare filet and a baked Idaho and then telephoned his office. Duck-Eye Ryan said it was good Cellini called because Ira Haenigson was sitting in a prowl car parked downstairs, waiting to pick him up.

Cellini had expected it. Max Cushman had warned him. He thought a moment, then told Duck-Eye to inform Haenigson where he was. If Haenigson wanted him he might as well see him because he had no chance to tie the case up if he had to hide out.

Ira Haenigson arrived ten minutes later. He watched Cellini eat for a while, then ordered a steak for himself. He was affable and overly gracious but he assured Cellini that when they were through eating they had some serious talking to do.

"I know the whole story," said Cellini. "You were messing around Nina Saunders all morning to see if you could find out something about me."

Haenigson's face lit up. "That Miss Saunders is a mighty fine woman. It was a pleasure to talk to her—even about you."

"Yeah," said Cellini. "She says you're a big, gruff darling."

Haenigson reddened. "She didn't mean it like that."

"Forget it. Haenigson, you're trying to revoke my license

and I don't give a hoot in hell. I'm not getting paid for this job anyway. What's the use of having a license if I can't make money out of it?"

"Now it's no use taking it that way," said Haenigson in a hurt tone. "I tried to be a friend to you. You betrayed me all along."

"Save it, Haenigson. You're after my scalp and you know it. You can't get the killer so you think you'll take it out on me."

"In a way you're right, Smith. Three people have been killed—a dick among them, and I'm still guessing. Maybe I'll never be able to prove that poor Ned Lyams' killing wasn't accidental but I know it. I keep running between the Turk and Nikken and his wife and everybody else and I can't figure out how or why. Naturally, I've got to take a serious view of it if you go and spoil all my important witnesses and don't play ball with me."

"So you're still guessing?"

The Homicide man stared morosely at the steak. "Sure. I saw Earl Nikken's wife today but that mixed things worse. Do you know about it?"

"Sure. Valeria Nikken decided to sue her husband for divorce, name Olive Fain as corespondent, and also sue her for alienation. So Earl got Ward to marry her for the simple purpose of scotching the alienation suit."

"Yes," said Haenigson, "and the way I figured was that Valeria Nikken killed Ward to make Olive Fain single again."

Cellini shook his head. "No. If Valeria does any murdering it will be Olive Fain and nobody else."

"I guess that's so."

"Besides, the fact that she married Ward wouldn't be wiped out by killing him."

Haenigson nodded glumly. "I figured that. Then I thought that Olive Fain might have killed her husband because he couldn't get it straight that the marriage was just for the books and made a pass at her."

"Olive Fain isn't the type you make passes at if she doesn't want to play."

"Then how about Earl Nikken? He might have gotten it into his bean that Jesse Ward was getting fresh with her."

Cellini tapped the table to emphasize his words. "Your whole line of reasoning is wrong because who married who and why doesn't allow for the murder of Miles and the assassination of Lyams. You're barking up the wrong tree if you're looking for a motive along that line."

"Maybe," said Ira Haenigson dubiously. "But I know I could have gotten something out of this Belle Polk and maybe out of Joe Lucca if you hadn't got at them first."

"That's all right. I got plenty."

"You mean you know who did it, Smith?"

"That's right. I've back-tracked, double-tracked and worked on everybody else. I've been eminently fair but I can't escape the conclusion. All roads lead to the same person."

"What'll you do about it?" asked the Homicide man slowly.

Cellini shoved his plate aside. "Now that we've finished eating I suppose you'll take me to the D.A.'s office where some phony deputy will give me a pretty speech about moral obligations and playing fair with the police department. Let's go."

Haenigson didn't move. "Can you prove it?"

"I think so. I think I can make Jesse Lee Ward's killing stick anyway and that ought to be enough."

"Who is it?"

Cellini said: "Damn this wax in my ears."

"All right."

For some minutes, Haenigson didn't speak. Suddenly he stood up. "Forget about the license, Smith. I'll give you till tomorrow. I've got to crack this case even if you get the credit. It's too important."

THE HANGOVER, CELLINI found when he arrived there, felt hurt collectively and singly. They'll send some Vassar girls over to fight them, will they? It was nothing new for wrestlers and fighters to express contempt for each other, but such talk just wasn't in the books. Though the place was crowded, the floor show was lethargic and lacked its usual bawdy, roisterous pace. The fighters, sullen and angry, crowded Earl Nikken's table though Nikken himself was not there.

Cellini Smith and Duck-Eye Ryan, ignoring the pointed lack of invitation, found two chairs and sat down with them. The fighters paid them no attention. Their minds were single-tracked and for the present their thoughts, obscenities, and emotions, were directed against the Turk. Smith would be dealt with at another time.

"We've got to do something," Kate Kelly, the club canary was exhorting them. "Everybody knows he killed Morton and now he's laughing in our faces."

"But how can we be sure he killed Miles?" said Tim Moore uneasily. "The cops don't think so yet."

Cellini asked: "When will you boys stop talking and do something?"

Hard eyes and faces turned on Cellini. "It's the rat who talks like a detective," one of them remarked.

Duck-Eye Ryan stirred resentfully. "And the guy who takes care of him," he muttered.

Cellini said: "Hold it, Duck-Eye. I meant it, guys. Why don't you do something tonight? Go down and wreck the Turk's joint."

"Why so interested?" asked the Sioux City Slasher.

"I'm just trying to be helpful," was Cellini's airy reply. "I've done my job—you do yours."

"You mean you know who killed Morton Miles?"

"Yes. I'm pretty sure."

"Who, Smith?"

Cellini grinned and shook his head. "Earl Nikken backed down on his promise to pay me for this job so I'll give out my information in my own sweet time."

"Suppose we take it out of you?"

"Go ahead."

"Hold it," said the Sioux City Slasher placatingly. "When will we find out who killed Miles, Smith?"

"Probably in tomorrow morning's papers—when everybody else does."

The fighters thought heavily for a while. Then the Slasher became their spokesman again. "Smith, if you're kidding us we'll put you in a hospital. We've been wanting to do it, anyway."

"I'm not kidding anybody."

"And if you're not we're all for you. What do you want us to do?"

"I don't want you to do anything," said Cellini. "I just suggested that if the Turk's been sending ultimatums to you, that you go down and bust his bowling alley open. You've always tried to prove a good fighter could beat a good wrestler and now you've got your chance to prove it. Get the boys together and go down there tonight."

Kate Kelly delivered a whoop of agreement.

"O.K.," the Slasher finally said. "You, Tim, Denver, and Tony get the boys together. Try the Olympic, Jeffries, and the Legion, but get them here. It ought to take a couple of hours and we'll be ready to go down there at twelve o'clock when the Turk won't be expecting us."

"Sure," approved Cellini. "And don't forget to beat it the back way if the cops show up."

"We're no dopes, Smith."

The Slasher continued to bark orders and when he was through they separated to their tasks. Only the tuberculous ex-announcer stayed at the table. He regarded Cellini and Duck-Eye humorously and asked in his hoarse whisper: "What do you get out of it?"

"I don't get you, Mike," said Cellini.

"They don't like you, you don't like them. Why do you come around with friendly suggestions?"

Cellini dodged the question. "Why should I like them? They've threatened to beat me, they've been tough, and they've been liars. They hired me, or had me hired, for this job, then wouldn't give me any of the facts. You too, Mike. You're in with the boys here and you must have taken part in the scrap-iron shindigs."

"So you found out," said Mike. "I was wondering if you would."

"Sure I found out—the hard way. How many times has that load of scrap on the *City of Kobe* been sold?"

"Four times."

"A sweet racket. If I had known it from the start it would have saved me a lot of hard work."

"How did you get on to it?"

"I kept asking myself how Morton Miles would work a racket in scrap iron with the kind of organization of bruisers he had here. That and a couple of other things. It's peculiar, though. All these bruisers going down to the docks and picketing the ship. Cauliflower ears singing the *Internationale!* How'd they take to it?"

The announcer smiled. "They loved it. They just kept yelling about me brudders in China' and waving placards. Is that why Miles was killed? Because the Turk found out about it?"

"No."

"The Turk certainly got a royal rooking," said Mike.

"The-rook-of-the-month," mused Cellini. "But the funny thing is," he continued, "that if the Turk could have known of the rooking he got, Miles and Ward and Lyams would still be alive."

AT ELEVEN THIRTY, Cellini Smith and Duck-Eye Ryan left the Hangover. They crossed the street to a nearby drug store and Cellini found a phone booth. He dialed the Terrible Turk's bowling alley, said, "Some boys from the Hangover will pay you a visit at midnight to bust your joint wide open," and immediately clicked off.

He left the booth and said to Duck-Eye: "Are you sure you've got it straight?"

"Uh-huh." Parrot-like, Duck-Eye reeled off: "I should wait outside the Turk's and when I see the Slasher and the other boys barge in I should call the cops and say they're blowin' the top off the Turk's alley and they should get there quick and cover the back way and I'm anonymous."

"That's fine, Duck-Eye, only forget the anonymous. That's between you and me. If I can bastille that outfit for thirty days I'll get some satisfaction out of this case."

As they got into the Plymouth roadster and drove for the Turk's, Cellini made Duck-Eye repeat his instructions twice more. A few minutes later they reached their destination. Cellini parked the car and entered the bowling alley alone.

On the surface, the noisy, active establishment seemed normal. But on closer scrutiny, the several beefy individuals who stood around the entrance, with heavy cue-sticks hitched under their arms, did nothing too intensely. Still others, wrestlers most of them, were deployed in small groups at strategic points over the acres of alleys. Some hefted bowling balls with great absorption and others held down picked pool tables and simulated play. The Siberian Adonis and the Manhattan Muscovite, apparently the appointed leaders of the star-and-crescent forces, sat at the bar, waiting. They had taken the telephone call seriously.

Cellini loitered at the bar for a few moments, then inconspicuously passed through the door into the Terrible Turk's quarters. The Turk was alone. His tall, wiry form was sprawled, as usual, over the mounds of cushions.

"This is the pay-off, Turk. I'm pinning a couple of murders on you," Cellini said.

"You're just a gag boy, ain't you, Smith?"

"I mean it. I'm pinning the murders of Jesse Lee Ward and Ned Lyams on you."

The Turk rolled and threshed about until he managed to sit up, his long legs under him crosswise. He stared at Cellini with his shiny black dots of eyes. He said: "So you mean it, do you? How's it you left out Morton Miles? Maybe I killed him, too."

"You didn't," said Cellini. "Everybody thought you killed Miles and he was the only one you didn't. That was Ned Lyams' job. Are you interested?"

"I'm listening."

"Then I'll talk. It took one little word, a description of you, to make me certain. Olive Fain—you probably don't know her—mentioned that you were tall. That's all I needed. Before that I didn't know where you fitted in."

"And now you know?"

"Yes. As careful as you were when you put up the dough for Miles to buy scrap iron to fill the Sawamura contract, you felt something stank when the ship couldn't meet the delivery date. So you hired Ned Lyams. Lyams, in his investigations, wrote a letter to the Bureau of Marine Inspection and found out that the *City of Kobe* had so much trouble with her gear that she couldn't have sailed even if she hadn't been sabotaged, that Miles never had any intention of letting it sail to meet the delivery date in Japan. From that he was able to figure out the racket Miles had worked on you, but he didn't tell you about it. He had other ideas.

"So Miles caught on that Lyams was checking him—as a matter of fact I told him—and arranged to meet him at his house that Sunday night. He phoned Lyams from the Hangover. When they met, Lyams showed Miles that letter from Marine Inspection and tried to blackmail him. Miles got scared that you'd find out, pulled a gun, and Lyams shot him in self-defense and ran like hell. Poor Ned was so excited he forgot the letter there and didn't even take the dough from the safe. I don't even think he remembered the letter afterward. But the important part is that Jesse Lee Ward showed up at the Miles house a few minutes after the killing. He showed up to talk over some offer he had from Nikken to marry Olive Fain, and he found Miles dead. He saw the letter which showed him that you were investigating Miles, and he saw a scimitar you had given Miles as a gift while Ward was vacationing in Palm Springs. That convinced Ward that you had killed his best friend, Miles. Right so far?"

The folds on the Turk's face spread out to form a grisly smile. "Talk."

"Then I take it I'm right. Jesse Lee Ward didn't tell anybody. He went home with the scimitar, which I later saw in his apartment, and the letter which was found on his body. The next night he called you over to his house and accused you of murdering his friend. Maybe it was the other way around because Ward wasn't a very brave man. I took the trouble to find out about him. Maybe you phoned him and went over because you heard the police thought he did it. Pinning it on him would, of course, have cleared you. Whichever the case, Ward did one of the few reckless things of his life because he really like Morton Miles. He told you about the scimitar and probably showed you the letter. He told you that he could prove you killed Morton Miles. You denied it, of course, but you knew that if Ward spoke up it meant curtains for you—if not from the police, then certainly from the Hangover outfit. And that gave you the most peculiar motive for murdering a man I ever heard of: You had to kill Jesse Lee Ward because he was able to prove that you had committed a murder of which you were innocent. Right?"

The Terrible Turk began to rock back and forth flexing his arms and shoulders. "Now I *want* you to go on," he said. "I want to find out how you figured all this. I want to find out how you think you can prove it."

Cellini continued: "Lyams and I drove up just as you plugged Ward. Lyams chased you out the back way. He didn't see you but you saw him. When you got home you started to think things over. That letter Ward had shown you or told you about proved that Ned Lyams had held out on you when he found that Miles had rooked you on the scrap-iron deal. And starting with that you were able to figure out that he had killed Miles— that he was the only one left who could have done it. Your own detective! The one you hired to prove you were innocent of the Miles murder had done it! So you had to get rid of Ned."

"So I killed Ned Lyams, too?"

"Of course, though not directly. You were too afraid to. It would have been straining your luck to do it yourself so you hired Joe Lucca and the Gimp to get rid of him in what would look like an accident. And they did."

"O.K. The door's shut so I don't mind telling you that maybe you're right about a couple of things but that you can prove nothing. Smith, this is the last slice of detecting you're gonna to."

"Do you want to hear the whole story I'll tell Ira Haenigson?"

"Sure. Only remember I'm giving you just about another minute or two."

"That's all I need," said Cellini. "About Morton Miles' murder, I've got a written confession from Ned Lyams but if the cops won't believe it and want to pin that killing on you, too, it's all right with me. Ned Lyams' assassination is different. I want you responsible for that. I can prove Lucca and the Gimp pulled it off and it's obvious they'd do something like that only for someone very important. Earl Nikken is the only other person involved in this, beside you, for whom they would have done a thing like that. But he's out as the murderer. He might have had motive to kill Miles and Ward but there was no reason for him to go after Ned Lyams. He didn't even know him. Which left you as the only other man to engineer that assassination at the Three Nuns."

"You think that'll hold water?"

"No," admitted Cellini, "it may not. Especially since Lucca and the Gimp will say that was all an accident at the Three Nuns to save their own skins. But I've got something better to tell the shams about Jesse Lee Ward's death. You told me yourself that Lyams was messing around Ward's home. If you had gotten that dope from the cops you would have known I was there with Lyams. But you saw Lyams chase after you out the back way. That's how you knew. Jesse Lee Ward never even met you—you said so yourself—yet he had one of your scimitars there and a letter from Lyams. I can prove he picked those up at Miles'.

"But what's more important," continued Cellini, "was the circumstance of Ward's murder. As soon as you shot him, you heard my car pull up in front of the house. You snapped the lights off but there was still a light from the burning clothing which you used to swathe the gun so as to deaden the shot. You had to cross the room past the half-open Venetian blinds to get out through the back door so you *crawled* past the blinds. Why?

Because you're so damned tall, Turk! If you had run or walked by the window your height would have been a dead giveaway. We thought you were searching for something but you were just trying to get away. We thought you were searching for something behind the sofa cushions because they were put back hurriedly the wrong end out. What I forgot at the time was that, phony Turk that you are, when you sit down *you only sit on cushions.* So you pulled them out and sat on them on the floor while you talked to Ward and shoved them back quickly, any way, when Ned and I showed up. That's one thing—"

"Damn you!" said the Turk. "I'll break every bone in your body!"

Cellini said: "All right. If you're spoiling for a fight come on. I could have gone to the shams with my story but I've got a score to settle with you."

The Turk's arms spread gorilla fashion and he slowly began to weave toward Cellini.

THE TERRIBLE TURK'S arm pawed forward tentatively as he approached. Cellini ducked under the arm, landed a stinging, slashing right into the pit of his stomach, and jumped back. The punch delayed the wrestler's cumbersome but steady approach for only a second. Cellini backed away and flanked him. "You weren't very smart," he taunted. "You should have taken the time to put those cushions back correctly in Ward's house. You like to think you're a Turk and you like to sit on your prat like one. Well—"

Cellini leaped in and put his whole weight behind a blow to the jaw. The Turk tossed his bony head impatiently as if shaking a fly off his nose and kept coming in.

Cellini laughed jeeringly. He thought it was fortunate that the Turk was too enraged to remember the scimitars on the walls. He said: "You're lucky you're getting stuck for murder because otherwise I'd stick you for Belle Polk. She's jail-bait. You forget I saw her here first, then later with the Gimp at the Three Nuns. That's another pair of deuces that made four and told me you engineered the assassination of Ned Lyams."

The Terrible Turk lunged forward with surprising agility. Cellini leaped sideways and stumbled over a cushion. In a split second the Turk was on him. His stringy, over-developed arms circled his chest with bone-crushing pressure. He gave a piercing cry of triumph.

Cellini's strength was no match. His breath began to come in short, stifled gasps. His ribs were meeting like the pincers of a crab and his eyes stopped focusing as the Turk's arms tightened yet more. He began to feel light and the Turk began to seem like a monstrous, inexorable, nut cracker.

Cellini's fists pounded with more protest than effect. He fought for a final lungful of air and his scrabbling fingers found the Turk's face. He felt for the pin-point eyes and dug a thumb into the corner of one of the sockets.

The Turk jumped up with a yelp of pained rage. He reached down, lifted Cellini effortlessly over his head, and hurled him to the far side of the room.

Cellini landed against a corner of the stetzl floor safe. For the instant of impact he lost consciousness. He felt the painful gash opened by the steel under his arm. He could feel the warm blood trickle down.

The Turk advanced. "I'll kill you like I killed Ward," he screamed insanely.

Cellini rolled over to ease the wound and the revolver in his pocket weighted his other side as though to remind him. He fumbled for the weapon. The Turk didn't pause. If he saw it he didn't care. Cellini supported himself on one arm and sighted with blurred vision. He pulled the trigger. A spot of deep crimson appeared on the Turk's trouser leg.

The door was pushed in and a frightened face appeared. The Turk wavered a second, then came on again. "I'll kill you," he screamed. "I'll kill you like I killed Ward!" The face at the door caught sight of the gun in Cellini's hand and the door slammed shut.

Cellini aimed for the other leg and depressed the trigger again. Through blurred eyes he saw the Turk fall and begin to crawl at him on hands and bloody knees.

The door flew open again and several burly wrestlers, the Siberian Adonis among them, bounded in. Before they could orient themselves there was some uproar outside and they disappeared again. In a moment a deafening tumult shook the alleys. The bruisers from the Hangover had arrived.

The Turk still crawled. When he was within two feet of him, Cellini took vague aim at one of the pitted, whipcord shoulders and pulled the trigger again. For thirty seconds the Turk rested motionless on hands and knees, like a Moslem on a prayer rug, then toppled over.

The gun slipped from Cellini's fingers. Between the recurring blanks of darkness he strained to hear the sounds of the brawl. It had been timed right, he thought. Then his knees buckled and he pitched forward on top of the unconscious Terrible Turk.

WHEN CELLINI SMITH came to, he was lying on banked cushions in the Turk's room. He was stripped and a doctor was applying the final pieces of adhesive over the bandage on his side. Ira Haenigson, several policemen, and Duck-Eye Ryan sat around in a semicircle, watching with interest.

The doctor gave a final pat and said: "There, Mr. Smith. Just stay quiet. I've done some nice hemstitching on you and it won't hurt so much now."

Cellini ran his fingers over the bandage. Only a dull throb remained. He said: "Give me my clothes."

"Give us a couple of more minutes," said Ira Haenigson, "to admire your torso."

Cellini didn't smile. "I asked for my pants."

"Take it easy, Smith," soothed the detective-sergeant. "Your drawers are dunked in blood."

Cellini asked bitterly: "So you managed to get in on the kill, didn't you, Haenigson?"

"Sure," replied the Homicide man. "You did a nice job, Smith. The way you had the Turk going, he yelled he fogged Ward so that everybody in the bowling alley heard him."

"Where's the Turk now?"

"The ambulance carted him to the hospital. You winged him three times—legs and shoulder. How'd you know it was him?"

Cellini said: "I explained to him."

"Tell me."

Cellini's brow darkened. "I'll tell you to go to hell. I work four days for nothing, give you the credit, and then you try to get my license revoked."

"There, there," soothed the doctor. "You must take it easy, Mr.

Smith. You may have a fractured rib. We won't know until we take X-rays tomorrow."

"We'll forget about that license angle," said Haenigson. "We've had a busy night. I've never seen a riot like the one here. Hammer and tongs. We've booked practically every crummy wrestler and fighter in town for rioting. Who tipped us off? You, Smith?"

Cellini made no reply. He stood up cautiously and was pleased to discover that he wasn't as weak as he had expected. Just that dizziness. He felt his way to a closet where he found a large stock of men's underwear. He took out a pair of flowered shorts and donned them, bunching the spare width into a knot. He felt his side and successfully essayed a few rapid steps up and down the room. Then he put on his clothes.

"Where are you going, Smith?"

"Away. I'm busy."

"I've got something to tell you, Smith."

"Go ahead."

Haenigson seemed embarrassed. "I'll tell you on the way out."

Cellini shrugged. He finished dressing and walked out, followed by Ira Haenigson. A large crowd of the curious stood about on the sidewalk, still discussing the riot. Cellini led the way to the Plymouth roadster and they got into it. "Well?" asked Cellini.

The Homicide man stuttered for a few minutes, then asked: "Are you going home?"

"No."

"Well, start driving. I'll tell you as we go along."

Cellini set the car in motion. "I said I'm busy."

"Sure you did. Smith, don't you want to tell me now how you knew it was the Turk?"

"I'll tell you tomorrow."

"Why didn't you let me in on it before?"

"I had to put it up to the Turk myself," said Cellini, "and get an admission out of him because most of my proof was my word against his."

"Then tell me this, Smith. That scrap-iron deal the Turk had with Miles. Was that on the level?"

"Of course not. That was probably Earl Nikken's brain-child after he got stuck with a boatload and a bad ship himself. When the Bureau of Marine Inspection found his ship unseaworthy, he organized a Japanese concern with a large capital and through the concern gave Morton Miles and Ward a large, fat contract to deliver scrap iron to Japan by a certain date. The concern put money into escrow and with that as bait Miles and Ward got suckers to invest dough to buy scrap iron to fill the contract. Two weeks after they got the dough from the sucker, Miles and Ward showed him his phony ship full of scrap but when it was supposed to sail they sent their outfit down each time to the ship to yell about their brothers in China. It looked legitimate and it worked four times—the last time on the Turk. Of course, when the ship couldn't sail in time to meet the contract delivery date in Japan they probably bought the scrap back from the sucker at one tenth the price."

Haenigson whistled. "Neat."

Cellini cut into the curb in front of the Professional Building and went up to his office—Haenigson following. Cellini turned on the lights and said: "For God's sake, why tail after me?"

"I've got something to tell you."

"Well, tell me!" Cellini opened the desk drawer and palmed the key to an apartment in the Sheraton Manor. "I've got to go now. What do you want?"

"Well," said Haenigson, "you know I'm a nice guy, really, and I admit I've been pretty rough on you all along."

"Let me kiss you."

"It's like this, Smith." A slight red appeared on the detective-sergeant's cheeks. "Bella—my wife—is a very fine woman and I think highly of her."

"Sure she's a fine woman, Haenigson. Hurry up."

"Well, Bella says that trust is the basis of marriage and—" The red deepened as his words trailed off. Haenigson, without further ado, thrust a hand into his pocket, silently handed Cellini a key.

The stamping on the brass check said: *Apt. 3-B—Sheraton Manor.*

About the Author

I AM TWENTY-SEVEN years old and much as I would like to hint at prospecting the Gold Coast or gun-running below the Rio Grande, I cannot. Simply, then: I have done nothing of especial interest.

I was born in Manhattan and raised on the South shore of Long Island where I attended the elementary and secondary schools.

I worked at carpentry and cabinet- and candy-making and drove an armored Post Office truck and carried (as per regulations) a Colt .45 that scared the living daylights out of me.

Then came "higher" education, at New York University. There, amidst the sylvan glades (Washington Square Branch) I studied Anthropology, History and English without neglecting the serial "cliff-hangers" at a nearby Eight Avenue grind house. Eventually I secured an A.B.

Armed thus with a degree and the intellectual assets of eye-glasses and a receding hair-line, I managed to become an outside reader for Fox Films and thereafter drifted into reading for Broadway play brokers.

For the next few years (when not visiting with my family in Hollywood) I haunted New York's theatrical byways, working as a casting director, at play doctoring, an assistant producer, and a stage manager. At one time I was stage manager for the Theatre Guild and at a lot of other times I wasn't.

During those years I stocked my shelves with rejected stories and articles.